Geeky Books © Copyright 2013. No part of this publication may be recreated digitally or physically without prior written permission from the publishers first. www.victorsbooks.co.uk

First Printing 2013 - Published by *Geeky Books*

Huge Thanks

Behind every writer are those special people offering support, wisdom and input into the project at hand. I'm no different. Without some of the folk who have helped me nurture this novel from infancy to completion, I'd never have managed it. I'd personally like to thank one person in particular for supporting me over the last 12 months.

Danielle Super - for listening to the story so many times you must know the characters better than I do. But more so for your input into how things play out and for being patience over the many long hours I spent on this book.

Thank you.

LIGHT OF DARKNESS

BOOK ONE: DAYS OF RECKONING

By Victor Wright

CHAPTER 1

July, 2003

"I'll be back before you know it, Poppy."

Even as her father spoke the words with a smile on his face, Poppy Applebaum felt uncertain, a premonition of something she didn't understand frightening her so she clung to her father's neck, wanting to beg him not to join the rest of his unit and get on the plane.

Catherine smiled down at her 5-year-old daughter as she gently hauled the girl back, allowing Richard to rise and kiss her, one last kiss, before he lined up in formation. She, too, felt oddly about this deployment to Afghanistan. Rich was due to end his contract with the US Army in just under a year, and they'd hoped he'd avoid another stint across the world. She knew he would want to be with his men this last time before retiring to the family business of Primrose Farm. However, his unit had been called in for a nine-month tour of duty, and she stood here, feeling strangely panicked about something her husband had already done twice before.

Richard cupped his wife's face in his large hands and kissed her with a bit of desperation. He could feel the concern his family had, and it made him jittery about leaving. "I love you, Cathy," he said to the beautiful woman with the long raven locks, memorizing her face as he had his daughter's.

With the call to come to formation, he said one more quick goodbye to his parents, rubbed the top of Poppy's hair, and jogged over to his place in the lineup.

Poppy swallowed hard. She was a big girl and wouldn't cry. Instead, she tugged on her mother's dress till she got the woman's attention and reached for her hand, squeezing tight and praying her daddy would be alright.

November, 2003

For a long moment, Richard couldn't tell if the explosions had left him temporarily deafened or if they'd come to a stop. They'd been ambushed, with their Intel less than stellar, and they hadn't been armed as heavily as they should have, expecting a safer journey. Now, though, there were more dead than alive for sure.

Richard breathed as quietly as he could, intermittently holding his breath as he crouched in one of the bunkers, gun in hand. Most of his unit was dead or injured, and he'd slowly made his way toward one of his fellow soldiers to see if he could help staunch the blood that squirted from his femoral artery before it was too late. He didn't know how the enemy had gotten inside the camp, but he intended to get out alive and take as many of his own with him as he could save.

He only had to make it another twenty feet to get to the soldier, who tried unsuccessfully to hold in his groans of pain, and he took a single step in the godforsaken sand, attempting to maintain the silence so the enemy wouldn't find him. He hoped they thought they'd gotten everyone and moved out.

Slowly, step by miserable step, he made his way over to the bleeding man, until he lowered himself to his knees and took the wadded up shirt from the man's hands and tore it to strips. He knelt on the wound, which he knew hurt like hell but held back the blood flow, while he created a makeshift tourniquet, then moved to tie the thing tight enough around the soldier's thigh to cut off circulation. Better he loses the whole leg and survives than die here in the middle of the damn desert, surrounded by miles of nothing but enemies.

The soldier bit into his leather belt to hold back screams of agony, and at one point, his eyes rolled back in his head as he almost passed out. But he held onto consciousness and nodded his thanks, his breathing so labored he couldn't speak. Finally, Richard reached into his own pack and pulled out a cloth and tore his belt from his waist, determined to bandage the wound as best he could. But as he covered the ragged bullet wound and drew the belt tight around the other soldier's leg, the leather strap fell from his mouth, and the soldier let out a piercing scream.

Richard slapped his hand over the guy's mouth as fast as he could move, but it was too late. If there were any enemy soldiers around, they'd be found in seconds. He froze, holding stock still and listening intently for several long moments, expecting the worst, but no one came, and he breathed a sigh of relief. He finished the job he'd started and whispered, "Let's get out of here."

The other soldier nodded, Richard bent down, throwing the guy over his shoulder and standing, stooped, readying to jog along the bunker toward some sort of safe haven, though god only knew where he'd find that. Tapping into something deep inside, he prepared to send up a prayer, but a battle cry struck out, and he found himself face down on the ground, the wind knocked out of him and pressure on his back.

He was yanked to his feet by the hair on his head and a knife held to his throat, and he didn't move. This enemy wouldn't think twice to kill him, and the only way to guarantee you'd make it out was to die. He still had a fighting chance. Five more of the bastards surrounded him, two of them dragging his fellow American to his knees.

A third stepped up, and before Richard could open his mouth to cry out in protest, the gun went off, and the body fell to the ground. "Silence," the one holding the knife said in his ear with a thick accent, "or you will join your infidel brother."

Richard assessed the situation. He was far outnumbered, images of Catherine and her beautiful face, his daughter Poppy with her childishly sweet smile and soft hair, his parents standing proud seeing him off, swam through his head. He couldn't get away, couldn't outrun their gunshots, and couldn't take them all down alone. There were no other members of his unit left who could fight with him. He was done.

And he wasn't going to die.

So, he stayed silent, even as they broke his nose with their fists, cracked several ribs kicking him to the ground, and threw a burlap bag over his head. Like the soldier he was, he'd bear it and wait for an opportunity to escape. The key to survival was to remain positive and never give up hope, no matter how hard it got and no matter how much pain he'd have to endure. And as they began marching him blindly though the desert, he knew very well the torture would be unbearable if he ever stopped thinking of his family.

Poppy sat, cradled between Nana and Mama, Papa sat on the other side of Nana, his arm draped over the back of the couch while they watched Mary Poppins. It was her favorite movie, full of fun, magical stuff like Mary being able to reach into her bag and pull out a whole lamp, and all of them going inside a sidewalk picture and going to the fair. It really was the best film.

Someone knocked on the door, and Papa paused the movie. She looked up and saw all the adults giving each other strange looks, and Mama and Nana felt stiff beside her. "I'll get it," Papa offered, pushing to his feet and heading toward the front door across the room.

When he opened the door, Poppy recognized the uniform. It looked just like Daddy's, and she jumped up and ran to see if, maybe, the army had brought Daddy home early. "Poppy!" Mama called, but she was already out of reach and standing just a couple of feet behind Papa.

"David Applebaum?" one of the two men at the door asked.

David nodded, a lump forming in his throat. The only thing that held him together was noting that neither of them appeared to be carrying dog-tags or a flag. "Yes, sir, can I help you?"

The man in front took off his dress hat and held it in front of him, the other standing at attention to his right. "Sir, I'm here to inform you that your son, Lieutenant Richard Applebaum, is *Missing In Action*. We don't believe him dead, as all but one of his troop was found, either dead or wounded, at the scene of the battle. However, we do fear that he was taken hostage."

A sharp pain tore through David's chest, and had he not known the difference, he would have thought it was a heart attack rather than fear and grief consuming him. "Is there any evidence that he's alive?"

The man swallowed visibly. "Yes sir. Two soldiers who were mortally wounded said they believe they saw him hooded and carried away prior to their expiration."

David tried not to shudder at the clinical terminology. This man had a terribly difficult job to do, and he respected that he had to keep an emotional distance to survive it. Still, his mind swirled with hope that his son was alive while he also feared he'd be tortured and killed before he could be rescued.

Poppy listened and sensed the change in the atmosphere. She also heard Mama and Nana coming toward the door now and knew something was very wrong. Whatever they were saying about Daddy, it wasn't good. In fact, it sounded very scary, and Poppy's heart started to flutter. "Mama?" she whispered, turning to her mother and tugging on the hem of her shirt.

Catherine put an arm around her daughter's shoulders, trying to stay calm and brave. "Shh, it's alright, sweetheart."

The man who'd been talking nodded at Catherine respectfully. "I want you to know the US Army is doing everything in its power to investigate the situation and find Lieutenant Applebaum. While we hold to the policy of not negotiating with terrorists, we will work diligently to get him released, assuming he has been taken hostage."

David grabbed his wife's hand as Jill reached for it and squeezed, nodding his appreciation. "I think I speak for all of us when I say thank you, and I am refreshed by your own courage. God bless you, sir."

The soldier nodded his appreciation. "Thank you, Mr. Applebaum. I hope to be in touch with you again soon with very good news." He saluted formally and turned to leave, his companion pivoting and marching stiffly away behind him. They climbed into the back of a car, and the chauffer drove away, leaving a trail of road dust behind.

Slowly, David shut the door and turned to his family. Tears streamed down Jill's face, and Catherine wore a stoic, determined expression. But the one he worried the most about was Poppy. He crouched down in front of her, reading confusion and fear on her face, and he gave her an encouraging smile, mustering up all the hope he had to make it sincere. "Hey, Pops. Do you understand what that was all about?"

She shrugged, not sure how to answer Papa. "The man said Daddy is missing. Does that mean they don't know where he is?"

David nodded, his heart breaking for his granddaughter. "It means they know he's not dead but they don't know who took him or where he is. But the soldier said they're looking for him, and they'll find him."

Poppy frowned. If she played *Hide & Seek*, and they weren't inside the house, there was always a specific boundary they didn't cross. That's why she could find people. But how was the army going to look for Daddy and find him if they didn't know where to look? It sounded like a very, very bad thing. "How are they going to find him, Papa? Isn't he in a big place?"

"Yes, Poppy, he is. But the army has lots of people whose job it is to find the places where the bad guys might be hiding him, and a whole other group who go looking for him there and rescue him." He put his arms around the small girl and hugged her tight to his chest. "Everything will be alright, Poppy."

Somehow, though, Poppy didn't think so. No, she felt the whole world collapsing around her and had no way to explain that or to stop it. Still, if Papa believed they would find Daddy, Poppy would believe it, too. And she would be a big girl and not cry, even if Mama and Nana cried.

March, 2004

If Richard counted right, it was sometime in March. He wasn't sure what day – he thought he'd missed a day or two along the way – but at least he was close. So far, he'd been lucky. He'd been questioned only once, and that had resulted in minimal beating that may have bruised or broken a rib or two and which had left his lips bloodied and his left eye swollen shut for a few days. After that, he'd simply been locked in this tiny cell that smelled of underground mold, with a bucket in the corner for defecating, a pile of worn, holy blankets to sleep on, and stale bread and water twice a day. No one touched him or talked to him, and he wondered if they'd forgotten he was here. The only contact he had was with the man who shuffled past twice a day to give him food and the other who came once a week to allow him to empty the rancid bucket. He wasn't a big talker, and it appeared several bones in his face had been broken and healed poorly, but when he did utter a word or two, it was obvious he was British by the accent.

His chains rattled as he passed, and with the rags on his body, Richard had to wonder how long he'd been here. But he never asked, afraid it hadn't been long and that he was doomed to such a pitiful existence in the next few months.

He'd rather keep his hopes up for some kind of rescue. Surely, someone would realize he was missing after all these months. While the army may not make the most aggressive attempts to free prisoners, they would at least be actively searching for him and then would start figuring a way how to get him back. Unless they thought he was already dead.

He still wore his dog-tags, which shocked him. It would be just like the enemies to take them and send them to someone to prove he was dead, and then no one would keep looking for him. But he wouldn't question his blind luck, not now or ever. He'd simply make the best of it and think about the future, when he'd get out and back to his beautiful daughter and his gorgeous, loving wife. They were his world, and they kept him sane so he could function in this 24-hour dark, sweltering hell.

June 2006

Strange sounds echoing from somewhere far down the long, dark corridor, awoke Richard to a semi-conscious state. He couldn't quite make his eyes open just yet, but he listened intently, trying to determine what was happening outside this dungeon. As he listened, he went back over his count, and cursed when he couldn't quite remember what month it was anymore. Was it April? May? He wasn't sure, but it was 2006. He did know that much.

Coughing hard, the rattle of his lungs temporarily drowned out the other sounds. But he strained his ears, so sensitive to sound now, and his heart sank.

Curled in on himself, he heard the arguing in a language he almost understood, then the sound of gunshots. All hell seemed to break loose, and he heard the door at the other end of the corridor swing open and hit the wall. This was it, he thought. He sent up a prayer that Poppy and

Catherine and his parents would be okay when he was gone, that the strength he knew his family possessed had carried them through this nightmare and would continue to carry them after his death.

He forced himself to straighten and gain his feet as the sound of someone running came closer and closer. Placing his hands behind his head, he faced the cage in front of him, waiting and almost welcoming the end of this nightmare. He didn't want to leave his family without saying goodbye, but at least from Heaven, he could watch over them, something he couldn't do here. How he longed to see the growth of his child, the maturing of his wife. He wanted to put his arms around them, to look at his father and hear how proud the man was of his son.

But none of that would happen now.

Braced for death, he inhaled deeply and stood, waiting. But rather than any of the Afghanis standing outside his cell, pointing a gun at him, he saw Americans. Soldiers, in uniforms, carrying large, American guns.

And he wasn't imagining it.

The relief was so profound, Richard sobbed a laugh and fell to his knees, weak and tired and hungry and grateful. "Lieutenant Applebaum?" one of them asked, and he gave a vague nod. "Stand back, Lieutenant, we'll have you out in no time!"

Richard crawled on his hands and knees to the back of the cell as the other soldier pointed his weapon at the lock and blasted it, pieces of metal flying everywhere. Richard winced, but when the door swung open, he was so thrilled he nearly passed out from the overwhelming rush. One of the soldiers caught him and hollered to another member of the rescue squad for a blanket. Someone draped it over Richard, wrapping him up, as the two who had found him half-carried him up the stairs and out into sunlight that fully blinded him.

He heard others hollering in cracked, hoarse voices about being freed, and Richard smiled. "You found us."

The soldier who'd first addressed him chuckled and said, "Yes, Lieutenant. It looks like we've got about twelve of you coming out of that hole, sir. All nationalities. You're families are going to be so happy."

That made Richard's heart pound. "My Catherine. And my little Poppy." He felt for the soldier's arm and squeezed it. "Take me home, Private."

August, 2006

Poppy sat on the steps at the front of the wraparound patio of the farmhouse, her chin resting in her hands and her elbows on her knees, staring down the lane and waiting for a glimpse of her grandparents' car. She wore her best dress and had asked Mama to pull her long locks that matched the shade of her mother's, back from her face into a slick ponytail with a ribbon that matched the midnight blue of her clothes. She wanted to look her best for her father.

She'd seen Daddy on the news just last night, one more interview where he'd talked about being a POW, which she knew meant a prisoner. He looked the same but different. When he left, he stood tall and wide, with shoulders and a chest that were like a big wall she couldn't get past. His hair had been dark brown and cut so short it almost wasn't there, and his face was smooth.

Now, he had what Nana called 'salt and pepper' hair, and he looked very thin. He was still tall; the heads of most of the other men on TV only came up to Daddy's chin. But he looked smaller, like maybe Daddy needed to find his strength again.

When she heard Daddy was coming home, Poppy hoped he'd make it for her eighth birthday, since he hadn't been there for the sixth or seventh. But he'd missed it by two days. Mama said it was the government's fault, and Poppy didn't really know why, but at least it meant Daddy hadn't missed it on purpose.

She could hear tires on the dirt road that led through the large Primrose Farm, and she stood, hopeful. As the nose of the car crested the hill ahead, still far but within sight, she ran up the steps and to the kitchen, where her mother stood over the sink, washing dishes. "Mama! They're home!"

Catherine Applebaums eyes grew wide as she looked down at her young daughter, then up out the window in front of the sink. Sure enough, her father-in-law's car was winding its way down the lane, getting closer and closer and causing her heart to pound harder and harder.

She turned off the water and tore off the apron, wiping her hands and touching her hair. She'd planned to do her hair, maybe put a little color on the few gray streaks that had appeared over the last three years as she'd cried herself to sleep and prayed for her husband's safe return, always awaiting news. But they'd gotten back sooner than she'd expected, and she stood here in faded jeans, a loose tank top, and a mess of hair pulled into a frizzy ponytail with strands flying around her face.

Did she even have time to run to the bathroom for some foundation and cover her crow's feet?

But she didn't get that choice as Poppy grabbed her hand and tugged, putting her whole body weight into it, so she had to follow the young, tenacious girl out to the front of the house to greet the arrivals. Admittedly, her daughter's excitement, contagious as it was, drew her out and made her chest tighten. She could feel the waves of glee rolling off Poppy, and that alone made her forget for a moment the frumpy feeling as she squinted to try to see Richard.

Poppy rocked up on her toes, but she couldn't see Daddy. Nana and Papa were in the front seat, and Daddy must have been in the back. So, as they finally arrived and parked facing directly at the front of the house, Poppy nearly screamed with her desire to see the man she hadn't gotten to hug in three years before the back door of the car opened and Richard Applebaum stood to his full height and smiled down at her.

She didn't hesitate but dropped her mother's hand and bounded off the steps, throwing her arms around the man as he knelt to hug her, squeezing her tight against his chest. "Told you I'd be back! Look how you've grown."

Poppy pulled away and touched his face, feeling the stubble that had grown overnight and the hollows of his cheeks. "I counted on the calendar, Daddy, and we learned multiplication in school. You were gone three times what you were supposed to be. So I'm three times as happy you're home."

Richard's heart swelled with love and pride. His daughter hadn't forgotten him, and while she'd grown in both height and beauty, she'd also proven a highly intelligent young girl. He hated how much he'd missed of her childhood but intended to make up for it from now on.

Patting her on the head and rising, his eyes fell on his wife. Escaped hair blew around her face, and she squinted into the sun as it shone around her, almost like an aura glowing as her smile melted him into the ground. How he'd missed her touch, her smile, her laughter. Slowly, he moved toward her, the picture-perfect woman in the country, until he stood only inches from her, their eyes on level because she stood two steps above him. "Hello, pretty lady."

She blushed. "I'm a complete mess," she laughed self-consciously tucking her hair behind her ears and smoothing her shirt.

But Richard grabbed her hands and stilled them, holding them to his chest. "You are the most beautiful sight I've ever laid eyes on." Leaning forward, he captured her lips in a kiss, and she sighed, all the tension that had built up over the last 33 months since she'd learned of Richard's imprisonment lifting from her shoulders. Her husband was home safe, and he still looked, tasted, felt the same.

Poppy watched them for a minute as Nana and Papa stepped up beside her. But she couldn't take it for very long. She wanted Daddy's attention, and she rushed forward, wrapping her arms around both her parents. They broke apart and looked down at her, both of them smiling brilliantly and seeming to shine with their own lights.

"What can I do for you, Popsie?" Poppy giggled at her dad's old nickname for her, which she'd almost forgotten over the last three years. He squatted down so he could look her in the eyes, his green eyes sparkling at her.

Suddenly shy, Poppy rocked side to side, looking up at her father through her long, dark lashes. "Daddy, I wanted to ask you if we could go to the candy store for my birthday.

23

It was two days ago, and I don't want a lot of stuff, but I want to go to the candy store with you."

Richard chuckled, shaking his head at the easy pleasure his daughter took in the idea of something so small. If only everyone could appreciate the small things in life that way, without being stuck in a foreign country, stowed away in what equated to dungeons that weren't fit for pigs. One thing was certain – he'd never take a moment of life for granted again.

"Yes, ma'am, we will go to the candy store in just a few minutes." He stood and looked at his wife. "And later when we get home, I'm going to take your mother on a nice romantic date."

Catherine blushed again, thrilled to have a chance to clean herself up first and even more excited to be alone with her husband for the first time in years. She couldn't express her joy, so she simply caressed his face with the back of her hand and kissed him one more time. "I'll get ready while you two head to the store." Poppy smiled up at her father as he took her hand in his large one, walking her toward the car and winking at Nana and Papa as they passed. Papa handed Richard the keys, and Poppy climbed over the center console rather than going around, not wanting to be that far from her father. She'd been without him for so long that he seemed almost like a ghost, and the further she got from him, the less real he seemed.

As Richard drove the few miles to the center of town, he gazed several times at his daughter, not sure he could process her growth since he'd last seen her. That had been almost the full three years before, when Catherine sent him her school pictures. She was such a beautiful child, and now more than ever, she looked like her exquisite mother.

Poppy bounced in her seat as they reached the candy store and Richard rolled to a stop. "How much can I have, Daddy?"

This had always been the first question on arrival, and Richard couldn't help but sigh in satisfaction at the way things never changed. He loved that he could come home, find his daughter three years older and almost a foot taller and still have the old routine fall right into place. It was the magic of youth, and the magic of Primrose as a home. The rest of the world changed, and Primrose and its keepers stayed almost unchanged.

He got out and waited for Poppy to skip around the front of the car, taking his hand and following him into the store. "I think you can get $10 worth today." That was double what he usually allowed, and her face lit up.

Almost beside herself with anticipation, Poppy moved swiftly through the store. She wanted a good look at everything so she could choose her favorites today. And of course, one thing for Mama and one thing for Daddy. That's the way she'd always done it. She wanted a piece of chocolate for sure, and maybe some gummy candies. And definitely a couple of pieces of sour candy that made her lips pucker so hard that Papa and Nana laughed until tears ran down their faces.

Poppy took pride in her dad following her around the store, and Richard loved pandering to the child who'd been half the reason he'd suffered through the worst moments of his life to see again. When she'd collected all her things, she looked up at her father and smiled brightly. "I'm done, Daddy. Let's go to the counter."

He nodded and motioned for her to lead the way, and she bounced to the front of the store. She watched in anticipation as the clerk patiently added up the total, then turned expectantly to her father to pay. Richard patted his pockets and frowned. "Wait right here, baby girl. I left my wallet in the car."

Poppy nodded silently and watched him walk out the door, still in awe of the big man that he was. She turned to the clerk and said, "My daddy just came home from the war. He just got back a few minutes ago."

The woman smiled at her. "Your daddy's a good man. We've missed him around here."

Poppy would have replied, but she suddenly had a sick feeling in her stomach. Something wasn't right. It was a lot like the way she'd felt when Daddy left for the war, only this time it was stronger. She sniffed the air. It smelled funny, but she didn't recognize the smell. Her heart fluttered and, as the sick feeling grew stronger, she noticed it was getting darker inside the store. Suddenly she began to feel scared.

She looked toward the front windows and the display cases, and even though she could clearly see the sun in the sky, the air seemed dark and thick, like she was in the middle of a dark cloud. The butterflies in her stomach reached her chest, then her throat, and her heart raced in her chest. Something was very wrong. "Daddy?" she whispered.

She looked up at the clerk, frightened, and wanted to tell her what was going on, but the lady didn't seem to notice anything wrong. She hummed to herself as she toiled behind the counter, waiting for her payment. Still, the air grew darker, the smell got stronger, and Poppy put a hand on her chest. She could feel her fear like static electricity. She had to go to her father, or something terrible was going to happen.

Running to the front door of the shop, she crashed through it and found herself in a dark world where the sun still shone. Her father stepped away from the car with his wallet in his hand, but froze like a statue after just a couple of steps. "Daddy!" Poppy cried out, and he reached out to her with one hand. But before she could get to him, a hot wind whipped around her, slinging her ponytail in her face, and a black, sticky cloud surrounded her father, swirling like a tornado until the entire cloud covered him.

It stopped moving and seemed to cling to her father. Her eyes wide, Poppy watched as the transparent mist grew thicker and denser, until she couldn't see her father anymore, could barely hear him. For just a moment, Poppy swore in the dark cloud she saw a shape, a face, with hollow eyes, and an evil grin with deadly sharp teeth. And within just a few moments, it dissolved, taking her father with it. There was nothing left, just an empty space where Richard Applebaum once stood, and Poppy panicked.

Unable to scream, she ran to where he'd been, trying to sense him, hoping she was dreaming, but there was no trace as the darkness around her subsided and the heat of the day returned. She turned a full circle, and then another, praying she was wrong, but in her heart she knew the truth before she looked down and saw the only evidence her father had even been here.

His wallet lay open on the ground.

Filled with despair, Poppy fell to her knees, grabbed the wallet and crushed it to her chest, wailing in agony.

CHAPTER 2

Jill Applebaum wrung her hands as she spoke to the officer who had responded to the call. When Catherine had answered the phone, she'd collapsed, and they'd barely gotten her into the recliner at home before she'd had to find the keys to the old Impala and rush out, leaving her husband to watch over her daughter-in-law.

Now, she glanced at Poppy, sitting on the wooden patio of the candy store, rocking back and forth with tears streaming down her cheeks, Richard's wallet hugged tight to her chest. "Mrs. Applebaum, there's no sign of any foul play, and the word of an eight-year-old doesn't give us much to go on."

Jill may have been worried, but that statement pissed her off. "Listen, Officer Grady, I want you to understand that whatever my granddaughter says is worth listening to. You can't just write it off because she's only eight. She's a smart girl with keen senses and intuition."

Grady sighed and threw his hands up in defeat. "Mrs. Applebaum, I'd love to take her at her word. But the girl says she saw a black cloud come and take her father away. She says the day went dark while the sun was shining, and Maud Letterman the clerk in the store, didn't see anything at all. I've got no corroborating witnesses and no evidence. According to Maud, your son walked out of the store to get his wallet, left his daughter inside, and disappeared. It sounds to me like the war got the best of him and he ran scared. Now, I don't want to believe that any more than you do, but I can't prove otherwise."

If only she could explain things to him, Jill thought, but even now, her inner voice told her she couldn't speak a word to this man. She looked back at Poppy, and her heart sank. The girl was devastated, and when she got home and found her mother catatonic, it was only going to get worse. She was a Daddy's girl, and it had nearly killed her childhood to be without him for so long. But at least she'd had her mother. What if Catherine didn't snap out of it?

And as for Richard…Jill's terror was almost tangible, like a big ball of yarn she could hold in her hand. Unlike the authorities – or anyone else for that matter – she believed every word Poppy said. She knew something foul had occurred, and Poppy had watched it all go down. She also feared her granddaughter would be scarred by it, that she'd never see her son that her daughter-in-law was down for the count.

A lesser person would have suffered a stroke or a heart attack right then and there at the hopelessness that overwhelmed her. But she had unnatural strength and faith, and she would rely on that. With a determination she hadn't tapped into in years, she faced down Grady. "It's alright, Officer. Your people handle this the way you see fit. In the meantime, I'm going to take care of my granddaughter, my daughter-in-law, and my husband. And our family will work together to find the answers your people don't see fit to seek."

She saw Grady gnashing his teeth, wanting to retort, but Jill stepped away with a small bit of satisfaction at having said her piece as she hurried over to Poppy, sitting down next to her on the dusty porch. "How you doing, baby girl?"

Poppy looked up at her Nana with the biggest green puppy dog eyes Jill had ever seen. It broke her heart, and she wrapped one arm around Poppy's shoulders, drawing the small girl against her side. She felt the silent sobs, and it brought tears to her own eyes. She cradled the child, rubbing a hand up and down her arm. "It's alright, Poppy, we'll find him. I promise we'll find him."

Poppy pulled away, still clutching her father's wallet tightly in her hand. "Nana, Daddy didn't run away. The police think Daddy ran away, but he didn't. I saw it. The black cloud took him."

Her Nana nodded. "I know, sweetheart. I believe you."

"What was it?" Poppy couldn't help but wonder if the thing would come back for her, or maybe it might come for Mama or Nana or Papa, or all of them. What if it left her all alone?

She read the concern and fear on her grandmother's face as the woman shook her head. "I don't know, Poppy. I can't answer that, but we'll find out. I won't give up until we do, and we'll never stop till we find your father."

But Poppy could hear the hesitation in her voice, the lack of confidence. She trusted her Nana, but if Nana couldn't believe, neither could she. It wasn't fair. She'd just gotten her father back, and something had taken him away, something no one else had seen and no one else understood. All she wanted was her parents and for things to be normal again.

Taking a deep breath and trying to sound like a big girl, she told Nana, "I want to go home and see Mama." She watched Nana's face change, the little wrinkles by her eyes get deeper, and she wondered what was wrong. But finally, Nana nodded and said she'd go talk to the police and find out if they could leave.

Catherine couldn't move. She could hear her father-in-law talking to her in the background, could see

32

David's movements, but they didn't register. Nothing registered beyond the voices in her head.

From the moment she'd answered the phone, they hadn't stopped. She was inundated to the point of not even hearing the voice at the other end of the line. Her knees simply buckled as the cacophony in her brain took over. From time to time, blinding lights flashed in her eyes, peppered with moments of complete darkness, all the while a legion of voices screaming at her, whispering to her, in a symphony of chaos.

She wanted to scream, wanted to grab her head and shake the voices out of it. She wanted to cover her ears and pray for silence. She could do nothing but listen and try to sort out the words, try to understand what each separate voice said.

If only she could get them to stop talking on top of each other, take turns speaking. She thought for the briefest moment of Poppy, of her husband, and she knew this would drive her mad, to the point she'd never get to see her daughter grow up, to cherish Richard's return.

And that's when one of the voices popped above the others, an insistent feminine voice. *They have Richard!*

Catherine gasped, and tears welled in her eyes. She didn't know who 'they' were, but she knew 'they' weren't friendly. Amidst the raucous came a keening, wailing sound and it plagued her. She wanted to comfort the person in such horrifying pain, especially as it grew louder, closer, more intense.

It was Richard.

You must stay calm, for you are our messenger, came another voice, this one with a warmer, soothing tone. With effort, she forced the sound to stop, only vaguely registering that David had a hand on her knee. She still hadn't moved, stared straight ahead as she sat in the recliner, her eyes fixed on some distant spot as if waiting for a vision to appear.

David stared at his daughter-in-law with a sense of hopelessness. Catherine was a strong woman, had been strong for her daughter through Richard's deployment, stronger through his imprisonment. He and his wife knew she cried behind closed doors, but she stood up and did what she could to keep Poppy happy, to take care of things with a determination that Richard would return. And when he had, she'd found an inner peace again, if only briefly.

Now, he feared the worst, that losing Richard a second time, with the strength of the love and bond between them, had broken both Catherine's heart and her mind. Worse, he feared what Jill would tell him when she returned home, feared what could have become of his son. Richard was an only child, and the idea that he was gone for good was beyond comprehension to David at this point. He'd always had faith before, but something was off, and everything was slowly crumbling around him.

And Poppy…well, she was eight years old, had already lived nearly half her life without her father's presence. Richard meant everything to that child, and she'd turned to her mother in his absence. What would she do without either of them to lean on? Certainly he and Jill would care for her, raise her best they could, but it wouldn't be the same, and David worried about his granddaughter. She showed too many signs, and she'd already suffered so much trauma.

As he watched, Catherine's jaw went slack, and her eyes lost focus. Unsure what exactly was happening, he tried to draw her back to reality. "Catherine, darling, can you hear me? Poppy will be home soon, and she's going to want you to hold her." No response, not even a twitch. Dammit!

He could throw a bucket of cold water over her, manners be damned. This was a dire situation, and she'd forgive him later, if that's what it came to. She loved her child and would never have consciously chosen to disappear into some internal hell. But he couldn't bring himself to do it, not yet. He'd wait until Jill came home, with Poppy, and he'd hold his granddaughter and pray for her safety and peace, then figure out how to help Catherine.

~~~~~~~~

Jill's lower lip trembled as she tucked Poppy into her bed. The small girl slept, exhausted and traumatized by the day's events, and while Jill was glad her granddaughter was resting comfortably, she worried about the nightmares she could almost guarantee would ensue.

And she had no idea what to do with Catherine.

Seeing her mother like that, unresponsive to any stimulation at all, had caused poor Poppy to start wailing all over again. Catherine sat, mouth open, eyes staring at nothing but the breaking of her own mind within, and nothing would raise her from it. Jill couldn't stand to see her like that, and it was unhealthy for Poppy as well.

"We can't keep her here like this," she whispered to her husband as she entered the other room and joined David in watching the woman. "It's only going to hurt Poppy more."

David wrapped an arm around his wife's shoulders, trying to comfort her with a sense of hope he didn't feel. "I think she'll come out of it. Let's give her some time."

Jill frowned. "How much time? David, we have to find out what happened to Richard, and we have an eight-year-old girl who has no parents. What time do we have to take care of Catherine? She needs to be here for her child, for her husband. I hate to see her like this. It makes my chest ache, and I don't want to send her away. But by all that is holy, we have to do our duty, and if she doesn't come around soon, we'll have to get her care elsewhere."

With a resigned sigh, he nodded. He and his wife were still young, but they only had so much to give, and if they tapped their internal resources, they might be able to accomplish a number of tasks they wouldn't achieve otherwise. Still, they couldn't be everywhere at once. Jill was right, and he hated to admit it. "Alright Jill. Let's give her a few days. If she's strong enough to break out of the cage she's put herself in, we can focus on Poppy and finding Richard."

Reluctantly, Jill nodded and leaned on her husband's shoulder. She knew they had a long road ahead of them, and no clues as to which direction to start. One thing the police had right was that there wasn't a single clue, a shred of evidence, as to what had happened to Richard. Their only hope now was to pray for answers. And to keep Poppy safe.

That was Jill's greatest concern. Something inside her was terrified of the possibility that none of this was about Richard, or Catherine. None of this had anything to do with them, except for the child. She couldn't explain the dread, the feeling of a coming doom that would steal their granddaughter away, but nonetheless, she knew never to ignore such premonitions. Because that's what they were, bits of foresight, warnings about the future.

This time, she'd be diligent, and she'd be cautious. She'd listen to her gut, to her inner consciousness, and she'd keep Poppy from ever learning anything that could potentially cause her harm.

With a renewed determination, she kissed her husband. "Let's move her to her bedroom, put her to bed. We'll keep her there until she regains herself so Poppy doesn't have to see. And if she doesn't come around, I'll call to find help or a safe haven for her."

Knowing something else bothered Jill, David simply nodded, not questioning anything. He'd felt her change in attitude, heard her thinking, though what her thoughts had been didn't come across. But he didn't doubt that his wife knew something he didn't. It wouldn't be the first time she'd made a decision that had saved lives. He'd pay attention and follow her lead, until she ran out of ideas or they both ran out of steam.

~~~~~~~~~

Sitting in the dark grew tiring, and even brief trips into the light were not enough to relieve the monotony, clear the doldrums of an eternal existence below the earth. But now, he watched the man in the reflective dome as he tried to investigate his location, to discover what had just happened to him. It really was quite amusing.

The man was thorough, feeling every inch of the dome, which appeared to be formed of mirrors from his perspective, looking for a hole or a crack or crevice that would give him some clue. Even the image of the tiled floor created for this purpose was flawless, and Richard Applebaum would find no means of escape.

Soon enough, he would wear himself out and settle onto the floor, curling his knees up to his chest and wrapping his arms around them while he rested his head on top of them in utter defeat. They all did, at some point or other. It was a weakness of all species of light.

And when all hope was lost, it would be time to step in. Easier to convince Richard Applebaum to enlist in service of a different kind. Or, if he refused, this time there would be no choice between cooperation and death. This time, he would be enslaved and forced into service.

He was a necessary part of this plan. A being that had already committed the worst sin, the death of an innocent person, yet was respected and honorable. With someone like him, it would be easier to approach the others needed, the ones who would create for the Darkness a way to walk and thrive in the light. Only with a way to extend the time above ground would there ever be a means to make it further. Yes, there would be feeding for strength, giving foot and substance to the Darkness in the world of Light. Permanently.

CHAPTER 3

August, 2011

Poppy sat next to her mother on the sofa, making sure that, despite her lack of communication, Mama ate her lunch. She didn't pretend to understand the catatonic condition. After all, she had her own pain at the loss of her father, but she'd never given up hope. She resented her mother's absence, felt like Mama had given up the day he'd disappeared. Still, Poppy had done her duty to the best of her ability to help care for her mother, not willing to see her put into a home, as Nana had suggested more than once.

The news played in the background, more noise than anything, as Poppy ate her sandwich and crunched her chips. She watched the images flicker on the screen, glancing at her mother from time to time, wondering if the older woman saw or comprehended anything. Poppy may not be the most talkative person these days, but she couldn't imagine being completely silent for five years, never focused, unable to enjoy anything.

Did Mama even realize within her private little world that they were celebrating her thirteenth birthday today? Doubtful.

Angry, she stood and walked away, pacing in the kitchen as Nana peeled potatoes to roast for dinner. Where was her father when she needed him? More to the point, why had he abandoned them? "It's your fault Mama's like this."

"What are you talking about?" Nana's tone was sharp, and Poppy looked up with a start, not realizing she'd spoken out loud. Putting down her tools and the potato in her hand, Jill turned to face her granddaughter, leaning back against the counter and crossing her arms. "Who gets the blame for the way things are?"

Poppy felt years of rage and pain well up inside her as she faced Nana. "It's Dad's fault! You know, he disappeared on us almost before he came home, and the day he disappeared Mama lost it. If he hadn't run out on us, she wouldn't be like this!"

Jill glowered at Poppy. "Since when do you believe your father ran off? Weren't you the one who refused to believe that before anyone else? Weren't you the one who saw what happened?"

"And who's to say I didn't imagine the whole thing? I was little, Nana! And no one else believes me. Why should I be any different?" The police had stopped their investigation years ago, and she hadn't seen her grandparents make any recent efforts to find out what happened. She was starting to feel like she'd truly made it all up because she didn't want to believe Daddy would leave by choice. "Look what all this has done to Mama. I can't even talk to her, Nana."

"That doesn't make it your father's fault. You more than anyone, Poppy, should know better than that. What does your gut tell you? Does it tell you he ran out on you and your mother? Would he really do that after fighting to stay alive while he was tortured to a degree that causes most people insanity?" Jill's emotions were getting the best of her as her voice shook and elevated in volume.

Still, Poppy stood her ground, gritting her teeth. "So? Maybe that's why he left. Maybe it did drive him insane."

But Jill shook her head. "That's not possible Poppy. He was the same man he had always been, and that's faithful and loyal. You saw what happened. You've told me many times. I believe you, and so does your Papa. We haven't given up. We're just out of leads right now." She moved toward Poppy, who was barely holding back from another outburst. "Listen to me. You can't blame your father for your mother's condition, and you certainly can't blame him for his disappearance. Ask your heart, Poppy. It knows the truth just as much as your mind and your eyes."

She wanted to believe, and she knew it was wrong to push blame on someone who wasn't even around to defend himself. But Poppy couldn't stand it anymore. "I just want one of my parents, Nana. Why does the world have to be so unfair?"

Hugging her granddaughter close, Jill squeezed her eyes shut and sighed. "That's just the way of things. If God meant for it to be easy, he wouldn't have given us free will, he would have just made us all the same."

Poppy stiffened. Nana rarely mentioned God anymore, but when she did, a bolt of lightning shot through Poppy, energizing her. She didn't know why, considering she had trouble with blind faith, which is the only way it was possible to believe in a higher being. And yet, there was something familiar about the idea that was both soothing and invigorating.

Feeling chastised and contrite, Poppy pulled away from her grandmother. "I guess you're right, Nana. I best go check on Mama, make sure she's eating." The older woman released her, and she returned to the living room, finding her mother's plate laying empty in her lap. She picked it up and started to take it to the kitchen when the news story caught her attention. She turned to watch and listen carefully.

"Police aren't giving many details, but it appears this is the second crucifixion murder in the last three months. If they aren't connected, it's entirely possible there is a copycat killer out there. Sources say both victims were avid churchgoers, and neither had any particular enemies that friends or neighbors were aware of. There are no witnesses coming forward, but police do urge anyone who may have useful information to call them."

Poppy remembered the first news story, and just like last time, she felt sick at her stomach over the murder. Who could do such a thing, and who would create such a religiously charged crime scene? It would seem like an attack on the church, but as she listened more closely, the two victims didn't even practice the same Christian religion. It was a gross act, whatever the reason, and Poppy turned down the volume, unable to stomach any more of the story.

As she pushed the button, she thought she heard her mother gasp, but as she looked at Mama, she saw no sign at all of a reaction, no movement whatsoever, and she put it down to wishful thinking. As she'd originally intended, she carried the dishes to the kitchen and washed them before drying them and putting them away. She had a routine, and regardless of today's date, she would follow that routine. And when they celebrated her birthday, she would try one more time to use the occasion to rip Mama from whatever black hole she lived in these days.

But something didn't sit right, and she couldn't quite place it. Reaching for the remote, she turned up the volume and ran the story back, pausing it at the start of the segment. "Nana, come here for a minute," she called.

She waited until her grandmother reached the archway between the kitchen and the living room. "Watch this." She pressed play and ran through the story again. She watched Nana more closely than the news, glancing at her mother as well to see if either of them had any reaction to what was said. Mama didn't move, her breathing not even changing, but Nana's face contorted, lines drawing across it and making her suddenly look older than her56 years.

Poppy narrowed her eyes. "What is it, Nana?"

Her grandmother turned to her with sudden, jerky movements, and she pasted a smile on her face, but Poppy could see through it, see fear somewhere beneath the façade. "Nothing, dear. It's just heinous, that's all. It's blasphemy, and it hurts my heart." She closed the distance between them, laying a hand – which Poppy noticed shook – on her shoulder. "Are you alright? What's on your mind, sweetheart?"

To her consternation, Poppy couldn't explain it. "Just a feeling, Nana. I don't understand it, but it feels like this is just the beginning, like it's going to continue."

"Well, if this is a serial killer, by all means, it's possible it's going to continue."

"It happened here, Nana, in our county." She shook her head, unable to describe her uneasiness. "Something about it feels familiar, and I don't know why."

Nana offered her a sympathetic look. "You're making it personal, Poppy. This kind of thing – killing someone by crucifixion – it's pure evil, and that's going to burn your soul because you're a clean, caring individual. But you can't personalize it. You can't make it your business." She held out her other hand. "Give me the remote, Poppy. Let's find something entertaining to watch that will take our minds off how sick the world is today."

Reluctantly, she handed over the control, but watching a sitcom did nothing to settle her anxiety. She tried to reconcile her issues, tried to decide if it had something to do with a book she'd read or a lesson in school, but nothing equated. Finally, she gave up thinking about it and simply sat; mirroring her mother's blank stare, barely processing what was on the screen. And when she tired of that, she went to her room to read. At least it was a distraction.

In the kitchen, Jill ran a hand over her face, turning to the ceiling with wide, frightened eyes. In the quietest whisper, she prayed for the souls of those who'd been so brutally murdered, souls she recognized as more than just regular people.

Something stirred, something evil, and she had to keep Poppy out of it. She would talk to David when he came back from working the crops, and they would look more closely into the murders Poppy suddenly seemed obsessed with. She was a smart girl, and it would take careful attention and sheltering to keep her from finding the truth.

~~~~~~~~

A single voice crept through the fog of many, and Catherine whimpered at the implications of the words.

"Souls are eaten, feeding strength, giving foot and substance to the Darkness"

If only she could share what she heard, Catherine thought. She'd been able to form her own clear mental patterns recently, but she couldn't voice them, still couldn't even control her own body. Every so often, her eyes would search the room, take in the view of her daughter, of her precious Poppy who assumed she'd lost both of her parents, and Catherine would nearly cry. But as she channeled these voices through her, she couldn't even shed a tear.

When she was able, she prayed that she not be forsaken, that she regains her senses and control of her own body. But every time she prayed for such help, she only heard more voices, louder, more insistent. And then she screamed internally at the irony and unfairness of life.

In a rare moment, she'd been in a semblance of silence, the sounds of men and women surrounding her no more than whispers, when the story of the crucifixions aired, and it

47

had wounded her. But what was more devastating was that it seemed to ignite a fire under the residents of her mind, and they began screaming until she developed a migraine from their continuous prodding. And finally, the one voice, a deep, resonating baritone, broke through the pleading crowd and all the wailing that had ensued, sending her the message.

"Souls are eaten, feeding strength, giving foot and substance to the Darkness"

The Darkness. The words themselves brought to her mind a blinding light, and then veils lowered over her eyes and a scenario played out in her mind. Richard stood, alone, surrounded by a black mist that enveloped him completely. It grew thicker and denser until she could see and hear nothing from him, and still she knew he screamed as he disappeared.

When the cloud dissipated, Richard was gone, and in his place stood her little Poppy, hugging his wallet with tears of blood falling down her face.

As if that wasn't torturous enough, she saw a beautiful young woman with Poppy's emerald green eyes, running from some unseen threat, a black mist surrounding her and clinging to her skin as she screamed for help. Her raven locks flew behind her as she raced against an enemy she couldn't escape, and the cloud thickened and ate her, as well. As she was taken, a deep, evil laugh rang out, shaking the ground and the buildings and the entire world with its force, and the sun disappeared.

Catherine tried to fight, tried to free herself from the chains that held her locked in place and allowed her no escape. But she couldn't breathe, couldn't lift a finger, and couldn't make a sound to catch anyone's attention. She needed to get free, needed to warn someone. This wasn't just a dream, wasn't just a manifestation of fear.

It was a vision. A premonition.

And suddenly, she knew why.

Resigning herself to her fate, she began, for the first time since she'd fallen into this virtual tomb, to listen to the voices, to really strain to try to make sense of it all. They were sending warnings, giving her important information, and she was determined to use what she could to assure her daughter wouldn't face the terror she'd just foreseen. She would get the full message, and then she would break free.

October, 2012

Poppy and her friend, Megan, giggled as the sitcom ended. In a rare move, Papa had agreed that Poppy could have a friend over to do homework together. They'd finished their schoolwork early, and with a quiet plea to have Megan stay for dinner before they drove her home,

Nana had reluctantly agreed. So, they'd popped some popcorn in the microwave and curled up on the couch to watch television.

As the show ended, a preview of the evening's top news stories teased viewers, and the reporter instantly had Poppy's attention. "A new victim, over a year after the last, has been found crucified in his home. Is this confirmation of a serial killer in our midst? More in just a few minutes."

"Whoa, that's so creepy," Megan commented, but Poppy held up her hand and shushed her friend, turning up the sound and sitting forward with rapt attention. She'd been waiting for this, and while she'd let her uneasiness fade with lack of new information, it jumped right back to the surface at this announcement.

She waited anxiously for the introductions, and the newscaster didn't disappoint as the lead story broke. "Felix Anderson of Bexar County was found murdered in his home this morning. Investigators say his neighbor hadn't seen him in three days, which was highly unusual, as they left for work at the same time every morning. Fearing Anderson was ill, his neighbor, who has asked that his name not be released, went to check on Anderson, only to find the door ajar. Inside, Anderson was crucified, his body nailed to a cross that had been formed on the wall.

"It's been fourteen months since the last crucifixion murder was discovered, and authorities say they are not yet ready to treat this as a serial murder investigation, as they have as yet not found any connection between the three victims. The first victim, Angela Radcliff, was found in April of last year, and Damon Frederick the following August. Aside from all the victims being residents of Bexar County, no other characteristics seem to form a pattern.

"However, due to the severe nature of these crimes and the threat of a murderer on the loose, the police do suggest county residents take extra care to protect themselves and assure that all doors and windows are locked at all times."

"Oh my god," Megan breathed.

Poppy nodded but didn't offer any other response, her mind spinning a million miles an hour. She didn't care what the authorities said. This was obviously the work of a serial killer, and it was very close to home. This was no coincidence, and it didn't matter how much they tried to lie or deny the truth to soothe the worry of the public. Nothing was going to hide the fact that a murderer was on the loose and was killing people on the cross.

That familiar unease crawled up Poppy's spine, and she recognized it this time. It was the same feeling of dread that had overwhelmed her the day her father disappeared. Somehow, it was all connected, and even though it had been over a year since the last murder, she clearly remembered her grandmother's reaction. Nana knew something, and she was trying to hide it from Poppy.

But why?

"I thought you were watching a show." Her grandmother's voice behind her made both girls jump as if they'd been caught like a child with their hands in the cookie jar. Turning to look at Nana, she saw the same drawn expression on her face and wondered just how long Nana had been standing there.

"We were," Megan told her with wide eyes. "The show just ended and the news came on. We were going to change the channel and look for something else, but then the news about the murder came on…" She trailed off, obviously shocked by what she'd heard.

Poppy ignored her, focused on Nana. She didn't speak, and neither did her grandmother for a long moment. Finally, Nana broke the silence. "Dinner will be ready in just a few minutes. Why don't you two young ladies help get Mama into the kitchen?"

The curt tone wasn't lost on Poppy. It wasn't Nana's angry voice. It was the tone she used when Poppy was hurt or sick, when something worried her. Narrowing her eyes, Poppy nodded and stood, excusing herself to go to her mother's room and help the woman across the house. Poppy had the feeling her grandmother would be watching closely, but somehow, some way, she was going to discover what it was about this string of murders that affected her grandmother so negatively.

Don't take it personally, Nana had said. It was hypocritical, really, when Nana took the whole thing to heart herself. Yes, this was definitely closer to home than even Poppy had guessed, and she was going to find the connection. Deep down, she knew it was related to her father's disappearance. She just had to find the means to prove it.

~~~~~~~

"No one's talking, Jill." David watched helplessly as his frantic wife paced back and forth in their bedroom. The house was quiet, everyone already in bed except the two of them, and they spoke in hushed, harsh voices in the midst of a heated argument.

"You're not trying very hard, then," Jill snapped, rubbing her forehead. "Someone must know something, and it's our job to protect each other. If they aren't talking, it's out of fear, which only makes it more vital. We have to find out what's going on, or there's no way we can protect Poppy."

David sighed. Honestly, everyone feared the news, and Jill had a point. But there was little he could do about it. He couldn't force anyone to tell him anything. "You know, Jill, Poppy is fourteen years old. She's ridiculously intelligent, and she's strong. And I guarantee you that those are the two biggest reasons she's so close to the truth. Maybe it would be better just to tell her."

Jill stopped moving and glared at her husband as if he had three heads, horrified. "Why on earth would you say such a thing? The less she knows the less of a target she is. And she has enough burdens without us placing anything else on her shoulders."

Frustrated now, David crossed his arms over his chest. "And what happens when she learns something on her own? Or maybe she gets attacked, heaven forbid. At least if we tell her, she'll be prepared for the worst and can take care of herself. If she were to get struck blindsided..." He trailed off, hoping he'd made his point.

But Jill just pursed her lips. "No, David, it's too dangerous. We have to keep her tucked away from all of it. No one has a reason to come after her if she's ignorant. And if they do, we'll protect her."

David knew quite well they couldn't guard Poppy 24/7. They couldn't follow her through school, and they couldn't deny her a life with her friends out of fear. But it was senseless arguing right now. David could only hope that his wife would eventually come around and realize what a mistake she was making. In the meantime, he'd take the steps necessary to prepare for the worst, with or without her help. "Fine. We'll do it your way. On two conditions. First, if by chance someone comes for her, we tell her the truth. And second, if things get worse here, we send her away to somewhere safe."

He could see Jill starting to protest, so he held up his hand. "Right now, it's confined. There are no reports like this anywhere else in the country. If we sent her away to school, she'd be safe."

Reluctantly, Jill agreed. She and David had always been equal partners in such decisions, and she already felt guilty for making demands. But it already seemed like Poppy found too much interest in the murders, and Jill intended to stop that obsession before it brought her granddaughter into grave danger.

November 2012

In a mad rush, Poppy ran from the convenience store, newspaper in hand, all the way back to Primrose, too excited to even care if she got in trouble for being in town alone. She'd been using Megan as a cover for awhile now, and typically, Megan was there. But after failing a math test, her friend was grounded for the next week, and Poppy still had investigating to do.

And today was her lucky day.

She flew into the farmhouse, waving the paper madly as she found Nana vacuuming the living room. "I knew it!" she cried triumphantly.

Nana looked up, startled, and turned off the loud machine. "Knew what, sweetheart?"

Even the suspicion in Nana's voice couldn't curb her enthusiasm. "It's all related, Nana. All the way back to Daddy." She spread the paper wide in front of her face, showing the headline reading, "The Crucifixion Killer: With A Fourth Victim, Police No Longer Deny The Connection".

Her grandmother sighed and shook her head. "Poppy, I can see the relationship in these horrible crimes. But what does that have to do with your father?"

Determined not to be shoot down again, she turned the paper around and found the paragraph she was looking for. She read out loud, "'Around noon on Tuesday, one witness reports having seen a black mist or vapor surrounding the house of victim Louise Stratton. Afraid the substance could be smoke and Ms. Stratton caught in a fire, the witness called 9-1-1. By the time authorities arrived, there was no sign of the alleged substance, but Ms. Stratton was found dead, crucified in her back yard. Investigators will search the house for signs of a leak or other means of producing the cloud-like mist seen by the witness as they look for signs of forced entry and clues as to who the serial killer is.'"

She tossed the paper on the coffee table and stared at her grandmother. "Now we have the Crucifixion Killer, and a sighting of the black cloud, all at the same crime scene. How are you going to tell me it's not related?"

Now, Poppy could sense real terror in her grandmother, though she tried to play it off. "Really, Poppy, it could have been a mistake. Or maybe the poor woman was just doing laundry and her dryer was making the smoke."

"That's white, Nana. I've seen it before. You only get black smoke from rubber or a very hot carbon fuelled fire, of which in this story there is no mention of a fire."

"Alright, I didn't want to have to do this, but I can see I have no choice." Nana strode over and picked up the paper. "I don't want you reading or hearing or watching or talking about this serial killer anymore. It's obviously unhealthy for you. Whatever happened here is unrelated to your father. He didn't die, he disappeared. He wasn't crucified, thank the lord. And none of this is any of your concern. I've asked you before, now I'm telling you. Let it go, or you'll be grounded for the rest of the school year."

Enraged, Poppy stormed out of the room and to her mother's bedroom, trying not to cry in her frustration. She threw herself at Mama, wrapping her arms around the woman like she did only when she was desperate. "Mama, please...I know you'd back me up in this. I know you'd take my side. I need you, Mama. I found a clue, and for some reason, Nana and Papa don't want me to find Daddy. Why can't they just support me?"

For such an independent, smart, almost-fifteen-year-old, Poppy suddenly felt like she was eight again, crying for her father, sobbing for the loss of a mother who was still here in front of her, only not able to form intelligent sentences. All she could muster was the energy to beg. Her spirit felt like it was breaking. She'd held on for so long, and now that something tangible appeared, she was being stunted by her own family. It wasn't right.

Of course, Mama didn't even turn her gaze from staring absently out the window. She didn't move or speak, and she didn't look at her daughter. Again defeated, Poppy followed her gaze out the window and caught sight of Webber, their old horse. She hadn't paid him much attention lately, and he could probably use a good brushing. And spending time with Webber would help calm Poppy.

Kissing her mother's cheek, she crawled off the bed and headed out to the tack room for grooming supplies. She brought them to where Webber stood grazing in a satchel on her side and greeted the horse with a pat on the nose. "Hey, boy, how you been?"

He snorted at her and nuzzled her head, making her smile as she started brushing him. And the longer she worked, the more she thought until she knew a way she could get around the rules, if she was careful. After all, she didn't have to read about the murders themselves. And she didn't have to actively hear about them when she would catch bits and pieces about them in the halls at school.

And she already had the names of the first four victims.

No, she didn't need to disobey her grandmother to continue looking for pieces of the puzzle. There were plenty of other ways to get information, and plenty of resources she could tap to get what she needed. She'd start by grabbing Megan in the morning and enlightening her cohort to the new, improved plan of action.

CHAPTER 4

January 2013

Poppy slammed the drawer full of clothes and glared at the barren walls surrounding her. She slumped onto the bed, arms crossed over her chest and brows drawn angrily together. Her roommate raised an amused eyebrow at her over the top of the book in which Poppy had assumed she was absorbed during the little tantrum. "I take it boarding school wasn't your choice."

It was Poppy's turn to raise an eyebrow. "Was it yours?"

The other girl laughed, but Poppy could hear the sarcasm behind it. "It never is. The kids who want to escape home are either oppressed or poor." She closed her book and put it down, turning to face Poppy fully. "My Mama says she can't handle me alone, and since my dad died last year, she sent me away with Grandpa's money."

Poppy grimaced. Maybe her situation wasn't so bad. "My grandparents sent me here because they seem to think I have an unhealthy obsession with the local serial killer. They wanted me to have a 'safe distance' from it." She made air quotes and rolled her eyes. "I'm Poppy, by the way."

"Abigail. You can call me Abby." She shrugged. "So, what you're telling me is that you were poking around about something, and your grandparents didn't like it. So, now you're here, far from where your grandparents can keep track of what you're doing. How is that not an improvement?"

Considering Abby's words, Poppy had to admit that, technically, she had more freedom here where she wasn't under Nana's watchful eyes. But she knew very well that, at this distance from her home, she wouldn't have access to the same information, and if they were allowed internet access at this school, it would be limited. She doubted she'd be able to access news feeds or any kind of restricted documentation.

She'd been so close.

Her research consisted of pulling every public file she could find on the four victims, including their birth certificates, school documents and diplomas, colleges attended and academic achievements, community activities, religious affiliations, and even some information on hobbies and clubs they were part of. She had just organized all the information to cross reference when she made the nasty mistake of not locking down her laptop before going out for a ride.

Of course, Nana had run across her little project and had freaked out. Apparently, it didn't matter that Poppy was a fifteen-year-old girl who could take care of herself. She was putting herself in grave danger. By researching victims of a crime? How? She wasn't actually taking any kind of action.

Still, it was trouble, and Nana insisted to Papa that it was time to get her away from the unhealthy habit and send her someplace safe, away from these murders and her morbid curiosity. So here she sat, in a tiny little dormitory at a boarding school in Seattle, which obviously catered to troubled teens through high school.

Dammit, she wasn't troubled, except for the trouble Nana gave her! Poppy just wanted the truth, and she was going to grasp onto any little lead she found, even now. But she didn't delude herself into thinking she would actually have the freedom Abby suggested. No, Nana would find a way to keep Poppy under her thumb, even from 2500 miles away. Scowling, she muttered, "Nana didn't used to be so controlling. I don't know what's gotten into her lately."

"She got old," Abby answered, uninvited, as she picked up the book again. "Don't worry; she'll be nicer now that you're at a distance. And it's really not that bad here. The food's good, we get to go on trips downtown to shop and stuff sometimes. In some ways, it's better than public high school, I think."

Poppy wasn't so sure. She wanted to be with her mother, and she wanted to look for her father. Something told her she'd never find him in this place, almost a foreign country compared to her home. She already missed Webber and couldn't imagine not having a horse at her disposal when she needed to clear her head.

"So, if you want, we can go to the deli around the corner and get some lunch." Abby seemed to be trying to cheer her up, and Poppy appreciated the effort. She reached into her wallet and pulled out the prepaid Visa card Papa had given her. She'd have $100 a week in allowance for miscellaneous things, so it wasn't like getting lunch would be a hardship.

"Sure," she agreed, and the girls went down, signing for a pass to go to the deli. Abby explained how that worked, and that if they didn't return promptly, they'd be in a world of trouble. Maybe they would have some freedom here after all.

By the time they got back up to their room with their sandwiches and chips, Poppy decided that, if nothing else, she at least liked her roommate. Abby was chatty, a little sarcastic, and had a sense of humor. If she had to share a tiny space with a stranger and hope for the best in terms of making friends, she couldn't ask for anything more. It would help her settle in better. After all, she had four long years to spend in this place, and she might as well make the best of it.

To her surprise, Poppy found she enjoyed the classes at the boarding school. At the public schools she'd attended so far, she'd been incredibly bored and felt like things moved at a snail's pace. Here, she had plenty of work to do, and the lessons were actually somewhat of a challenge that made her think. She figured the idea was to keep the girls occupied, so they wouldn't get into trouble. After all, several of the students had behavioral issues, and the structured environment and tough curriculum were either punishment or rehab for them.

For Poppy, it was like learning to live. She didn't realize how caught up she'd been in her home life and the tragedies she'd suffered. Here, she found excitement and caught herself smiling more, being more open with people. And she barely thought about the serial murders or the information she still sought. When it did come to mind, she was typically in the middle of something else that seemed more important, whether that was soccer practice, writing a paper, a math assignment, or reading her history homework. She'd tell herself she'd find time for her investigation later and set the thoughts aside.

In December, the entire class made a trip to Pioneer Square to see the decorations in the park, and then they traveled down to Pike's Market and broke up into small groups so they could shop for Christmas gifts to send to loved ones. She found a beautiful hand-carved wooden angel brooch for Nana, a tooled leather belt for Papa, and a knitted shawl for Mama. While she was at it, she grabbed a leather-bound notebook for Abby, who seemed to journal a lot. She'd been saving back some of her allowance every week, which gave her plenty of cash to play with for the season.

They stopped by the Crumpet Shop before they left, then climbed on the bus and headed back to the school, most of the girls jabbering about the experience. Poppy, however, grew silent, remembering Christmas as a child, with her mother and father. The holiday had lost some of its sparkle over the last few years, and she often reminisced to the point of dragging herself down.

She didn't want to feel that way this year, but this would be the first time since coming to Seattle that she'd had any real down time, and she couldn't help the negative thoughts swirling around her head. It brought her back to her research, and she decided she just might make use of the free time to finally work toward finding a common link between the murder victims that she could also trace back to her father. For all she knew, in the last four months, there could have been another one.

"You okay?" Abby asked beside her, nudging her with an elbow.

Poppy gave her a smile she knew didn't quite reach her eyes. "I'm fine, just a little homesick."

"That's pretty common this time of year, especially for first-timers. It gets easier." She put on a bright smile. "And the good news is, we're in it together. Mama doesn't visit, and I'm not going home for the holidays, either. We can have Christmas together."

That brightened the prospects significantly for Poppy. She'd have a friend, and just maybe, she could wrap Abby into her little investigation and have a partner in crime. Feeling a little better, she returned a genuine smile. "Sounds like a good plan to me."

~~~~~~~

Only burning torches illuminated the deep caverns. Any life calling it home had long since vacated when it had been altered into a haven of terror. It provided the perfect combination of discreet protection and easy access to the world above. So far, it had worked, and great success and accomplishment came from diligent efforts. He was so close to his goal being able to unleash his evil, vile plan, to walk the plains of the Earth and attack the Heavens above. Still, the key to the locked door eluded the hunters, and frustration grew.

Stalking in the Darkness, he was surrounded by his *Legion*, wanting nothing more than to unleash his reign of terror, proving his worth to those that had failed before him. His stench so disgusting even the strongest of stomachs would heave violently. Seribulous raised an eyebrow as he looked down at the nameless servant who lay prostrate before him with a modicum of interest. He yawned and crossed his arms over his broad chest. "Have you news for me?" His deep voice rattled among the crystal formations in the cavern, echoing and booming with power.

Raising little more than his eyes, the servant replied in a weak voice, "Y-yes, my lord."

Seribulous snarled, his jaw full of razor sharp teeth glowing in the dim light and causing the servant to cower even more. He despised weakness, and he wouldn't suffer a servant who was frightened by his own shadow. "Stand up, you fool," he hissed, narrowing his black eyes at the kneeling figure. "Show a backbone or face the consequences." To emphasize his point, he swirled his finger in the air as if stirring a cup of coffee, creating a small black cloud.

The servant's eyes widened and he was instantly on his feet. Content with the reaction, Seribulous offered what he thought might be an inviting smile but actually screwed up his face in such a way that he seemed even more monstrous, with his leathery skin, obsidian spikes on his skull, and pointed chin. He could easily take any form, beast or being, but there was no need to waste the energy, especially when his natural form intimidated his subjects ever so much more. "Tell me."

With a quick nod, the servant began. "The concentration of energy pulse has diminished here, but we are still tracking two families that are promising, as well as following leads on several more in other areas of the country."

A low, rumbling growl came from Seribulous's chest. "You call that news? Perhaps you are unaware of the meaning of the term."

"My lord, there is more." The sniveling idiot was now desperate for approval, and Seribulous basked in his fear. "There is a farm in the area where we can confirm at least two generations. It is well masked, but we found it, and we simply need to find a way in."

Second generation could possibly fulfill his needs. Thinking it over, Seribulous considered what might lie within the confines of the grounds. After all, his targets could be lying in wait with some type of bait to draw them in. Thus far, the enemy had not been prepared, but he could sense the shift in the atmosphere, the change in the energy, and he knew that would no longer work in his favor.

In the end, he asked, "Do you know the origin of the blood line? Or at least have a family name?"

Eager to please, the servant nodded. Yes, my lord, the family goes by the name of Applebaum."

In a shocked silence, Seribulous stared at the servant before him for a long time. And then, he began to laugh, a sick, choking sound at first, then a hiss escaping through the knives that were his teeth, and finally out loud with such volume that several of the stalactites fell from the roof of the cavern. This was almost too good to be true. Calming enough to address his servant, he asked, "Have you spoken to anyone else of this?"

He shook his head. "No, Dark Lord, I only share information with you, unless otherwise directed."

"Excellent. I had a mind to end your existence, but it seems you have redeemed yourself with some very valid information." The servant stood there, wringing his hands, which irritated Seribulous, and he bellowed, "Dismissed!" The beast scrambled away, and Seribulous chuckled. He enjoyed his affect on others; it fed his ego, which only made him stronger and more confident in his other pursuits.

With a sinister smile, he sent out a thought that reverberated through the network of caverns, the piercing vibrations making several of his servants cover their ears in agony. But he sought only one with his singular beckoning. "Richard!"

~~~~~~~~

CHAPTER 5

"Are you sure we did the right thing?" Jill worried her hands, twisting them and fiddling with her fingers, a worried look on her face. She stood in the kitchen, beside the sink, with David still seated at the table, sipping coffee and eating a slice of pecan pie.

He raised an eyebrow at her over his cup. "You were the one who felt Poppy would be better off away from here. You made every argument that she'd be safer if she was far away."

"I seem to recall you making it one of your conditions. If things got worse we were to move her out of danger, that's what you said. I just agreed with you."

Jill pursed her lips. Of course she had agreed. She knew of the danger more than anyone. The number of crucifixions in the area was steadily increasing, and there were few reports from anywhere outside of Texas. It seemed the heart of the problem was here, in their area, and Poppy's interest was too strong. She was going to get herself in trouble.

"I just think that, at school in Seattle, she'll be distracted. And it puts her away from the majority of the issues going on." She shook her head. "But I have this sense of dread, like she can't outrun this mess, no matter how hard we try. And being so far away, she doesn't have any kind of protection like we could give her."

David rubbed his eyes with forefinger and thumb. "Jill, you had two choices, according to your reasoning. You could send Poppy away, to somewhere you felt she'd be safer, or you could put Catherine in a home, where someone else could take over her care, and put Poppy on what equates to house arrest. That second option would have done nothing other than upset everything in Poppy's life and make her hate us. By sending her to Seattle, we've given her a life and a lot more freedom than she's ever had here. You do realize she'd stopped making friends and started spending all her time taking care of her mother and watching for new murders? She needed to be removed from the situation or she would have found out."

Jill was well aware of the poor quality of life Poppy led. It was what had cemented her decision. Of course, she'd requested David's opinion and approval, but he'd passed on making the final choice, leaving it on Jill's shoulders. And it was probably for the better, even though Poppy probably hated her, and Catherine would be angry beyond words, if she even knew what was going on.

But something still felt wrong. Jill knew the epidemic would spread, and with Catherine keeping her hands full at all times, Jill couldn't investigate the source of the murders closely enough to discover anything of consequence. There was evil afoot, and that's as much as anyone knew.

With a sigh, she reached for her husband's empty dishes, rinsing and washing them by hand, something she did to keep herself occupied and give her hands something productive to do. "Can't you just tell me everything is going to be alright, David?"

Standing, he moved up behind his wife and ran his hands up and down her arms comfortingly. "I could, but you would tell me I was a fool to believe that. Something's wrong, Jill, and we both know it. We just have to hold on, hope for the best, and take every development in stride. And we have to keep up hope that this will all end without anyone else getting hurt."

~~~~~~

A piercing pain shot through Catherine's chest, and she gasped as it took her breath away. She wanted to reach out to someone, to ask for help or comfort or a doctor. But she still couldn't communicate. She could hear all the words in the world, feel someone else's pain, but she couldn't speak, and she couldn't fix herself.

The stabbing pain dulled slightly but left an ache behind, as if someone were squeezing her heart, and her husband's name screamed through her mind. Richard!

He was alive. She knew it in her heart, and he was hurting. Where was he, though? She had no way to find him, no way to rescue him from whatever plagued him. He was trapped, with no way to escape. Another voice spoke, loud and clear.

"Richard supplies the connection. Richard is the trust and the heart of the Darkness, whether by will or by force. He must be stopped."

What in the name of God did that mean?

Jill handed her a bowl and a spoon. It must be some mealtime or other. Which she didn't know, and at the moment, didn't care. Food was the furthest thing from her mind. She willed her arms to cooperate as she attempted to throw the food across the room, just to grab the attention that had long since vanished.

No one expected anything of her anymore. They just went through the motions, being sure she was cleaned and fed, that she slept and got out of bed in the morning. If only she could find a way to get these messages across, to share the knowledge that had been imparted onto her. She'd been chosen, and she had a duty to do. It was unfair she found herself unable to do it, unable to function beyond the most basic of motions. The most she had moved in years was when her body allowed her to raise a fork to her mouth to feed. That's wasn't everyday though. She longed to be normal again.

At least Poppy had still spoken to her, held regular conversations as if Catherine could talk back to her daughter. But she was gone, sent away. For her own protection, Jill said. To keep her safe, David muttered. Didn't they realize this was the safest place she could possibly be? Here, at Primrose, where they had strength in numbers? Wherever she was, Poppy was alone, and that was the most dangerous place of all.

With every ounce of willpower she had, Catherine sent up a plea, a prayer to anyone who was listening, that she would be released from the prison her body had become. Perhaps, if she put everything she had, every ounce of energy she possessed, someone would hear her. Someone might answer her. This time, it was vital. In her heart, she knew her daughter's life was at stake. And maybe, just maybe, in saving her daughter, she could also find and save her husband.

The hooded figure prowled in the shadows of the trees and outbuildings, careful not to cast a shadow of his own. He moved in preternatural silence as he committed the lay of the land to memory. Dim light shone from several windows of the quaint farmhouse, like knowing eyes staring him down. He sensed the prey inside, and he drew in a deep breath, enjoying the scent on the air.

He crept closer, almost slithering through the darkness, wanting to identify the sweet, pungent smell mixed in that drew and pleased him so greatly. If he didn't know any better, he'd say the aroma struck familiar. Yet, he'd never been sent to this place before. It was serene, fresh, memorable. And he had no recollection of such a place, in all his time hunting.

His eye twitched, a seizing pain blinding him on one side, and he pressed his fist to it, willing it to stop. But it continued, bringing him to his knees as it pulsed through his mind.

Previous life...not hunter...

Clips of phrases came like waves crashing over him, but it was as though the water filled his ears and leaked into his brain so he couldn't hear the rest, couldn't put together any lucid connection and meaning. Growling ferociously, he lay on the ground writhing, wishing it would stop, until the voices and the pain finally subsided.

Slowly, he gained his hands and knees, then pushed to his feet, which proved heavy as anvils as he trudged a few feet closer. He tried not to dwell on his little episode – they happened so infrequently he didn't put any stock in it. However, none of them had ever been so instant, so strong as this one, and a part of him couldn't stop thinking about it, even as he focused on this recon mission.

Staying just outside the beam of light coming through one window, he stood off to the side, looking in. He faced a kitchen, decorated in country blues and yellow and kept spotless, though it held an air of use that no amount of cleaning could remove. The wooden kitchen table was worn and slightly scratched, and the chairs, while sturdy, were a little beat up. Cozy would have been the word for it, had the term not made Richard wrinkle his nose in disgust.

Creature comforts were a weakness.

He inhaled sharply and took an instinctive step back further into the black of the night as a woman entered, tucking a strand of graying hair that had come loose from her bun behind her ear. She wore simply cotton pajamas – a sleeveless top and pants – and moved to the sink, rinsing a dish she carried. He felt a rush at the energy she held just before the pain erupted in his head again, crippling his thoughts momentarily.

But for once, he fought against it, not wanting to let the excruciating feeling play itself out. There was something trying to come through, some thought, and he knew it was vital, if he could just bear the pain long enough to grasp it. Squeezing his eyes shut, he willed the pain to shrink, imagining not destroying it but hiding it in a vile and putting a stopper in the top so it was still there but contained.

And then images began to flash on the backs of his eyelids. A boy on a swing that hung from a tree near a stable. A young man, smiling and sliding a ring onto the finger of a beautiful young woman in white. A baby, just birthed, crying wildly as it drew its first breaths of air. A man in chains, his face so bruised and bloody his face was unrecognizable. A black cloud swirling, stinging like mosquito bites from head to toe. Spiked horns like a crown above a flattened face and sharp, terrifying teeth.

The images were followed by a string of names. Mama, Dad, Jill, David, Catherine, Poppy, Seribulous.

No! No, Seribulous didn't belong in that list. As he watched the woman in the house disappear through a door he presumed – no, *knew* – led to the living room, it all made sense. In his previous life, he'd been a good person, with a family. He was a father, and he had a wife and parents. He'd been strong and healthy and hadn't lurked in the dark or lived in a cavern beneath the earth. Seribulous wasn't his family.

The woman he'd seen, her image clear in his mind, was his family. She was his mother.

And his family was Seribulous's next target.

CHAPTER 6

Poppy stood and cheered with the crowd as their team scored yet another touchdown. They were stomping all over the competition, and it was thoroughly entertaining. The night was crisp, and she was thankful for the windbreaker she'd bought last week.

"Every guy's rear should look that good in tights," Abby commented, her cheers louder than most, blasting in her ear.

Poppy giggled as she considered the tight end – no pun intended – to which Abby referred. He was a handsome guy with a great body. But just the fact that she'd traded in her worries to lead a halfway normal lifestyle by attending the Friday night high school football games was a feat. She had no interest in dating.

And as she thought that, she grimaced, sensing a disturbing presence next to her, sidling up a little too close. She wrinkled her nose as she realized Eric Vaughn had found her in the crowd yet again. "Great game, huh, Poppy?"

She shrugged, not looking at him, wanting to in no way encourage him. "Yes, it is." As few words as possible, she thought, praying fiercely he'd just go away and yet knowing better.

"You know, a couple of friends and I are going to grab some burgers after the game. You and Abby should come along. I've been dying to spend a little time with you." He sounded so anxious, so hopeful, and Poppy just hated disappointing him, despised the fact that she had no interest in him and his group of lackeys at all.

She glanced at him out of the corner of her eye. "Look, Eric, I appreciate the invitation, but I've got a lot of studying to do, and I'm already getting tired."

"We won't be out late. And if you're having any issues with any of your classes, I'd be more than happy to study with you over the weekend."

Now he was just trying too hard, and Poppy groaned internally. But before she could say anything, Abby popped her head around and faced Eric head on. "Listen, my friend here is trying to be polite, but what she really means is that we have no intention of going for burgers with you and the other idiots you hang out with. Nor will we be joining you for a party or any other date-like invitation you provide. And on top of that, you should know that, you might be the dweeb with all the brains, but I can guarantee you that Poppy doesn't need anyone's help with studying, and her GPA is probably running circles around yours. So sod off."

As she spoke, Poppy watched Eric's face turn red and his embarrassment showed in the dulling of his eyes. He was a cute boy, but again, she wasn't interested. At least she hadn't been the one to beat him down. He nodded silently and moved away, and Poppy gave Abby a bemused but withering look. "You didn't have to break his soul."

Abby shrugged. "He doesn't have a soul. He's got electrical wiring. He's nothing but a human calculator who's desperately infatuated with you, and it's sad. All I did was give him a shove into thinking about real life instead of a career as a lifelong student." She put her fingers in her mouth and whistled as the ball was intercepted. "You should be more assertive. You might do someone like him a favor."

Still shaking her head in disbelief, Poppy chuckled and returned her attention to the game. With one last jab at her friend, she said, "I bet you wouldn't have bit his head off if he was the tight end whose posterior you're so fond of."

"Damn straight!" Abby returned without missing a beat.

~~~~~~

May, 2016

Brendan O'Malley looked up as a uniform officer knocked on the open door to his closet of an office. The man's face was grim, and Brendan had an idea why. He'd heard the news on the radio as he came into the office, and he would have bet his last dollar on the reason for the visit.

"Detective O'Malley, I've been instructed to speak with you regarding this new case, brief you, and turn over the file." His voice was gravelly, and Brendan guessed he'd been at the crime scene since the wee hours of the morning, or maybe longer. He wasn't sure when the body had been discovered, but it was definitely time for this officer to be off duty.

Nodding congenially, he motioned for the man to sit down across the desk. "Sorry there's no space in here."

The officer shrugged. "It's not an issue." He held out his hand. "Officer Elliot Longmire. I was first on the scene at the crucifixion."

As he thought. With a nod, Brendan said, "Tell me what you know, Longmire."

Longmire heaved a tired breath. "Next door neighbor called in, reported that every night, around 8:30, the victim would come out and sit on the patio, drinking coffee or tea or something and sit for an hour. On Friday, around 7:30 pm, a dark cloud surrounded the victim's home, not touching anything else. The neighbor thought maybe he'd imagined it, but he didn't see the victim that night or the next two, and the victim's car didn't move from its spot, despite the fact that he should have been at work every day. So, he called us in to check on the guy."

Longmire hung his head and shook it, a profound sadness obviously overcoming him. "I reached the scene around 10:30 last night, and the front door was open. There was a rotten smell coming from the house and no response when I called to the victim, so I went inside." His breath shuddered now as he spoke. "It was right there in the living room, with flies buzzing all around. There were metal railroad stakes through his wrists and feet, pinning him to the wall, with dried streaks of blood running down. That was it, nothing else. No weapon, no fingerprints, nothing."

Brendan ground his teeth. "Do we have an approximate time and cause of death?"

Longmire swallowed as though he were trying not to puke, which told Brendan he was likely a traffic beat cop, not someone used to finding dead bodies. "Yes and no, sir. The cause of death has yet to be determined by autopsy, but the approximate time of death was between 6:00 pm and 10:00 pm Friday night."

Which is why the neighbor's testimony as a witness proved important. Brendan wondered about this supposed black cloud and figured he'd look for other instances of such sights. Perhaps this was a method of simply controlling lighting and that would help narrow down a suspect list. Regardless, Brendan had just been involved in the notorious crucifixion murders, something he'd hoped would never reach his city.

"Thank you, Officer. And listen, Longmire, feel free to let me know if anything else pops into your head that sticks out about the crime scene or the body. I know the first response officer can sometimes get a little overwhelmed at first, but I'm sure you're a good cop, which means that you'll eventually start to remember things you didn't even know you knew."

Longmire looked like he wanted to respond but hesitated. Brendan raised an eyebrow, prompting him, and finally he sputtered, "Detective, is homicide always this difficult?"

That was a tough question to answer. "Well, Longmire, I've been on homicide for four of the years I've been on the force, and I'm not going to tell you it really gets easier. What I will say is you become desensitized, which means it doesn't feel as personal. But it's almost always gruesome."

"Then I think I'm pulling my hat out of the ring."

Brendan offered him a sympathetic smile. "Homicide isn't for everyone, but then, neither is vice. But I think you have the heart for it, just not the experience. Don't discount it right away if it's what you want. I'd be happy to take you for a ride along any time, see what you really think."

With a quick nod and a handshake, Longmire stood. "Thanks, Detective. I appreciate it."He laid the file on Brendan's desk and rushed out of the office, his face a little green, and Brendan assumed he was likely going to finally get sick. Of course, it had happened to all of them at some point. Brendan had thrown up the first six cases he'd taken upon visiting the crime scene. He'd barely escaped it during the examination in the morgue a couple of times. He certainly didn't think any less of Officer Longmire.

With a sinking feeling in his stomach, he opened the file to see the full frontal image laying on top. He grimaced and ran a hand through his hair. This was definitely going to be gruesome. He flipped through the pictures, read the statement of the witness from Longmire, and thumbed through all the other preliminary information.

He'd obviously have to do a lot of research to find the similarities between this and some of the other crucifixion murders. Somehow, he got the impression that no one had cross-referenced the murders in the various locations, and he was determined to find something to crack the case wide open. And he wanted it done fast. He didn't know how much of this shit he could handle.

January 2017

Abby tossed yet another letter toward Poppy, raising an eyebrow and wearing an amused half-smile. "Dartmouth. How many acceptance letters have you gotten now? Or maybe a better question is, how many colleges and universities have you applied to?"

Poppy smirked as she tore open the notification of acceptance to Dartmouth. "I don't know, let's see." She reached into her desk draw and pulled out the file of letters, counting them one by one. Duke, North Carolina, Texas A&M, Rice, Brown, USC...

She looked up at Abby sheepishly. "I've got twelve acceptance letters here. I applied to, I don't know, maybe 25 or so?" At the ghastly look on Abby's face, she threw up her hands, exasperated. "I didn't know where I wanted to go, Abby. Should I limit myself when I can have all these options?" She spread them on the bed for Abby to see. "The worst part is, I think I've made up my mind, and the one I really want isn't here yet."

"Oh really?" Poppy didn't miss her roommate's evil grin. She hadn't lived with her best friend for nearly four years to not be able to read her now. "Maybe there's another piece of mail for you."

"Don't toy with me, Abby." Poppy's heart pounded in her chest. Abby knew very well which letter she'd been waiting for, and this was just cruel.

"I'm not. I thought you wanted to go home to Texas anyway."

Originally, that had been the plan. But over the last four years, Poppy had lost her love of the place she'd once called home. She resented being sent away, but in many ways, she felt now that it had been for the better. She'd broadened her horizons, and she'd become strong and independent. She'd also received a much better education; felt challenged, and still managed to pull of an excellent GPA that had colleges beating down her door.

But most of all, she'd fallen in love with Seattle, and she'd become a huge Huskies fan. The University of Washington was the first application she'd turned in, and she had been waiting anxiously for a response but not received it. Now, she was ready to scratch Abby's eyeballs out if she didn't turn over the damn letter.

"Relax, we both got letters from U-Dub today." She flicked her wrist, sending the letter flying at Poppy at such an odd angle she had to duck as she caught it to keep it from scratching her face. They tore into the envelopes at the same time, but Poppy hesitated to read hers, noting the look of foreboding on Abby's face as she unfolded the paper inside. Abby's grades were nothing to balk at; she'd studied with Poppy and would graduate in two months in the top 15% of the class. Still, she knew how much it meant to Abby, and the girl was terrified she wouldn't be accepted.

Waiting with baited breath, she watched Abby read her mail, and then read it again. Finally, Abby looked up at her with wide, shocked eyes. "I'm in. I got in!"

Poppy squealed and hugged her friend, beyond elated for her. It had been Abby's dream for years to get into UW, and it only excited Poppy further to think about the possibility of continuing to go to school with her best friend. With that in mind, she unfolded her own letter and read. With relief and joy, she announced, "Pack your bags, Abby! We're moving to UW!"

The two celebrated over lunch, and when they returned to the dorm, Poppy called Nana to give her the news, spewing words at lightning speed in her giddiness.

"Congratulations, Poppy. Papa and I are very proud of you." Nana sounded pleased, but there was something else in her voice Poppy couldn't quite explain.

Frowning, she asked, "Is something wrong, Nana?"

The woman was silent at the other end of the line for so long Poppy looked at her phone to make sure she hadn't lost the connection. Finally, Nana spoke in a sullen voice that carried just a hint of fear. "It's your mother. She's okay, but there's something going on with her. She's started mumbling incoherently. I don't know what she's saying, or if it's even words she's sputtering, but every time I walk by her, she grabs my arm and looks up at me like she's pleading with me to understand."

Poppy gulped. She tried to remember Mama as she'd been before Daddy disappeared, but this conversation reminded her of all the bad parts of the last ten years. Her mother hadn't spoken a word since that day, and she'd been falling further and further from health over the last couple of years. To hear this she was heartbroken.

Shaking her head, Poppy tried not to believe it, but she couldn't help thinking Mama had finally gone completely mad. Frustrated that she could never receive good news without it being tempered by negativity, she scowled. "Nana, I love Mama, but maybe it's time you put her in a home. She needs more care than you and Papa can give her, and she may even need to be medicated now."

"I can't, Poppy. I just can't do that to her." She heard the defeat in Nana's voice, and it broke her heart for a second time.

With a sinking feeling, she said, "I also got an acceptance letter to Texas A&M. it's not next door, but it's a short drive away. I could go there and be close, help you out."

"I won't allow that, Poppy." Now, the stubborn woman she knew replaced the hopeless voice on the other end of the line. "You have a life to live, and I won't see you put your dreams aside for this. Your Papa and I are old enough to have lived our lives. You're just beginning. I want you to have every opportunity, and if you don't go to the school of your choice, you'll never be happy."

An overwhelming guilt drew the muscles in Poppy's stomach into knots. She desperately wanted her freedom. She'd been through so much as a child, had helped care for her mother before she'd been sent away, and then had been forced from her home in the name of saving her from her meddlesome behavior. But didn't she owe it to her family to be there for them?

"I won't argue with you on this, Poppy. You'll go to the school of your choice." Nana said it with finality, and Poppy knew better than to retort. "I love you, Poppy. Be sure to call back when Papa's home to give him the news. He'll be just as proud as I am."

She said goodbye and hung up, feeling down, but with the boisterousness of Abby's excitement, it didn't last long, and she was soon busy planning for the future.

~~~~~~~

As Jill hung up the phone and turned toward the front door, she jumped, having not expected her husband to be standing in the doorway. "David! You scared me. I didn't think you would be home for another hour."

His face was grim, and he looked tired. "Sorry, Jill. Who was that?"

"It was Poppy. She's been accepted to the University of Washington and couldn't be happier. I think we made the right decision, sending her to Seattle." David nodded in agreement but didn't smile, as if something weighed so heavily on him it dragged him down into the ground.

There was a long pause then taking a deep breath and bracing herself for the answer, Jill asked, "All of them?"

Gravely, David nodded. "Every last one of them. And more than we thought, too. It's spread, Jill, and it's happening everywhere. I don't think they have a bead on Poppy yet, but it'll happen eventually."

Jill's lower lip quivered, and her heart ached. "How many?"

David shook his head. "Too many. Dozens of them Jill. Missing, crucified, murdered. Some are sloppy, others seem to be messages. Others left no trace, as if they never even existed. But according to the records, dozens. Who knows how many unknowns have been killed?"

Jill covered her mouth to hold back a sob. "What are we going to do?"

"Nothing. We're going to do nothing at all but keep up appearances. No one seems to have traced us yet, and no one seems to be able to trace Poppy. Until our personal safety is threatened, there's nothing we can do." He wrapped his wife in his arms, desperate to feel her warmth and her touch after the cold of his investigation. He'd wanted to be home with her so bad but had dreaded telling her what he'd found. But at least there was a small silver lining, even if it was temporary. And he'd do everything in his power to keep it that way as long as possible. He was done getting involved. He and his family were going to fall off the map.

~~~~~~~~

The absolute rage on Seribulous's face would have made most of his servants piss their pants, but Richard had an advantage. In order for his master plan to succeed, the spawn of the devil needed him, and they both knew it. While Seribulous would destroy anyone else who stood up to him this way, he couldn't afford to do so to Richard.

"We are on the precipice," the monstrosity roared. "Why have we still not broken through these barriers and harvested our reward?"

The truth was, Richard had beaten the wards years ago. Primrose was his home, and even when he hadn't known himself, the land had recognized him and allowed him to breach the invisible shield that surrounded it on his very first visit. But Seribulous, like most creatures of the dark, had no sense of time by the standards of men, and over the past four years, had simply taken Richard at his word.

And mostly, Richard had spoken the truth. Every night, he'd gone to Primrose, and he'd watched his mother and father as they'd discovered an evil that seemed to be creeping into the world, one small step at a time. They still hadn't found the origin, but they'd begun to string together clues that would eventually lead them to the truth. Richard wanted desperately to help them.

But while he could keep some things from his master, he could not directly disobey or betray Seribulous, for fear of reprisal against his family.

Instead, he'd simply watched and yearned. He'd seen what had happened to his wife, his precious Catherine, and it nearly shredded what was left of his heart into small pieces. But he also felt that, over time, his presence had given her strength, and she was starting to recover. He'd also learned that Poppy, as precocious as she was, had been sent away because she'd been on a treacherous path that would have led her to a horrible truth, one that would have gotten her killed.

She was now far removed from the base camp, but with activity all over the country and seeping into other parts of the world now, she still wasn't safe, and Jill and David were just learning that.

With the information he'd gathered simply watching his family; Richard was able to provide half-truths that, till now, had satisfied his master. Today would be no different. "The place is a stronghold, and with so many entities hailing from it, Primrose is virtually impenetrable." He smiled to himself, an expression which he knew Seribulous would take for deviousness. "But I am getting closer every day."

Frustrated, Seribulous lashed out in anger, setting fire to three of his *Legion* as they screamed in agony. The pungent smell of burning flesh filled the air. At one time, it would have gagged Richard, but he'd grown used to it. "And what of the entities within? Have you found a purebred?"

Not a question Richard wanted to answer, but he fielded it as best he could. "Not yet. But the one who is ailing is on the road to recovery. Attacking before she has returned to herself could be quite a waste, since you would lose what she has to offer."

For the first time since he'd been taken, Richard felt the brunt of Seribulous's rage turn on him, and the being wrapped a reptilian hand with long, sharp claws around his throat. "Do not test me, Richard. I can and will replace you if I feel you are not earning your keep. I suggest you work more diligently and get me what I want. Otherwise, regardless of how useful a servant you've been, I will crush you like the insect you are."

Struggling to breathe, Richard met his master's eyes that were like black holes. "I will accomplish the goal."

Seribulous bared his teeth, narrowing the slits of eyes, then released him with a shove that sent him sailing against the wall behind him. Richard rubbed at his throat, taking deep breaths. Yes, he would accomplish the goal at hand, but that goal was no longer aligned with the war Seribulous waged. Rather, he intended to protect his family as he had been for the last four years. And even more importantly, he meant to keep Seribulous from finding the purebred he sought so desperately. For if he found his target, nothing could stop the apocalypse.

Only the summons Seribulous had received drew him away from his attack on Richard. Damn the man! Seribulous could threaten him for all eternity, and they both knew nothing would ever come of it. Richard wasn't scared of him, and if he actually destroyed Richard, he'd lose his skeleton key, the one entity that could open any door for him.

Turning his irritation and ire toward this meeting, he shoved open the iron door and stomped into a chamber so hot, so desolate, that even he lost all sense of hope. He glared at the man before him as he bowed, down on one knee to show his fealty. A fealty ever waning as his father failed to acknowledge his worth. "You called?"

With a laugh more sinister than even his, the beast before him shook his head. "My unworthy child. Have you nothing to show for yourself? After all this time, walking amongst the mortals, living in a hovel under the ground, you have not even made a dent in the army of the enemy. Tell me, are you smitten with the mortals? Is there a reason you do not return to me and ask for my assistance? After all, at least I manage to collect the prizes I seek."

Seribulous held back a snarl as he righted himself. His father forever goaded him, forever chose to degrade him. It wreaked havoc on him to know that his father thought him valueless, as if he had nothing to offer and never would. In the eyes of his father, he was nothing more than a pre-pubescent failure.

And what had begun as a way to earn his father's praise and love had become a journey of vengeance, a chance to impress his father and to show his own prowess. Of course, he had eternity, but so did his father, and he didn't want to suffer his father's disapproval for the rest of all time. He needed things to move faster.

Now he met his father's gaze and said, "I, too, am collecting my prizes, Father. I hunt, and I reap the rewards from my prey. You should not doubt me."

But his father simply crossed his bulging arms over his bare chest and grimaced. "Oh, but Seribulous, I do doubt you. You were to be my greatest creation. Instead, your lack of ambition has caused me embarrassment to the point of denying you as my flesh and blood, hiding you in the dark where no one can see you." He raked a disgusting look up and down Seribulous. "You are an abomination to me."

Fuming, Seribulous hung his head and spoke in a low voice he hoped would not belie his absolute hatred for his father. "I apologize for causing you embarrassment, Father."

"Get out of my sight!"

Gladly, he thought, turning without question and exiting through the iron door and slamming it behind him. He had nothing to apologize for, except that he'd bowed down to his father so long. The world would see what he was capable of, as would his father. And when Seribulous conquered the heavens, his father would be the one bowing down to him.

~~~~~~~~

CHAPTER 7

With a contented sigh, Poppy laid back on the bed in her new dorm, finally settled in after a long moving process. "It's amazing the crap you accumulate over the years," Abby muttered from her side of the room.

Poppy laughed. "Four years is a long time. I have a new appreciation for the things I left behind in Texas. It would probably take the rest of my natural born life to move all of it!" She grabbed her phone, found Facebook, and began scrolling through her feed. Nothing noteworthy grabbed her attention, so she clicked over to her news app and froze.

The top story had her pulse throbbing in her ears at a deafening volume. "You must be kidding."

"What?" Abby asked, her interest captured by the disbelief in Poppy's tone.

Poppy sat up with a jolt, scrolling down the page and scanning the article for a few particular facts. "I have to call my grandmother."

Abby huffed, frustrated. "What are you looking at, Poppy?"

She moved across the room and moved back up to the title so Abby could see.

Seattle Man Crucified In His Home

"It's spreading. And listen to this." She pulled the phone back and found the paragraph with the information she wanted. She read aloud, "'One witness claims to have seen a black cloud descend over the small house on Capitol Hill just hours before the body was discovered, pinned to the wall, where a cross had been drawn and nails driven through the palms and feet of the victim.'" She shook her head and met Abby's gaze. "This isn't just a local serial killer anymore, Abby. There's something bigger going on."

Returning to her phone, she dialed the home number and waited for Nana to answer. When she got the antiquated answering machine, she growled. "This is why I keep asking them to get cell phones." The beep sounded and she spoke into the receiver. "Nana, it's me, and it's urgent. We need to talk. Call me as soon as you can."

She pounded the button to hang up. "I can't believe this is really happening."

"Me, either. Look, I'm not saying I thought you were crazy or anything, but it all seemed pretty far-fetched, and you were totally obsessed. I still don't know how it's related to your father, but it must be, right? I mean, how many people report something that sounds as ridiculous as 'dark clouds descending' on a murder scene?"

Poppy was only half listening, trying to figure out what she was going to do. She needed to talk to Nana. This was too much, and she intended to hand it up as proof. She'd let the subject go for a long time, but now, she'd distanced herself for so long she was sure she'd missed something along the way. "Let's go," she said, suddenly jumping up and slipping her feet into her worn flip-flops.

Abby looked confused. "Where are we going?" Even as she asked in a suspicious manner, she followed suit.

"To the library. We're going to reference any case in the last ten years that involves reports of a black cloud or a crucifixion. We're not stopping at a local search, we're going national. And we're investigating disappearances too, not just murders. I want to know the name of every victim, dead or alive. I'm going to find the connection."

As she rushed out the door, Abby was right behind her. "Poppy, wait. Shouldn't you talk to your grandmother first?"

"No," she said firmly, continuing down the stairs. "Nana's been against me on this from the start. She knows something she's not telling me, and if I tell her what I'm doing, she's going to find some way to stop me from learning anything. I have to do this on my own. But I'd like some help, if you're up for it."

"Of course I am. But that doesn't mean I'm not nervous about it."

Still, she followed Poppy out of the building and halfway across campus until they reached the library. She gave Abby the reins to the internet, knowing what a whiz she was, while she took the microfiche files, searching keywords that might pull up articles not indexed online. They worked for hours, Poppy scrawling on blank scratch paper with article index numbers while Abby printed and highlighted at a frantic pace.

They were so enthralled that, when Poppy's phone rang, she jumped. She didn't answer it – she was in no place to talk to Nana right now – and continued her work. Giving half the articles to Abby, they requested the microfiche they needed and dominated the machines, writing down dates, names, and related circumstances until Poppy's hand was cramping from the effort and the tension she felt. Finally, they confiscated a table at the back of the library to spread out their findings and put them in chronological order.

Abby whistled. "There are more than 50 cases here, Poppy. This is huge."

Poppy nodded as they sorted through dates. Of course, she wasn't surprised her father's disappearance wasn't among them. After all, she assumed no one had ever recorded her statement about seeing the black mist. The whole thing seemed like a cover-up in retrospect. "I can't even imagine how many more never made the paper, or the reports were filed without details. And how many on top of that have no witnesses at all?"

Dozens had been killed and crucified, and nearly twenty included a sighting of a cloud, mist, or other black shroud of some kind, and that was out of the articles they'd found. There weren't as many disappearances, but seven related cases was still a high number, even over a ten-year time span. As they looked at the dates, Abby frowned at her. "It looks like there was never a time when even six months went by without a case. And they're scattered across the country."

She was right. The timing was a distinct pattern, with four and six months between each death or disappearance, and they came in groups. But there was no rhyme or reason she could find to the various locations, other than the largest number of them occurring in Bexar County. They stretched from Texas to Georgia, back to California, into Idaho, up to New York, and again in Texas. Only recently did the epidemic seem to spread into the Pacific Northwest, but over the past three years, there had been a total of six cases in the area, with three of them directly in Seattle.

That hit hard. If Nana had followed this at all, she would know Poppy wasn't any safer here than she was at home. Did that mean Nana and Papa just didn't want her around? Did they find her mother such a burden that they didn't have anything left for her? She hoped that wasn't the case that Nana and Papa had simply chosen to ignore the news.

From now on, Poppy would do no such thing.

Hours of staring at small print and logging names, dates, locations, and any other pertinent facts took their toll, and Poppy's eyes hurt. She noted Abby rubbing hers and cleared her throat. "We've done enough for today. Let's pack all this up, and we'll start the next round later."

Abby gave her a wary look. "And what would the next round be?"

"Finding out who these people are and what they have in common. There has to be some link for them to be targets. It doesn't make sense for this to be so random." She scooped up and straightened the papers while Abby stretched and yawned.

"So, I feel like we should reward ourselves." Poppy gave her friend a doubtful look. Typically, when Abby had such an idea, it involved some sort of taboo or crazy indulgence. Abby laughed out loud, getting dirty looks from several serious studiers around them. Lowering her voice, she said, "There's this club up on Capitol Hill I've heard a lot about that I want to check out. We should go dancing and burn off some steam."

Poppy rolled her eyes. "We're under 21. Who's going to let us in?"

"This one's 18 and up. We just get our hands marked so the bartenders won't serve us alcohol." Poppy was skeptical, but Abby pouted her bottom lip. "Come on, it'll be fun, and if it's not, we'll leave."

With a sigh of resignation, Poppy stood. "Alright. Let's take this stuff back to the dorm and I'll change clothes. There's no way I'm going to a club in worn out jeans and a ragged tank top." Maybe it would be fun, she thought. She'd rarely had a chance to dance before, and she certainly had a lot of frustrated energy to release. Maybe a club with energy and lots of people was just what she needed to calm down.

She'd have to consider the implications of what they'd found with a clear head. She couldn't let stress affect her judgment. And she realized, as she dug for something a little more trendy and attractive to wear, she was justifying her fun. Dammit, she was 18 years old. Why should she have to justify living her life? Even in the midst of all the confusion, life had to go on. She might as well make the most of the time she had.

Brendan wanted to toss the case folders across the room and let the contents scatter and get mixed up. It's not like he could find the connection he needed anyway. How anyone could pull off the complete masterpiece of what accounted for dozens of deaths across the country and still have no pattern or evidence left behind was inexplicable. One strand of hair, one partial fingerprint, anything would help. Even something that connected the victims would make a difference.

His phone rang, and he saw it was Officer Longmire. They'd been hashing this thing out for a while now, with small bits and pieces coming back from the street cop over time.

The victim had an entire dresser covered in idols, mostly angels and such representing heavenly devotion. It made sense, coupled with the crucifixion and that the piercing in his side had been the cause of death.

The killer had chosen a man of faith and sentenced him to the same death the Bible told for Jesus. The same cause of death was reported in every other instance he'd gained access to. If only all the departments stricken with a crucifixion murder would cooperate with his efforts. If he could get every file he'd made reference to in his research notes, he was sure he'd find the missing link.

But some cops were too proud to admit defeat, or to let anyone else touch their cases, even when they had become cold cases. Essentially, that's what was building the majority of Brendan's research – cold cases. When they'd found no evidence and what they deemed 'no viable witnesses', the other departments had seemed to throw up their hands and file the murder in the unsolved cases drawer, forgetting about it until Brendan called. Maybe just his reminder of their inability to solve the murder made them not want to cooperate. Still, he thought they should be happy to have someone outside their jurisdiction and payroll working on solving a case for them.

Realizing he was overthinking this, Brendan rubbed the bridge of his nose with his thumb and forefinger, then ran his palm over his face to scrub it of the frown he wore. He needed to get out of the house. He hadn't been out in months, and if he was going to keep his sanity, he needed to socialize with someone or other, even if they were just short chats with complete strangers.

He just knew his patience and concentration were running low.

Something had to change, whether a break in the case came or he simply distanced himself from the entire cluster. He was spending far too much time fretting over the case, and it was bound to send him to an early grave. His father and uncle had both let the job eat them alive, and a couple of cases in particular had gotten to them. His father had been involved in a homicide investigation he couldn't seem to get a grip on when he'd had his first heart attack at 40. And his uncle had been undercover in vice at 44 when he'd had his.

Brendan wanted to follow in their footsteps; they were legendary on the force. But in terms of health and dying young, he desperately wanted to avoid that sort of ending. He planned to have a long, healthy life, find a wife and have kids some day, and watch his grandchildren grow up. Maybe they were lofty dreams, but they were his.

And if he ever hoped to get there, he knew he had to change his course. He couldn't let the job bring him to this high of a stress level. He had to start relaxing, taking time for himself, rather than throwing himself into his work and becoming a workaholic just to avoid the lack of a life he had.

His mind made up, he pushed away from the desk and stared at his hands for a moment, trying to decide what to do. He could pop the top on a beer or two and have a movie marathon, but considering he had no one to enjoy it with, that almost sounded more depressing than staying wrapped up in these damn murders. No, he needed some other sort of distraction.

He turned off the lamp on the desk and stalked off to the bathroom. He'd take a shower and find some place out to go tonight. Maybe he'd get this forsaken case off his mind and he could start fresh tomorrow.

~~~~~~~~

The music boomed inside Poppy's chest as she and Abby let loose on the dance floor. This had been a fantastic idea, and she was enjoying herself. It was nice to be out, doing something normal, something that every other teenager and college kid in the world did. Sure, she had large X's on the back of her hands instead of a drink in them, but she didn't need to drink to have a good time. She was happy to be surrounded by activity and a level of energy she hadn't seen often in her life.

Abby moved up close to her and shouted into her ear over the din, "There's a guy to your right, hot as summer in the Gobi, staring at you like he wants to lick whipped cream off every inch of your body."

A tingle ran down Poppy's spine, and she turned to look where Abby directed as she kept moving, trying to look inconspicuous. Sure enough, her gaze met that of a pair of gorgeous baby blues set in a handsome, clean shaven face. His dark hair was styled in a messy faux-hawk, and his smile was seductive with full lips. He was cut but not bulky in his muscularity, and something warm swirled in Poppy's stomach as he indicated for her to come over with a jerk of his head.

There was no question in Poppy's mind what she was going to do, even if it was entirely out of character for her. Keeping eye contact, she leaned over to tell Abby, "I'm going to go check him out. Are you okay without me?"

"Oh, trust me, I've got my eye on one, too," came the response, and Poppy couldn't help but snicker. Yes, apparently, this was going to be a good night. Something just felt right about it, and while she still didn't think she'd be interested in dating anyone or complicating her life with the addition of a boyfriend, she felt the need to explore her options, at least tonight. It was like something drove her forward relentlessly, as if it was something she absolutely couldn't refuse. Squeezing between gyrating bodies, she made her way over to where the hunk of eye candy stood with an intrigued smile.

"Hi," he said, his deep voice resonating like a vibration through her, even over the ridiculous volume of the music. That was it. Just 'Hi'.

With a short laugh, she said, "Hi."

"Can I buy you a drink?" he asked.

She shook her head. "No, but you can tell me your name." The last thing she needed was to get in trouble for underage drinking.

"Brendan. Brendan O'Grady. And might I have the pleasure of your name?"

"Poppy Applebaum. It's a pleasure to meet you, Brendan." She held out her hand and, rather than shake it, he took it and raised it to his lips, placing a light brush of a kiss on her knuckles that sent sparks up her arm and straight through to her core.

"You've never been here before." At her raised eyebrow, his grin broadened. "I would have remembered your face. You have incredible green eyes."

Was she really blushing? "Thank you."

He started to respond, but his brow suddenly creased, and he reached into his pocket. With a quiet curse, he gave her an apologetic look. "If you'll excuse me, it's work. I have to step outside for a moment."

Poppy watched him walk away, wondering what on earth he did for a living that he would take calls while at a club. Several thoughts went through her mind – high dollar lawyer, doctor on call, and with a bit of a laugh, she even considered he might be an escort. Curious – and not wanting to lose him in the distraction of an unavoidable call – she followed him toward the door that led to a smoking deck outside. She waited patiently, hanging back slightly around the corner from where he stood speaking in a frustrated tone, but couldn't help overhearing his end of the conversation.

"Did they come from the same batch?...I see...No, unless we can get a sample from one of the other investigations, or find something in the case records we've already pulled that matches, there's no way we can connect them...Right, well, I'll be in early tomorrow...Of course the area was canvassed immediately...No one saw anything that wasn't written in the report, Casey...Look, I'm out right now. Let's talk about this in the morning. Goodnight."

He hung up and turned, looking stunned to see Poppy standing there. But Poppy didn't retreat or make apologies. Instead, she focused on some of the things he'd said and tried to prod through general conversation. "I would ask if you were a lawyer, but it didn't sound like those were the case files you were referring to."

He smirked. "No, I'm a cop. Well, an investigator, if you want to get technical. Sorry about that. When duty calls, I have to answer, especially when it's a big case." He didn't look pleased at the news he'd received, but he had Poppy's attention fully.

She raised an eyebrow, playing it coy, even though intuition or something like it told her she already knew the answer. "What kind of big case?"

His face scrunched up in frustration. "An impossible murder case. A case that is more likely a serial murderer or possibly more than one killer, though I'm still working on proving that."

Poppy's breath caught in her throat, and her heart jumped out of her chest. Could he possibly be connected to the one murder case that held answers to all her questions? "That's intriguing. Is it something I might have heard about on the news?"

Brendan seemed to think it over, as if trying to decide how much to divulge. Screwing up his face, he moved closer to her. "I'm sure you've read about the crucifixions. Who hasn't?"

Holding her breath to keep from screaming in triumph at her good luck, she nodded emphatically. "I've been following them for awhile." Turning on the girl-charm, she gasped and laid a flirtatious hand on his arm. "Oh my gosh, are you heading up that investigation?" A part of her felt ridiculous for acting this way, but she was willing to do anything to get more information from a reliable source. And who would be more reliable and closer to the case than the man heading up the investigation?

"Unfortunately, yes." He seemed chagrined, and it was no wonder. Whatever was going on, there weren't many clues, and while she and Abby had yet to really dig into it, she could almost guarantee there were no obvious connections between the victims. Of course, this was Seattle, and O'Grady was likely only following up on the local occurrences. But he'd mentioned pulling other files. How much did he know? And if he didn't have all the information, all the connections, how could she give him direction without looking like she'd plotted bumping into him?

A small part of Poppy wanted to let it go and just enjoy the company of a handsome man. She considered that for just a moment, reminding herself how much fun she was having just letting loose and not thinking on the biggest mystery in her life, but the part of her that needed answers pursued the issue. Hesitantly, she asked, "Are you treating it like a serial killer?"

He looked uncomfortable, and then sighed with a heavy frown. "A lot of people don't want it handled that way. That's one of the biggest issues I'm having. The powers that be are letting me run with it, but I'm not supposed to make the assumption. Honestly, I don't see any other way to look at it. There are too many similarities. And if all the local cops across the country would cooperate, we'd have this thing solved in no time. It's possibly a cult."

Still playing the role of the ignorant girl, she tilted her head as if confused. "What do you mean?"

He checked around, as if worried someone was listening, then stepped closer so they were almost touching. "Everything I tell you is between you and me, and if you're a reporter, I swear I'm going to tear your story down like an old condemned building."

Poppy let out a genuine laugh at that. "No, I'm a college student. And I'm not even enrolled in a journalism course. Or anything related. I just find it intriguing." She blushed. "Plus you have a nice voice." She figured she might be laying in on a little thick, but it could also be a nice added touch to gain his confidence.

He nodded. "Listen, I have 18 case files from various places across the US, and I'm finding similarities in the murders no one else has noticed because no one's bothered to cross-reference their local cases against national news. And there are at least 12 more cases I want to get the files for because I suspect I'm going to find the same clues, the same M.O., but I can't get cooperation from the department. Neither my own or those that have the cases locally."

Poppy's breaths came in short pants. The fact that she'd somehow managed to stumble on the man with the most information about the murders had to be more than a coincidence. It had to be some sort of intuition, had to have something to do with the way she'd felt drawn to him from the moment she'd seen him. After all, she'd found men attractive before, and she'd had no shortage of attention from guys she wasn't the least interested in. But this was the first time she'd pursued one, and it had to be something above and beyond desire, since she had no room in her life for romance.

Brendan might be the key to solving the riddle. At the same time, listening to him, he was missing so much. There were disappearances he wasn't considering. She wanted to tell him that, but she didn't dare for fear of him suspecting her of seeking him out. Admittedly, she actually liked him and wanted more from him than just answers, even if she couldn't define her interest.

She needed to be able to get more out of him, such as the similarities he'd found so far. But she doubted he'd give her that much information. After all, she was just some girl he'd met in a club. She had no right to give him the third degree about anything. And he had no obligation to her, either. He'd just taken a liking to her and the way she danced. That meant nothing in the realm of reality and trust.

She had to find a way to get the files for herself.

Putting on her best smile, she touched his arm. Flattery seemed to have been a good choice for her thus far. She'd keep it up until it failed her. "So, are you gonna come in and dance with me or what?"

With a charming grin, he took her hand and led her back inside. "I can't think of a better way to spend the rest of my evening."

~~~~~~~~~

Brendan had come out to find distraction, and Poppy definitely filled the bill. He danced with her, but mostly, he watched her move. She was slender with just the hint of curves in all the right places. He could tell she didn't get out often, but she wasn't inhibited, and she moved with grace and style. It was a sight.

At the same time, her interest in the case was confounding. She obviously wasn't as dumb as she let on, but he couldn't see any ulterior motive in her questions. In a setting where they could hear each other again and carry on a conversation as they had earlier, he'd ask her what she was studying. He'd be willing to bet it was law or something of that nature. Hell, she might even be in psychology and interested in being a criminal profiler, which would explain a lot. He'd certainly never thought he'd meet someone sincerely curious about his career.

Of course, he also realized she was really young. It bothered him slightly as he looked at the X's on her hands and added up the fact that she was under 21. She'd said she was a college student, but he got the impression she was younger than even he would have thought at first. If she was a freshman, he'd kick himself in the ass because he found himself having all sorts of untoward thoughts about how satisfying she would be.

For now, though, he'd just be content to spend the evening in her company, pressing against her on the dance floor and watching her. It put him in a much better mood and lowered his stress level. And the more time he spent watching her, the more he wanted to know about her.

She'd come with a friend, and he caught them looking at each other across the large room with big smiles. Her friend seemed to have latched onto a college frat boy herself and was having the time of her life. So, he didn't feel like he was being too incredibly selfish by usurping Poppy's attention. In fact, he got the impression it was good for her, too. She seemed like she was releasing stress that had been weighing on her shoulders for ages. He watched her get lighter and lighter as the night wore on.

The question was what happened when they were finished here? Would he say goodnight and walk away? Would he at least get her number? Or would he break down and invite her home with him? It was a decision he didn't feel like thinking too hard on just yet.

Maybe he'd just let the chips fall where they may and go with the flow. He hadn't done anything like that in years, but somehow he thought it would shave a few years off his age.

~~~~~~~~

At one point, Poppy escaped to the ladies' room and shot Abby a quick text. Her friend joined her in no time. "So how's it going?" she asked in a nosy fashion, her own cheeks flushed and lips swollen, likely from a rough make-out session. "Is he still hot, or is he a creep?"

Poppy's eyes were bright as she spoke. "Not only is he hot, Abby, he's useful. I can't believe it, but he's the lead investigator on the crucifixion murders in Seattle."

Abby blinked several times. "You're kidding me, right? Doesn't that seem like a huge coincidence?" Her suspicion came through in her tone, and Poppy couldn't blame her. But it was a ridiculous statement.

Poppy rolled her eyes. "Maybe, or maybe it's fate telling me I'm on the right track and that I need to keep searching for the answers. Maybe this is the way to find my father." Abby didn't look entirely convinced. "Look, there's no way he could have targeted me as connected to any of this. It's not like he has information on my father's disappearance, and it's not as if we broke into the FBI database and our paths have been traced. Thinking anything of the kind is giving into paranoia." She took her friend's hand and squeezed it. "I just need to know if you can get home alright. I'm going to see if I can get into his

116

place and find the files he's got, copy the information. Or something."

Abby's eyes widened with shock. "You're going to go home with him? Poppy, you just met the man. Do you really think it's safe to just go sleep with a stranger?"

Ignoring the fact that Abby apparently assumed she was planning on sleeping with the guy, Poppy shook her head. "He's a police officer, Abby. He's not going to hurt me, and I'll be home in a few hours. I wasn't planning to stay the night. And in case you've forgotten, I'm a virgin, and I'm not going to lose that over a one night stand. I have money for a cab. Just don't worry about me and let me know that you're safe and in good hands."

At that Abby giggled. "Oh, I'm in good hands alright. Tommy has great hands, actually."

Poppy stuck out her tongue mockingly. "Too much information. And obviously, I'm not the one thinking about sleeping with a stranger" With a smile, she hugged her friend. "Thank you, Abby. This could be the end of it all. I might finally get my father back." Leaving the restroom, Poppy searched the crowd in the dark for her date, finding him leaning against the wall just a few yards away, watching her with an intense look. Good, she thought. It shouldn't be that hard to convince him to take me home.

Slinking up to him, she let him put an arm around her waist and hold her against his side. "So, how much longer do you want to stay here?" he asked toying with a strand of her hair.

She shrugged, moving in closer so their noses touched as she spoke. "I could leave any time. My friend's ditching me for some guy over there, and that means I've got to catch a cab." She gave Brendan a pouty face.

Suddenly sounding much less confident than he had earlier in the evening, he told her, "Well, you know, if you want, I have my car, and I could drive you home. I mean, if you don't mind hitching a ride with a cop." He gave her a crooked grin. "I promise, it's not a marked car, and I won't stick you behind the cage in the back seat."

Raising an eyebrow, she asked, "Did it look like I had a problem being seen with an officer of the law while we were dancing?" She actually made him blush and realized with a sense of relief just how easy this was going to be. "I have a better idea," she cooed, toying with the back of his neck with her fingernails. "Why don't you give me a ride to *your* home instead?"

He looked surprised and maybe as if he was going to turn her down. Poppy prayed she was mistaken and ran her other hand down his chest. She could feel his elevated heart rate, and as she waited impatiently, begging whatever god was listening to be on her side, she sensed his resolve failing. "Sure. That sounds nice."

Poppy had always thought it was easy to seduce men. After all, most of the guys she knew practically begged her for attention and thought more with the head between their legs than the one on their shoulders. Apparently, some of them had some sort of resolve that had to be broken, some sense of moral conduct. It gave her hope for humanity, even though it made life more complicated at the worst times. Leave it to her to find one that was difficult. Still, they left the club, and he led her out to one of the paid parking lots, his hand on her lower back making her skin tingle. His car was modest, a late model Hyundai, but it was nice and clean, which earned her respect.

He also opened the passenger door for her, and Poppy found it refreshing to actually have a gentleman around. She had assumed she'd left them all in Texas, so it was quite the find.

"Your mama taught you some manners, didn't she?"

He shot her a boyish, shy smile. "Just because I'm not a good old southern boy doesn't mean I don't know how to treat a lady. My mom, my grandmother, and one of my aunts had cops for husbands who acted like cavemen most of the time. They made sure I was raised right."

Poppy giggled and got in the car, shaking her head. "So, chivalry hasn't died."

He made as if tipping a hat. "No, ma'am, it hasn't."

There wasn't much chatter on the way to his place, and Poppy watched out the passenger window, getting her bearings. He was headed to Cherry Hill, which meant he'd have a nice home and a great view of the city. He pulled into a driveway in front of a garage at the bottom of a house on a hill. "I share the house with two other people. The basement's been renovated into an apartment."

The house itself sat a story above them, but Brendan had a private entrance on this basement floor, and he unlocked it, leading her into what was again a modest but clean space. Looking around, she suddenly realized that, if he was some sort of creep, he could easily make her disappear right now. She probably should have asked to see his badge. After all, anyone could have studied up on the murder cases and used them like a line. Not that she would have known the difference between a real badge and a fake one anyway.

Now, she was here, and there was nothing more to be done. All he had to do was take out a roll of duct tape, wrap her up, and shove her in his closet, and no one would ever know where she was.

But of course, she gave him the benefit of the doubt. After all, he was a cop, and even if there were corrupt cops, he didn't seem like the type. She imagined evil intent would have a certain smell, and that pungent odor was nowhere on him. He only smelled of aftershave and musk, the scent of male. And maybe something else. Maybe desire? Poppy wouldn't know, but whatever she smelled on him now, it wasn't dangerous.

If you say so, a little niggling voice in her head responded. Someone who smells like that, is drop dead gorgeous, and has information you want, and you think he's not dangerous? Stop kidding yourself, Poppy, and think about the giant storm you just created and stepped into. But then, she had felt that draw, and she didn't think she could have denied the drive to follow the exact path she'd taken with him so far. Maybe it was her mind trying to justify her actions, but it all *felt* right.

Too late to turn back now, she decided, looking around the main room with interest. He was obviously a book lover, with the walls lined by shelving that ran floor to ceiling, covered in volumes and volumes of books. He had simple taste in décor, with a small black couch, matching recliner, small glass coffee table on a black rug with gray plaid, and a gray and black lamp. To her right was an archway that looked as though it opened onto an office, where she could just make out a simple work desk that – to her delight – was stacked with dozens of file folders.

Hoping those were the case files, she turned her attention back to Brendan, trying to figure out how she was going to manage to get her hands on them. "Nice place." For the first time all night, she got a slightly awkward feeling, and she hoped it would pass quickly. What did you say to a man who brought you home, especially if you weren't planning to sleep with him?

He shrugged. "It's small, but it's enough for me." He motioned toward the couch. "Have a seat, make yourself comfortable."

With one more glance toward the study area, she sighed internally, knowing it was going to be a project to get at those files, and settled in on the comfortable furniture. For the moment, she would relax and spend some time with her host, get to know him. After all, he was a great looking guy, and he was nice. And on top of that, the closer they got to each other, the more likely she'd get the information she wanted. She knew with every ounce of her being she could gain that sort of trust.

~~~~~~~~

If Brendan was honest with himself, he wanted Poppy to spend the night. He found her not only to be absolutely gorgeous and magnetic, but also intriguing in her personality. Now that she was here, he didn't care so much about her age or the fact that she seemed absolutely innocent and inexperienced. They laughed together, and she found his work interesting and exciting, whereas most women seemed to blow it off. He had a feeling they were quite compatible, and he wanted to explore that possibility more deeply.

But, when it came down to the moment of truth, he flaked and took her home, reminding himself just how young she really was. He could ease into things with her, given the chance. He had never been one to rush into anything, After he dropped her off, he drove back home and flopped down on his couch, exasperated with himself, unsatisfied, and knowing he still had a mountain of work to do. He'd shirked his responsibilities for a night to go have a good time, and the distraction had been exactly what he needed. But now, he had to focus again. The reality was, people were dying, and it was just a matter of time before more gruesome pictures of dead, crucified bodies hit his desk.

Still, something about Poppy held him captivated, and he couldn't get her out of his head, even as he tried to go to bed. They'd exchanged phone numbers, and he planned to call her, if he ever had time again. But it took all of his willpower not to pick up the phone at this ridiculous hour and call her, just to hear her voice one last time, just to say goodnight and assure himself she'd had as much fun as he had. He'd never been so drawn to anyone.

He wanted to protect her, which was crazy because Brendan could tell from what he already knew of her that she could certainly take care of herself. She was a bit of a loner and used to handling her own shit. She was strong and confident, like few women he'd met, and there was a quality in her he couldn't quite place that spoke of a spirit that wouldn't die, no matter what sort of nightmare you put it through. Nonetheless, he felt protective of her, as if he wanted to be with her at all times. Which was even more insane when he looked at things logically and recognized he'd only known her for a few hours.

Growling, he rose from the bed and pulled on a pair of pajama pants before plodding into the study he'd made out of the small alcove space. If he couldn't sleep, he might as well get somewhere on the case. He made a quick side trip into his kitchen to brew some coffee, which was probably the last thing he needed but sounded good, before he sat in the chair in front of the stack of files, heaving a sigh as he flipped on the lamp and looked up at the dry erase board where he'd made dozens of notes. His brows drew together, thinking that it would have made so much more sense if these truly were religious murders, if some fanatical lunatic had targeted people he or she deemed sinners and sentenced them to death on the cross.

He'd read enough about fanaticism to know the pattern. This particular string of murders looked a lot like a copycat of those sorts of crimes. They all looked the same, acted the same, and followed a perfect pattern. And yet, the motive didn't fit, no matter which way he turned things or how deep he dug into the lives of every one of the murder victims.

The victims across the country weren't even close to being from the same religious sects. The only thing they had in common was that they did all apparently regularly go to some form of church or other. However, there were Baptists of three different kinds, Methodists, a practicing Hindu, a Pentecostal minister who had converted to Buddhism only a year ago, and a Mormon, just to name a few. None of them had more than a speeding ticket or two anywhere on their records, and many of them had been active in their community and were described as faithful friends and caring family members.

There were men and women, young and old, single and married – some with children, rich and poor, straight and gay, and every other iteration of lifestyle there was. It seriously threw him for a loop. Serial killers had a type. They had a profile and they stuck with a single type. Even if they weren't entirely predictable, every single incident made sense when compared to the others, and they all seemed related. It was textbook criminal profiling, and they didn't veer from the course, especially one as methodical and ritualistic as this one. So why couldn't he find a connection?

He reached for the top file on the stack, ready to browse through all of them again, looking for some tidbit of information he'd missed along the way the first fifty times he'd scoured them, some gem to mine from all the bullshit he'd trudged through like wading through a swamp in boots and coveralls over and over again. His hand landed on the file, and there was a post-it he didn't remember sticking there. Curious, he pulled it off and narrowed his eyes at the girlish scrawl written across it.

Have you looked into disappearances?

That's all it said, and since there had only been one woman in his place in the past, oh, five years, he picked up his phone and pulled up Poppy Applebaums number. Of course, he couldn't call her yet, but he could wait impatiently, an irrational anger swelling in his chest. He felt stupid for assuming she'd had any real interest in him, when she'd obviously been using him. He should have known he couldn't find the perfect woman – someone who would like him *and* his job.

And still, he couldn't help but listen to the investigator inside. Grudgingly, he rolled over to where his laptop lay on the floor, reaching down and opening it up. While he didn't appreciate the invasion of classified information, and he was more than a little bit hurt that she'd apparently been more interested in his case than in him, Brendan answered the call of the cop in him and decided to follow up on the advice, just in case there was something he could use.

"Leave no stone unturned, and follow up on every lead," he muttered in irritation, downing the rest of his coffee and preparing for a very long night.

~~~~~~~~

As Poppy dressed for bed, a tingling sensation crawled up her spine, and her stomach constricted as a smile crept across her face. She couldn't remember the last time she'd had this pure sense of contentment, and all of it came from having spent the evening with Brendan. He was an incredible man, and she was sincerely interested in him.

And on top of that, she had made a move that could be the biggest revelation of her entire life. Could Brendan really be the key to finding her father? Had she really stumbled onto the answer, just by following her gut?

Of course, that left butterflies in her stomach as she realized the chance she'd taken by leaving him that note. Her nerves were on edge as she laid down in the dark, silent room where Abby snored softly and nothing else moved. Maybe she'd get her answers, but it was entirely likely that, in the process, she'd piss off the one man she'd ever had any interest in.

She imagined the worst, that he'd feel used and never speak to her again. That he'd find the clues and put them together to get the answers but not share them with her out of spite. That he'd hate her with every ounce of his being. And the lighter part of her pictured the happy ending, where she and Brendan started dating, investigated these things together, and found the truth about her father's disappearance and, ultimately, these horrific murders. And, in that paradise ending, she'd get her father back, safe and sound, from whatever nightmare he'd been living for the past ten years.

She couldn't fall asleep, and she picked up her phone, scrolling to where she'd saved Brendan's number, wondering if he was experiencing the same euphoria she was after their pseudo-date. Was he sound asleep and content in his dreams? Or was he lying in bed, awake, those gorgeous eyes staring up at the ceiling and picturing her face, thinking what it would have been like to kiss her?

She wanted with all her being to dial his number, to find out. She even considered sending a text. After all, if he was asleep, he probably wouldn't hear it come through and no harm would be done. And if he was awake, he would get it and know she was thinking of him.

But she didn't want to push, and she didn't want to read more into things than what was there. She'd wait patiently for the morning, and she'd let things happen as they were intended. She believed in fate ,and if they were meant to be friends or something more, everything would work out, no matter what he thought of the little clue she'd left to point him in the right direction.

Frowning, she turned over on her side, leaving her phone behind, and hoped that he'd at least give her a chance to explain and to show that he meant more to her than just a connection. Brendan was special, and with that thought, she let herself ease into a peaceful, although light sleep.

~~~~~~~

CHAPTER 8

After a long conversation that had broken his heart, David stepped away and took a brief walk around the house. He understood Jill's concerns, and that's why he'd finally relented, and agreed to her proposition, even though he felt it was wrong from the bottom of his soul. He needed the fresh air. It had been a very long time since he'd felt the urge to cry, and he wasn't going to give into it now, however much the turn of events hurt him.

And even though he was going to go through with it and had been given his own duties, David had refused to be the one to call Poppy. He'd adamantly insisted that Jill be the one to do so. She'd raged at him, the entire conversation breaking down into a screaming match. They hadn't yelled at each other since they were in their twenties, and that only made the situation worse. But in the end, David had refused to change his mind on that one aspect, and Jill had reluctantly agreed to take on the responsibility.

Of course, she'd insisted that Poppy not know until after the deed was done, and while David felt that was wrong, he knew Jill had her reasons, whatever they were. He wanted to trust his wife as he had for the last forty years, but he was finding that increasingly difficult as her personality seemed to change. He realized it was all related to the same business, but he was afraid of what it was doing to Jill.

And a part of him also knew that Poppy would find a way to change Jill's mind, which would only lead to more misery for everyone involved. David already spent most of the time he actually got to talk to his granddaughter assuring her that her grandmother still loved her and only wanted what was best. All of this was bound to make the girl hate Jill, and he foolishly hoped that, maybe, if it was all said and done, Poppy would be able to forgive them for it.

As he rounded the back of the house, David heard a strange noise, almost like a deep inhalation, coming from the thicket of trees a few yards away, and he stopped, standing stock still and listening with all his might. But all he caught was the sound of cicadas croaking and singing. He moved forward again in his slow pacing, and this time, he was sure he caught a shadow out of the corner of his eye, just the briefest motion, amidst the trees. It moved with the speed of light, and he couldn't whirl fast enough to see anything head on. But a shiver went down his spine, and after waiting just a little longer for some other strange occurrence, he hurried back in the house.

It was time to do his due diligence.

As David walked into Catherine's bedroom, prepared to break the news to her whether she could hear him or not, that they were finally going to move her to a home, he stopped in his tracks, frozen in place, his jaw going slack. Catherine stood by the bed, looking around the room, her whole body trembling. He started to speak but wasn't sure of her state of mind and didn't want to startle her too much.

As he watched, her mouth moved, though no sound came out, and he thought about calling to his wife but, again, was afraid to break the spell. Finally, his daughter-in-law's eyes landed on him, and she stopped moving, stopped trembling, giving him a look that mirrored his own shock. "David?" she asked in a weak voice, hoarse with the lack of use and barely recognizable as hers.

Dear God, she was awake.

Before he could respond, her eyes rolled back in her head, and she collapsed to the floor.

David ran forward, this time shouting loudly for Jill and a cold, wet rag as he lifted the frail woman into her bed, laying her back and checking her over, noting a fine sheen of sweat coating her soft skin, which felt loose over her frame, that had grown thin and almost gaunt over the years. As soon as Jill put the cloth to Catherine's forehead, giving David an expectant look, Catherine's eyes popped open again, staring straight into his with crude, evident desperation. "David?"

"Yes, Catherine, I'm here." He heard Jill gasp and place a hand over her mouth, while David squeezed her hand to reassure her everything was alright. "It's good that you're here."

She gave a short, slow nod. "Where's my daughter?"

"She's at school, Catherine. We'll call her later."

Catherine tried to comprehend that statement, coupled with the fact that it was dark outside, but the messages swirled in her head over and over, and she had to keep them straight. She couldn't let anything muddle her brain until she got to Poppy. "David, I need to see my daughter."

"We'll take care of that as soon as we can, Catherine. I need you to relax and tell me where you've been all this time." David sat on the edge of the bed, wiping her hot face with the cool cloth to help avoid her falling out on them again.

"Listening."

David exchanged looks with Jill, who didn't know what to say. Pursing his lips, David turned back to his daughter-in-law. "Listening? To what, Catherine? What were you listening to?"

She gazed into space and scowled. "Voices. Voices in my head that told me what I needed to do. And now I have to see Poppy. I have to see her before it's too late." Suddenly, her scowl turned to a rabid grimace. "Why didn't you say anything, Jill? I know you know what I'm talking about. Why didn't you tell her?"

Jill gave her husband a sidelong glance, hoping she wasn't guessing correctly about Catherine's meaning. "I'm not sure where you're going with that, Catherine. You aren't making a whole lot of sense. Maybe we should get some food and water into you, get you cooled down before you try to explain what you're saying."

Furious, Catherine leveled a hateful gaze on Jill. "I don't need you to take care of me anymore, Jill, and I don't appreciate you patronizing me. I'm making perfect sense, now that I know the truth. God forgive you for what this may have done to Poppy." She looked at David. "David, I have to get these messages to Poppy. It can't wait. It's already been too long."

David looked to his wife, who refused to meet his gaze and held her lips in a tight line. She also wouldn't say anything. Of course, if the voices and messages in Catherine's head meant what he thought, Jill would have to get over herself, and Catherine would have to stop hedging and being belligerent until they could sort through the information. It was the only way to keep Poppy safe.

Clearing his throat to get everyone's attention, David said, "No need to fight, ladies. We just need to clear some things up." He gave Jill a look that asked her not to speak up until he had what he wanted from Catherine. "Now, Catherine, were these voices telling you to do something?"

She shook her head. "No, they were telling me..." She stopped, not trusting anyone right now. As much as she loved her father-in-law, she felt betrayed by Jill, and neither of them was important. Not compared to Poppy. She had to get to her daughter. "I'll explain it when we see Poppy. Where the hell is school? And why is she there this late? Can we go pick her up?"

Jill couldn't hold back her tirade any longer. "Oh, for heaven's sake, you know she moved to Seattle. We sent her there to keep her out of danger, and if what you refuse to tell us has anything to do with her future, I think it's better she doesn't know anything. It's safer that way."

This time, though, David cut in. "Jill, hold on. You may be right, but we don't know the whole situation." He turned back to Catherine, praying the answer would be no. "So, these messages – they were meant for Poppy?"

Catherine shook her head. "No, they were meant for all of us. But the danger is with Poppy, and I have to get them to her as soon as possible. They're somehow about Poppy, though I'm not sure how, and in order to protect her, she needs to know about the visions. And if we don't hurry, it could be too late." She was adamant, and it didn't matter how many times she had to say it – she insisted.

Standing and nodding, David said, "Okay, Catherine. If it's that important, I'll see if we can book a flight up there tomorrow or the next day. I'll get you to your daughter."

"That's insane!" Jill argued. "We can't just up and leave like that with no warning."

David held up his hands in surrender. "I don't have a choice, Jill. I have to believe what Catherine says, and I'm more afraid of what I won't find if we wait too long than about causing Poppy a little pain or finding nothing at all if we go now. You can go or stay. Catherine needs to get to her daughter, and I'm going to take her there."

Jill's lower lip trembled. "I see. Fine, I'll pack our bags. And send up a prayer that a bad decision doesn't ruin everything we've done."

Catherine pushed herself to a seated position as David left the room and glared at her mother-in-law. "Listen, Jill, I may have been in another place for a while, but she's still my daughter. I can't believe you sent her away. You, of all people, should have realized the danger she was in and kept her close. I already lost one of the people I loved because of all this. And I won't let anything happen to Poppy. I sure as hell won't sit by and watch her lied to any longer. She deserves to know the truth. And that's going to be her ticket to survival in all this. Did you know about me Jill? What I am? I know you have suspected it for a while, so why didn't you say something or have you chosen to ignore it like you did with Richard and Poppy?" She pointed toward the door. "Get out of my room right now, Jill, and give me a little time in peace to adjust."

Turning on her heels, Jill stormed out. She already had things to do. Obviously, she would have to cancel the pickup tomorrow, since it was certain Catherine wouldn't be going to the care facility. She'd also have to call the bank and stop the funds from being withdrawn. But once those things were taken care of, she'd sit back and analyze the situation, determine when and where she'd lost her edge. She'd gain back control of this situation or she'd risk the loss of yet another family member. She wouldn't let the rash decisions of a couple of people who listened more to their emotions than to their brains get her granddaughter killed.

~~~~~~~~

Poppy woke up smiling, much as she'd fallen asleep the night before. And despite her misgivings last night, she was also proud of the subterfuge she'd pulled off in the process. He'd only been out of the room for a few minutes, using the restroom and then pouring a couple of sodas, but she'd used the time wisely. She'd very carefully and briefly flipped through those files without upsetting the stack, to find exactly what she'd expected. He'd only followed up on murders and not disappearances.

She'd found herself unable to resist playing detective and leaving him a clue, and while she'd worried terribly that he'd never forgive her for her actions last night, today it didn't seem to matter. She wasn't going to let her concerns drag her down.

She started to roll back over and doze just a little while longer, but her phone rang, and Abby threw a pillow at her with a grunt, apparently unhappy with her own sleep being interrupted. Heaving herself out of bed, she reached for the cell and nearly choked as her mouth went dry. Okay, perhaps leaving the note for Brendan hadn't been the smartest move. A phone call this early wasn't likely going to be about thanking her for a grand time or for giving him the lead he needed to solve the case.

"Hello?" she answered, attempting not to yawn.

"Would you like to explain yourself?" Brendan's tone was irate, clipped, and demanding. His irritation was almost tangible through the phone.

No, she definitely hadn't made the best decision. "What would you like me to explain, Detective?" she asked in her most innocent voice.

"Don't play coy with me. What's your interest in this case? And don't tell me you don't have one. It's obvious you know something, and you came over just for that purpose. I don't take kindly to being used, and I'm always suspicious of liars. Now, if you can't give me a logical reason for all of this, I'm going to have to consider you a suspect."

She almost laughed. "First of all, Brendan, you came onto me to start with, so it's not like I set you up. And second, put me on your suspect list all you want. Come question me. I'll tell you everything I know. And if you look it up, you'll find that I've hardly left Seattle in the last four years." She sighed, her shoulders falling as her indignation dissipated. "And no, I wasn't only interested in your case. I liked you the instant I met you. The fact that you're involved in this particular case just turned out to be a bonus."

He didn't respond immediately, and Poppy's disappointment overwhelmed her to the point she actually felt tears sting her eyes. She hadn't expected to react so badly, especially after the resolve she'd felt this morning. She'd ruined the first chance she'd had to do or be anything normal in years, because she still held onto her obsession with the case, regardless of how long she'd managed to push it down.

"Brendan, please don't be angry with me. Check into the files from Bexar County, Texas, ten years ago, looking for mysterious disappearances before the crucifixions started. You'll find a whole new plethora of information for your case." She wrinkled her nose, blinking back the tears. "I'm sorry, Brendan. Hopefully, that helps."

Before he could respond, she hung up, and buried her face in her arms, propping them on her knees as she drew her legs to her chest. She didn't understand why she felt such a desperate ache right now. It was as if she'd lost someone close to her, but Brendan had never even been close to belonging to her, so she couldn't lose him. It was really ridiculous. How could she ever have let herself hope this hard? And why would a stranger she'd just met cause this sort of pain in her heart, like someone had stuck a knife in and twisted it round and round in a circle?

When her phone rang again almost immediately, she started to ignore it, assuming it was Brendan calling back to ball her out some more. But a tingle of warning crept down her spine, and she opened one eye to peer out of it at the caller ID. She gulped and grabbed it immediately, seeing the home number. Something had to be wrong.

"Nana?" she asked as she picked up the phone.

For a second, there was no answer. Then, a voice that wasn't her grandmother's came over the line. "No, Poppy, it's not Nana."

Even with the scratchy, raspy sound from not having been used for so long, Poppy knew that voice. "Mama!" She almost started crying right then and there, only the shock of the situation keeping her from doing so.

Even Abby sat up in bed with that exclamation, her eyes wide with disbelief. But before Poppy could say anything to her, Catherine Applebaum spoke again, her tone urgent.

"Poppy, we have to talk. I'm going to fly up there with your grandparents tomorrow, and we have to meet somewhere quiet, somewhere safe."

All Poppy could think was that something had turned up about her father, and she tried hard not to think the worst…or the best, for that matter. But whatever her mother wanted to talk about, she was talking, and that elated Poppy. It went a long way in relieving the pain that had welled up inside her moments ago. "I would love to see you, Mama. It's so good to hear your voice." She choked up at the end, no longer able to hold back the tears she'd almost cried a few minutes ago.

She heard the stutter and the tremor in Catherine's voice as she replied, "Oh, Poppy, I've been here all along. I'm sorry I couldn't say anything. But now it's important for me to tell you everything. There's a lot of important things to talk about, and all I want is for you to be safe." There was a sniffle. "So we'll fly into Sea-Tac Airport early tomorrow morning, and we'll rent a car. Papa will drive us up there, we'll be with you before lunch."

Poppy glanced at Abby thoughtfully. Her mother's words were ominous, and she couldn't begin to imagine what she referred to in talking about Poppy's safety. But she was so ecstatic about being able to see, hug, and speak to her mother, she'd take anything she could get without asking questions. "You can tell me whatever it is here in the dorm. My room is safe and quiet, and no one but my roommate can get in."

"Good. We'll see you tomorrow. And Poppy, I love you."

"I love you, too, Mama." She hung up and stared at Abby in complete shock. "My mom's snapped out of it, Abby. She's awake and lucid and functional. Well, at least, it sounds like she's functional."

Abby threw herself across the room and flung her arms around Poppy. "I'm so happy for you! And it sounds like she's coming to visit."

"Yeah," Poppy said, feeling a little out of it and staring off into the distance even as she returned the gesture. "She said they want to talk to me someplace safe. I'm not sure what's going on, unless they have some update on my father."

Abby pulled away and smacked herself in the forehead, scrunching up her face. "That's right! You were checking into that last night, too, weren't you? How'd it go with Officer Charming?"

Poppy came back to herself and shrugged, hanging her head. "I made a mistake. Things were going well, and I messed it up. I should have left well enough alone and just enjoyed the company, but it's too late to change things now. I'll be lucky if he follows up on my suggestion and gets any more information. And even luckier if he actually shares any of that information with me." She took a deep breath and forced a smile that almost reached her eyes. "But then again, I guess Mama might know something, or maybe Nana and Papa." Suddenly, she squealed. "I've got my Mama back!"

Giggling with her, Abby nodded. "Well, one parent is definitely better than none." And she was right. Poppy definitely felt positive about the way things were going, even if she'd suffered a minor devastation. Tomorrow, she'd actually get to hug her mother for the first time in seven years. That, at least, was something.

~~~~~~~

Catherine Applebaum saw the world through new eyes as she rode in the back seat of the car, headed toward the airport. That is, when she bothered to look. The colors were brighter, more vivid, and her sense of smell proved more potent as well. But her mission distracted her, the desperation to get to Poppy as soon as possible overriding her appreciation of these powerful changes to her life.

Nothing overrode the safety of her precious daughter.

She'd shared some of her revelations with Jill and David, and they'd listened intently before hitting Catherine with their own surprise information. But she hadn't even begun to share the majority of the information overload she'd experienced over the past ten years. It wasn't that she wanted to hide it from them. It simply worked out to a matter of priority. She wanted to motivate them to get moving as quickly as possible without delay, which additional conversation would have caused, and she also wasn't sure she could handle going through such weighty information twice.

And she had to tell Poppy.

So they would hear the rest of her message when they reached Seattle and the safety of Poppy's dorm room, a place Catherine couldn't wait to be. If this had been hard on her, she could only imagine how difficult it had been for Poppy, not to have a mother or a father to hug, to talk to, to rely on, for ten years. And on top of the tragedy of missing her father for the previous three years?

It was a wonder Poppy was a sane, well-adjusted 18-year-old. At least, that's what she appeared to be. Jill and David seemed fairly confident in that assessment, though she could tell they were concerned on some level they weren't readily explaining. But she'd figure out what their hesitancy was soon enough.

For now, she focused on the messages she had to relay, and how she would do so. It was like a data dump from a full database swirling in her head, and she needed to organize her thoughts and make sense of it all. She understood most of it, but there were still holes in the overall idea, and she could only hope that sitting down with Poppy and her in-laws would help her fill in the missing pieces. Only then could they strategize and form a plan of action that would keep them all safe.

~~~~~~~

CHAPTER 9

Brendan cursed himself as he slammed his laptop shut and stormed across the house. How could he have missed this? He had the files from the murders in Bexar County, but he'd never considered checking into disappearances. And as soon as he'd taken a look, he'd struck gold. It looked like the entire pattern had begun there.

With a Richard Applebaum. Imagine that.

The file stated Poppy, as an eight-year-old child, reported seeing her father disappear in a 'black cloud'. The investigating officer had blown that off as the manifestations of a young, creative child who didn't want to accept that her father suffered from PTSD and had run off. To the rest of the world, that sounded like a plausible explanation, and it was easy to see why that would have been the more acceptable one.

But from his own research, Brendan knew better. Far too many of the murders mentioned a black fog or mist, a cloud of some sort, and while he couldn't come up with an explanation for the phenomenon, he certainly couldn't discount it with so many witnesses in agreement, especially since it was one of the few things that now connected so many of the cases.

And something that wasn't regularly reported by the media.

Yanking on a pair of jeans and hoodie and shoving his feet into a pair of sandals, he grabbed his keys and headed out. He chided himself for being a typical Seattle-ite on a typical dreary Seattle day, realizing it would only be worse if he'd worn socks with his sandals.

Getting in the car, he thought he might regret this, but he had to follow up any and all leads, regardless of how shady or confusing the source. Poppy wasn't shady in the least, but he still felt used by her, and he didn't like that. He wanted to believe she truly had interest in him, but he couldn't quite accept that yet, and the idea of being near her with that sort of perception made him cringe a little.

Nonetheless, she had perhaps the closest perspective of anyone he'd spoken to on the matter and maybe the most vested interest in the entire case. As far as he could tell, her father was the first recorded disappearance, and it meant she'd literally been there from the beginning. And she knew a lot more than any other civilian source he could tap. After all, she'd pointed him in the right direction to make a new connection that could actually lead to a break in the case.

With a grumble, he took off, headed straight for U-Dub and Poppy's dorm. He'd call her when he hit the parking lot and pray she answered his call. He'd been more than a little rude to her, and he wouldn't be surprised if she blew him off. One way or the other, he had to try, and he pushed the gas pedal to the floor, fighting the other idiots on the road until he found his opening and took off.

~~~~~~

Dressing after a satisfying shower, Poppy frowned when her phone rang yet again. "I am not this popular," she muttered, as much to herself as to Abby, as she reached for the infernal piece of technology. Sometimes, she wished she didn't have a cell phone and finally understood her grandparents' complaints about the 'good old days' when people couldn't always reach you wherever you were. Poppy couldn't imagine being disconnected like that but today she thought it might be kind of nice.

Her frown deepened into a scowl when she saw the number. "Great. One bitch session wasn't enough, apparently." She wasn't sure she could handle another run-in with Brendan, especially now that she was in a much better mood and had something to look forward to.

Exasperated, she answered, clenching her jaw. "Yes?"

"Can you come downstairs to talk? I'll buy you a coffee and some breakfast." Brendan's tone hadn't returned to a pleasant friendly one but it had certainly improved over the bitter, biting one of an hour ago.

She narrowed her eyes, suspicious of his motivation. "What, are you going to give me the third degree and then arrest me?" She realized she was being just as sharp with him, but she didn't really care. He'd been a complete jerk on the phone, and if he wanted her attention now, he'd have to earn it.

"No, I'm not. But I got your father's file, and I want to talk about this with you. Are you free?" He sounded sincere, but she wasn't sure she bought it and didn't respond at first. "Look, Poppy, I'm sorry for my overreaction earlier. I promise, this is just a brainstorming session to try to resolve some of my Intel with what you know. I think maybe, if we hash this out a little, I might make a break in the case."

That got her attention. "Sure. I'll be down in ten." She hung up and turned to Abby, a bit bewildered, to tell her what Brendan had just said. "I don't want to speak too soon, but I feel like things are starting to look up."

"It certainly sounds that way to me. I mean, worst case scenario, he's really interested in you, and after being such a ridiculous ass, he couldn't think of another way to get you to give him another chance." Abby returned to painting her toenails, and Poppy shook her head, smiling at her friend's assessment. Of course, she had a point. When men were desperate…

She started to go downstairs, but reassessing her appearance, she wasn't pleased. Sure, she was clean and didn't really have a lot other than the jeans and t-shirts she typically wore, but her face seemed a bit bland. That wouldn't do at all. She added some mascara and just a hint of blush to bring out her color and the brightness of her eyes, then grabbed her keys and phone. "I guess I'll be back later."

"Go get him, girl," Abby called after her with a laugh.

Skipping down the stairs, she pushed out of the dorm and looked around, finding Brendan leaning against a tree to her left, about 50 feet away. He had that handsome just-rolled-out-of-bed look, except he looked too tired to have actually slept. Walking up to him, she asked, "Did you sleep at all?"

He gave her a half smile. "No, I was thinking about you for a couple of hours, then about the case, and when I went to look back through the files, I saw your note and spent the rest of the night thinking about you *and* the case until I could call you without looking like a total creep."

She raised an eyebrow. "You were pretty harsh anyway."

"I was pissed off. You butted into my case, and here I was thinking that I was simply that charming that you found me and my career interesting."

Poppy threw up her hands. "You had it all right there, out in the open. All I did was point you to something you were missing. And again, I didn't come onto you last night. You hit on me. So, it's not like I was stalking you because of your job."

His face scrunched into an expression of consternation. "Give a guy a break. I was up all night, your note could easily have been mistaken as the killer toying with me, and I was all but hurt about feeling used."

She rolled her eyes. "Listen, Brendan, if you knew how little experience I had with men actually flirting with me, you'd realize I wouldn't even know how to use someone. Now, can we get past this? I told you I was sorry."

He nodded. "As am I. Let's start fresh." He straightened and started walking, motioning for her to follow. Poppy saw where he was parked and headed after him, climbing in the passenger seat and waiting to see where he planned to take her. In the back of her mind, she hoped it was somewhere they could find a little privacy. Something about her mother's insistence on being in a safe place rankled her and made her paranoid. She didn't want to discuss the case in a very public setting.   .

To her relief, he pulled into a small café that didn't appear very busy and led her to a small booth in the back corner, where they were pretty far removed from the rest of the small crowd. It didn't get much quieter than this at a restaurant.

Brendan didn't start talking until after they'd ordered coffee and their food. "How comfortable are you talking about your father's disappearance?"

She shrugged. "It's been ten years. I still remember it like it was yesterday, but the pain has subsided somewhat. Plus I finally have my mom back, so I'm in really good spirits today."

He frowned at her, confused. "What do you mean, you finally have your mother back?"

She sighed. "When Daddy disappeared, Mama became catatonic. She ate and breathed and slept and sometimes even walked or moved, but she wasn't much more than a really depressed lost soul. And that's lasted for ten years. But she called me today, and she's awake and functional and headed up to see me tomorrow. It's a huge deal, and I'm sort of focused on that, so talking about Daddy won't be hard today. What would you like to know?"

"Everything." Something seemed particularly odd with the part about her mother, but he was focused on the case, so he didn't follow up on that. He had priorities, and he needed to stick to them. He thought again about his heart and the condition it must already be in with all the stress of this case. He didn't need to add yet another mystery to the mix. "What you saw, what you felt, who was there, and anything else you might find relevant to that particular occurrence, even if it's just a gut feeling."

It was the first time anyone had ever asked her for such an in depth account of that day. Even the officers who were supposedly investigating hadn't asked her that much. Partly because she was so young, she guessed, but also certainly because they assumed she was a just a little kid upset about her father running out on her.

"I was still in the store when it started. There was a chill in the air, and all my nerves tingled. I felt nauseous, like I'd eaten bad food, and I could still see the sun shining in the sky, but it was dark outside the big picture windows at the front of the store. Daddy had gone back to the car for his wallet, and I knew something was really wrong, especially when the store clerk didn't notice anything."

Brendan nodded. "So, you went outside to see what it was." It was a statement rather than a question. Poppy was a precocious female; he could only imagine how much more so she'd been as a child.

"Yes, I did," she told him in an unapologetic tone. "My father was the most important person in my life. And when I got out there, my dad looked at me, his mouth open like he was screaming but nothing was coming out. The black cloud swirled around him and got thicker until I could barely see him, and then both the cloud and Daddy started

to fade until it was all gone and all that was left was this."
She pulled out her wallet – the same one her dad had
dropped when he'd disappeared. She'd carried it as her
own ever since she'd been old enough to put something
important in it. "When it was over, the day got brighter
again, and it was like nothing happened. Everyone
assumed he'd just run out on me because, after being a
POW for three years, he couldn't hack coming home to his
family." Her voice carried an edge of disgust.

"But you knew better."

"You're damn right I did. My father was thrilled to be
home. I know for a fact that, through the entire
rehabilitation process the army uses for POWs, he did
nothing but beg to come home. He wanted to be with me
and my mother and his parents. He was supposed to be
gone eleven months, and he'd been away for three years.
He was a strong man with tender emotions. He would
never run out on his family." She scowled, looking down
at her drink and stirring it absently before adding quietly,
"I also knew I wasn't delusional. I hadn't imagined it,
there was a face in the mist and I had this strange feeling,
like nausea."

Brendan stopped the conversation while the waiter
delivered their food and refreshed their coffee, then
asked."A face? "

"Yes. It wasn't my fathers. It was something else.
Something I can't explain."

"Have you felt that strange sensation again at any point?"

"A few times. Every time I heard about one of the crucifixion murders on the news, I felt it, just not as strong." She took a bite of her eggs. "Of course, when I heard the first one with a witness who saw a black cloud, I knew it had to be related, and that feeling was stronger. But my grandparents didn't want me dwelling on my father's disappearance or spending time getting involved following this serial killer or whatever it is." She shook her head. "I think they still have some sort of notion as to what's happening, some strange connection they're aware of they aren't sharing, but I don't know what it is."

Brendan considered that for a long moment. Several of the witnesses had given statements to the interviewing officers regarding a feeling of being near or surrounded by 'evil', of the sensation of bugs crawling on their skin or electricity shooting down their back. All of those who had mentioned the black substance surrounding the crime scene talked about a 'sticky' feeling or one of doom. Many also felt nauseous during the episode. A few had even commented on the area surrounding them looking dark, despite a cloudless sky with a bright sun.

It all added up, but to what solution? That was where everything got tricky. If Brendan believed in the supernatural, all of this would make a hell of a lot more sense. But he was a cop, and cops worked with fact and tangible evidence in the corporeal world. Magic and evil entities were not things to be considered in investigations.

Stepping out of his comfort zone, he asked a question leading a different direction, hoping he wouldn't make Poppy as uncomfortable as he was about to make himself. "So, tell me, do you have a theory? And if you do, does it involve an evil plot or just your average serial abductor and killer?"

She scoffed. "Average, huh? Is there such a thing? I mean, look at history. Every serial killer who's been caught has a different MO, a different reason and motivation, a different perspective. I don't think there's such a thing as an average, run of the mill serial killer."

"Okay, you got me. But you know what I'm asking. Do you think there's something outside of human actions involved in all of this?" He felt ridiculous even asking and it took a lot of effort not to blush.

Wrinkling her nose as she thought that over, she considered the distinct possibility that Brendan was purposely trying to rule her out as a viable, reliable source on the grounds that she was some lunatic who believed in what they referred to in Harry Potter as the Dark Arts. While she very much believed in evil, she wasn't sure how to answer his questions. "I'm not sure what you're looking for here, Brendan. If you mean, do I believe in witches around a cauldron churning up wicked potions? Or monsters under my bed trying to eat me? I don't. But evil exists, or we wouldn't have things like serial killers."

"Fair enough," he hedged. "I guess what I'm asking is this: a black cloud or mist or substance of some form or fashion surrounds a victim and he or she disappears, or it hovers around the area and the person inside is crucified. Now, is there a logical or scientific explanation for this cloud, or is it something supernatural?"

Poppy couldn't believe she was having this conversation at all, much less with a virtual stranger who also happened to be a member of law enforcement. It was so surreal she laughed. "Hocus pocus, abracadabra. I hate feeling like a child who's watched The Hobbit too many times." She felt better when he smiled with her, but she still sobered quickly. "I don't believe in unicorns, so I don't know that I can believe in ghouls either. But even the Bible talks about demons, and I guess if I believe in a God above, I sort of have to buy into demons and the devil, don't I? Otherwise, I'm a bit of a blasphemous hypocrite."

He didn't respond, and she gave him a testy look. "So, what do you believe in, Brendan? Because the look on your face expresses your opinion of me and my crackpot theory quite clearly."

He laughed this time and shook his head. "No, Poppy, you're reading it all wrong. That's my thoughtful expression." Getting serious, he leaned forward, lowering his voice slightly. "Look, I've been trying to reconcile this for months now. And I'm a pretty rational guy who is pretty good at explaining things in a natural, scientific way. I believe in shifting of energy, controlling it to make things happen. I believe the universe runs on force of will, and science has proven that energy never disappears, just changes. So, who's to say you can't put certain energy out there and cause it to rain, or make some other such thing happen? That, I guess, could be similar to a spell."

He stopped and took a bite, thinking about his next words and feeling that frustration that always built in his chest when he came to the conclusion that he was getting nowhere. "But I can't seem to find a way to make the 'black cloud theory' fit into that same box. And yet, I have to believe it because so many witnesses saw it. It' hasn't been covered by the media in most cases, so it's not like people can fake it. And even when it has been mentioned, the details of how it comes and goes and acts while it's there haven't been divulged, and every witness who's seen it gives an almost identical account of it." He waited a breath and sipped his coffee before adding, "And you were the first."

Brendan's words filled a hole in her chest she hadn't realized she'd carried all these years. Being validated felt good, but that wasn't the only thing about his statement. He'd also verified that this whole string of occurrences had started the day her father had come home, the day he was taken from her all over again. He had been the first to confirm that, the first to truly believe her, the first for a lot of things that Poppy didn't want to evaluate just yet.

She cleared her throat to keep her emotions in check. "Is there significance to that?"

He shrugged. "Don't you think so? Why Richard Applebaum? The reason he disappeared, or was taken, or whatever happened to him, has to link all the others after him. It's the key to solving this case, and all the cases across the country. Hell, for all I know, this is global." His eyes danced with excitement. "And if that's the case, I can pretty much guarantee we don't have one serial killer on our hands, we have some sort of mass movement, whether human or other. I seriously doubt we are dealing with one person. Its happened too many times in too many states. Could be copycat killers of course."

Her heart pounding, Poppy put down her fork. "But what is it? Who's doing it, and what's the pattern? It's not genocide, or a religious zealot going berserk." Her father had sometimes attended the nondenominational church with her family. They'd never bought into a particular sect, and they weren't avid churchgoers. And as far as she could tell from the various cases she'd researched, none of them had been part of a pattern that would have been created as a vengeful act against a particular sect or god.

Brendan sighed, throwing his hands up in defeat. "And that's where I don't have answers. But it's also where your father comes into play. If we find out the facts there, we can piece this together." Why had Richard been taken? Where had he gone, and why had he been the first? Was there something about him that wasn't quite understood, something that rolled over and created the pattern? It only took one small trait to link everyone together, and Brendan prayed that Richard Applebaum held the answers that would put that chain together.

Poppy remained focused on Brendan's words, not quite sure she'd understood correctly. She gulped at his insinuation. "Did you just say 'we'?"

He grinned, but no mirth reached his eyes. "Neither of us has found the answer on our own, have we? I can't exactly hire you, but I know your interest in this is far more vested than anyone on my payroll. I can't pay you, Poppy, not like I could someone on my team or a source on my list. But if you'll work with me, I'll help you find your father."

Her heart soared. This was the best news she could remember getting in ages. She wanted to throw her arms around him but didn't, restraining herself, in case it wasn't welcome. Blushing a little, she told him, "I have information on every disappearance and every murder across the country for the last ten years that might be related. Any crucifixion, any disappearance with a witness who saw a black vapor, cloud, mist, whatever. I have dates, locations, names…all I'm missing is profiles on the victims, which is what I need to try to cross-reference any kind of connection."

He smiled. "I can get that, if you can get me the list." Oh, yes, they'd make a great team, and he'd become a national hero when he solved this case. In the meantime, he'd help Poppy find her answers and have the attention of the beautiful, charismatic woman who intrigued him so. "It's a win-win situation."

Poppy couldn't agree more.

~~~~~~~~

CHAPTER 10

Jill watched her daughter-in-law while David filled out the paperwork to rent a car. She seemed mostly like her old self, though her nervousness drew deep lines across her beautiful face and she wrung her hands constantly. She'd taken the news well, all things considered, but she had her own demons to contend with, and with the hell she'd lived for ten years, stuck in her own personal prison, she was fragile, whether she realized it or not.

Jill wasn't quite sure how yet, but she knew she could use that fragility to help put herself back in the driver's seat as it were. She could use Catherine's weakness and David's status as an outsider, even if it was cruel, and she could regain control of the situation. She knew best, and she would have things her way. She was determined it was essential to saving all of their lives.

In the meantime, she'd play the fool.

Catherine had insisted on three things after they'd sat down and discussed the turn of events. Her most adamant demand had been to get to Poppy as soon as possible to tell her the truth. Jill had balked, fought that request tooth and nail. She knew they would simply be disrupting the life her granddaughter was leading, free of pressure and worries. She also feared they'd be leading trouble right to Poppy's door.

David had taken Catherine's side, said they'd kept the truth from Poppy too long and, now that she was an adult, it was likely she'd start experiencing inexplicable changes in her life that would drive her mad without any understanding or support. Jill couldn't remember a time when she'd felt that way, and Richard had certainly never exhibited such traits. And neither of them had been aware of their true state of being. Jill argued that Poppy would be no different. But again, the two of them had sided against her. Defeated, Jill had quietly packed a bag and followed along, keeping a close eye on Catherine and her frailty.

The other two requests had been simpler, and Jill had been happy to assist, considering she had no choice in traveling. Catherine's figure was easy to shop for, and they'd found a new outfit for her to wear today as she greeted Poppy in less than an hour. She'd also helped Catherine color her hair, just a bit of black dye to cover up where some of the roots had gone gray. It didn't take much, since her renewed vitality seemed to be bringing more and more color to her on an almost hourly basis, but Jill understood the small vanity and complied.

The drive from the airport to the dormitories would only take about 30-40 minutes, and Jill found herself holding her breath most of the way. Traffic proved dangerous and slow-moving, with a mist making it appear foggy and all the bright colors of Washington State washed out and gray. For once, Jill felt terrible about having sent Poppy away. She had ended up in a place where everything was black and white, like an old film, and the days were dreary, the nights cold. How could she possibly keep her head up in such a depressing place? She'd come from the land of heat and sun. Jill could only imagine what Poppy had become over the years. She imagined her granddaughter as a vampire.

When they exited the I-5 and headed toward the U-District, Jill could sense the relief from both her husband and Catherine, and she, too, let out a long breath. They'd made it off the freeway safely. But even the streets and avenues were crowded and difficult to navigate. Jill had never spent much time in Seattle, but it seemed like rush hour was an ever-present state, much like the rain.

As the school loomed in the distance, she turned to Catherine. "You should call Poppy and let her know we're here. I don't know exactly where her dormitory is, and she'll come down to meet us."

Catherine nodded and pulled out the cell phone. Jill had been very short and clipped since the decision had been made to come to Seattle, and it angered Catherine that her mother-in-law wanted to continue hiding things from Poppy so badly. Didn't she understand the danger that put Poppy in?

Holding back a biting remark, she dialed her daughter and waited while the phone rang in her ear. "Hello?" came Poppy's voice, sounding anxious and nervous.

"Hello, darling. We're pulling up to the school in a couple of minutes and have no idea where to go."

"Are you on 45th? You should just pull into the parking lot at the Catholic center." Catherine squinted, seeing the Prince of Peace Catholic Newman Center coming up on the left and directed David towards it. "I'll meet you down there in just a few minutes."

"You good?" Abby asked as Poppy checked herself in the mirror for what had to be the twelfth time in less than five minutes. Poppy knew she was fidgety and flighty, but she deserved that right, talking to her mother for the first time they'd been able to talk in ten years.

She nodded and smiled reassuringly. "I'm great. I'm just...nervous. It's going to be great, you'll see when they get up here." Poppy knew that she was partially trying to convince herself as much as she was trying to convince her roommate. She loved her family, and she was so glad to have her mother back, but she felt distanced from her grandparents and still a little hurt that they'd sent her away. And what if Mama wasn't the same after all these years? Traumatic experiences could change a person. She knew that firsthand.

Abby looked sheepish. "Are you sure you don't want some privacy? I mean, I can easily disappear for a few hours, if you want the time and space." She looked lost, and Poppy couldn't help but feel bad. She may have her mother back, but Abby would never feel like she had hers back with the disconnect they had. She wished she could take that pain away from her roommate. "I really don't want to intrude."

Poppy rolled her eyes and laughed. "Come on, Abby. I've told you at least six times that's not necessary and I want you and my family to meet. You're my best friend, and you've been my only family for years while my blood relatives had what was apparently far too all-consuming going on with them." She didn't want to be bitter, and she forgave her mother and, most likely, even her grandparents. But that didn't mean she was any less hurt by being shuffled off across the country, even if she did prefer it here, to be completely honest.

Taking a deep breath and preparing for the meeting, she gave Abby a quick hug. "You stay here, and I'll be back with my family in a few minutes." She squealed for a second, unable to help herself. "Oh, Abby, they might have some news about my dad."

Abby gave her a sympathetic smile. "Don't get your hopes up too high, okay? I don't want to see them dashed if they don't have news or, worse, if the news is bad."

Poppy understood her sentiments, but there was no reason to worry about bad news. Somewhere, deep down inside, Poppy could still feel Daddy, and she knew that, against all the odds, he was still alive. And even if her family had nothing to tell her, she now had Brendan as an ally, someone who truly believed in her and was willing to fight to help her find her father and bring him back to her. Either way, it would work out, and she couldn't look at things negatively.

With a quick nod and a wave, she hurried out the door and downstairs, racing across the campus and then down the street toward the Catholic center. She wrinkled her nose at all the Frat and Sorority houses she passed, wondering what about people made them need to fit in so badly.

But those thoughts were pushed from her mind instantly as she saw her mother, standing under an umbrella at the back of the car, watching for her as if she was more anxious than Poppy. The sight of Mama there fueled her, and she sprinted the rest of the way, throwing her arms around her mother's neck and laughing with delight. "Mama!"

Catherine wrapped her arms around her daughter with a contented sigh. She couldn't believe how good it felt to be able to do something so simple. Maybe this wasn't the little girl she remembered, but Poppy had grown into a beautiful young woman and still looked and felt like the daughter she loved. She couldn't have asked for anything more. "Hello baby. I've missed you so much." The hug was desperate, and Poppy felt all the love her mother carried for her seeping through her touch, into her bones. She reveled in it for several long, heavy breaths as she fought a wave of tears that threatened to crash down her face.

Finally, Poppy stopped squeezing her mother so tight and leaned back to take a good look at her. Confused, she stared in wonder. When Poppy left for school, Mama had been getting wrinkles, and her hair was starting to turn gray. She had aged quickly and, as far as Poppy knew, that aging process hadn't started to reverse itself for the four years she'd been gone.

But today, Mama looked very much as Poppy remembered before Daddy had ever left for the war. She was young and vibrant, not a line on her face, her hair returned to its natural shimmery black, just like Poppy's. Her eyes also glowed the emerald green Poppy had inherited, and she couldn't believe the change in her mother. In fact, it was quite possible that, if the two of them went out together, people would be more likely to believe that Catherine Applebaum was Poppy's sister than that she was her mother. It was an incredible shift. And while she still sensed some sort of fragility underlying all of it, Poppy was too glad to see this remarkable recovery to question that too much.

"I've missed you, too. Mama, you look incredible!" She smiled in wonder, searching her mother's face, even as the older woman looked away, suddenly not making eye contact.

For the first time since she'd come down, Poppy looked over at her grandmother, who was sending Mama some sort of pointed look she couldn't understand. She couldn't make herself truly greet Nana, not when the older woman had so severely hurt her. Nodding curtly to Nana but not going over for a hug, Poppy turned to Papa, giving him a broad smile and jumping into his outstretched arms. "Hi, Papa!" He was the only one that appeared to have aged, and while he didn't particularly look old, there were more creases at the corners of his eyes, a few around the edge of his lips, and the skin on his neck had begun to sag a bit, whether due to age or weight loss or both, Poppy wasn't entirely sure.

"Don't you look all grown up?" David greeted his granddaughter, amazed at the time that had passed, now that he saw Poppy. She looked utterly amazing, the spitting image of her mother, and while she'd kept her relaxed style, her body had matured, as well as her face, and she was ethereal. It was a wonder boys weren't crawling all over her, he thought grumpily, but let it go in favor of the joy of a reunion and the desperate times that had brought them here.

Poppy blushed under Papa's praise, as she always had. "Look, why don't we all get in out of the rain? I know it's just a drizzle, but it's a little cool outside right now, and there's plenty of space, it's dry and warm in my dorm room. And I can't wait for you to meet my roommate, Abby."

She didn't miss the dark expression on Nana's face, although Mama and Papa didn't seem to think anything of her statement. What had happened to Nana? Why was she so negative and disapproving? It hurt Poppy to think of how close they'd been and how much it seemed she didn't even know her grandmother now. Certainly she'd been away from her whole family long enough to feel a little bit estranged, but it was worse with Nana than even with her mother, and they'd been separated a lot longer.

Determined not to let Nana's judgment get her down, Poppy took them the shortest route through the campus back to her dorm building, and for the first time ever, she called the elevator, not wanting to make the rest of them climb the stairs.

Catherine didn't say anything and tried to keep her expression stoic, but she was insanely relieved to use the elevator. She had gained a great deal of strength, but after so long of not using her body, the muscles had weakened immensely, and she was physically exhausted from this long journey she'd taken. Of course, Jill was looking for almost any excuse to put a stop to all this, so Catherine did her best to hide it, but just like she could sense her mother-in-law's angst, she knew Jill could sense her exhaustion.

As they stepped into the corridor leading to Poppy's dorm, her mother and grandfather followed eagerly, while Nana lingered behind. Her actions made Poppy uneasy, and for that reason alone, Poppy couldn't wait to get to the bottom of things. Whatever bothered Nana, she was allowing it to affect the way she treated everyone around her, so Poppy actually felt like maybe she hadn't wanted to come. Forcing herself not to say anything that might ruin the pleasant parts of this visit, Poppy pasted on a smile and opened the door to her room.

"Mama, Papa, Nana, this is Abby. She's my roommate and best friend." Poppy made introductions as they filed into the room, hoping to avoid any kind of awkwardness that might ensue. Right now, she wasn't sure who she trusted anymore, especially with the friction she could feel in the air.

Abby gave her most winning smile and extended her hand to each of them in turn. "It's great to meet all of you. I've heard so much about all of you that I feel like I know you already."

Catherine smiled at the young girl. "It's wonderful to meet you, too, Abby." She stepped back as David offered a friendly greeting and frowned as Jill offered a curt nod, a touch of fingertips, and stepped away. Really, the woman was being ridiculous, and it was creating a tension between all of them that was useless. As if they weren't all stressed enough!

Clearing her throat as if to clear the awkward moment, Abby turned back to Poppy's mother. "Wow, you two look so much alike! Ms. Applebaum, you are a beautiful woman."

With a shy smile, Catherine nodded. It had been so long since anyone had told her that, and while it made her miss her husband even more, it also made her feel better after such a long time. "Thank you, Abby."

Poppy and Abby pulled the folding chairs they'd borrowed from downstairs out of the closet and set them up so everyone could have a seat. When Poppy set up the fifth chair, her grandmother's eyes bore a hole in her. "Are you planning on making family business public knowledge?" she snapped.

Tired of the attitude she couldn't for the life of her understand, Poppy felt the anger gather in her chest and responded in kind. "Abby's not a member of the 'public', Nana. She's been more family to me over the past four years than you have. Maybe, if you weren't so stiff and determined to make this an unhappy occasion, whatever it is we're going to talk about, you'd realize that."

Jill opened her mouth to respond, but David pointed to a chair, his face less than pleased. "I love you, Jill, but this is not your situation to control. You've played your part, as have I. Now, it's time to sit back and shut our mouths and simply offer support where it's required."

"Really, Jill, what's gotten into you?" Catherine asked in exasperation as she took her own seat next to where Poppy stood. "You've been nothing but belligerent since I came out of my catatonic state. If you're angry because life was easier while I was out of it, please say so because I thought we had a better relationship than that."

As Poppy turned to Nana, looking for a response, she saw tears in the woman's eyes and an expression that said she was about to explode. Poppy held her breath and waited for the eruption. She wasn't disappointed. "We have protected Poppy all this time, just like we did Richard. And now, you're doing everything in the world to ruin the protection we've built to keep her safe! Coming here when the idea was for her to be untraceable, wanting to tell her everything when Richard was just fine never knowing."

"Just fine!" Catherine cut her off. "Maybe if you hadn't held back the truth, he would never have disappeared. Did you ever consider that, Jill? Or maybe, if my parents had told me, I might not have slipped into a virtual coma for ten years and might have been able to handle things more adequately. Then, you never would have had to carry that decision on your shoulders, and we wouldn't have needed to make this trip you seem to think is so dangerous and such a mistake."

Poppy gulped, hearing the venom in her mother's voice. She desperately wanted to know what they were talking about, but she didn't dare interrupt either one of them in their tirades to ask. She started to feel embarrassed and glanced at Abby, but noticed she was desperately trying to follow the enraged conversation with incredible interest.

"My choices were made with everyone's best interest at heart," Jill came back. "And I took care of you every day while you were…sick. I made sure you were fed and cleaned and everything – it was hell, but I did it because I care. How could you possibly insinuate that I didn't want you to come back?"

Catherine scoffed. "Just because I was unresponsive doesn't mean I couldn't hear. It just meant I couldn't always process immediately and I couldn't defend myself. Such as when you told your husband that I was too much and I needed full time care in a facility that was created for that purpose."

"You what!" Now Poppy was livid. It hurt bad enough that she'd been sent away, but to realize that she'd been the one caring for her mother most of the time and that, as soon as the responsibility fell on Nana's shoulders, she was ready to pass it on royally pissed her off. "Nana, who are you? All my life, you were this charismatic, loving, attentive person with a smile on your face and love in your touch. But now you're crass, hateful, cold, and can't even accept responsibility for your own family. Tell me, once I was out of the house, and you got Mama into a home, did you plan on making Papa disappear too? In fact, maybe you're to blame for Daddy's disappearance, too. After all, it fits the pattern."

"Enough!" David roared, drawing all of their attention. "Sit down and be quiet. This is not what we came for. Now, there are several questions that are valid and need to be answered, but that has to come after we clear up a few other things, as we planned." He took a seat between his wife and his daughter-in-law, hoping to be a bit of an obstacle for the tension and hate between them at the moment, and turned to Abby, who was sitting quietly next to Poppy, watching the fireworks with wide eyes.

He gave her a sympathetic smile. "Abby, I'm sorry about this. I can't remember the last time we all broke into a fight like this. In fact, I think we've always gotten along. But there's a lot of stress on all of us right now, and I think it's affecting our communication."

Abby nodded. "It's okay, I understand. Besides, people who care about each other passionately are the first ones to argue with the same passion. Love and hate are flip sides of the coin. I know that better than anyone."

Poppy caught the sad reference, knew Abby wanted nothing more than a good relationship with her own mother, and it made Poppy feel terrible for acting this way in front of her. "I'm sorry, Abby. We'll keep things to a dull roar in the future." Abby simply nodded and smiled, and Poppy turned her attention to her mother. "Okay,

Mama, let's have it. Obviously, this is something very important or it wouldn't be such an arguable matter."

Jill started to say something, but seeing the warning look on her husband's face and the combative posture of pretty much everyone around her, she pressed her lips together. She wanted to beg Catherine to reconsider, to tell Poppy anything but what she'd come here to say. It was the last chance to keep her off the radar. But she knew she'd get backlash, and she'd already been outvoted, apparently, so she sat back and sat on her hands, just listening to the train wreck that was about to happen.

Not knowing where to start, Catherine sputtered for a moment. How did you divulge this kind of information to someone? If she didn't have firsthand experience, she wouldn't believe it, either. "Poppy, when I was...unresponsive..." she trailed off, looking for the right words. "I wasn't just tuned out. There were other things going on inside, in my head and in my soul. It wasn't grief that sent me to that place, either, or weakness. I think it happened when it did because, somehow, the messages had to come through, and those messages were triggered by your father's disappearance."

That made no sense whatsoever to Poppy. "Mama, I don't understand what you're saying. Are you saying that it wasn't Daddy disappearing that put you in that trance?"

"Well, yes and no. It wasn't the news that sent me spiraling down. It was...something connected to it. Like I said, when he was taken from us, someone had to hear these messages, and I guess I was chosen."

Oh, now this was a bit ludicrous. "Are you telling me you're some sort of medium or prophet or something?" Poppy giggled nervously, hoping her mother would deny it. Otherwise, she was beginning to understand why Nana was upset – she didn't want to admit that Mama had gone off the deep end.

"Not exactly, no. I'm a messenger." Sending a desperate look to David, Catherine got his nod of approval, and she took a deep, fortifying breath. "Poppy, not everyone is what they seem on the surface. I'm sure you know that in a metaphorical way, but it's also true physically." She huffed, feeling like this was coming out all wrong. "Honey, what I'm trying to tell you is that the voices I heard...they're angels, and they fed me information that I have to share, with you, and with your grandparents."

That was it. "Mama, that's insane!" She started to get up, but Papa motioned for her to wait. "Is this what you came 2200 miles to tell me? That you *hear angels* or the *voice of God*?"

"Poppy, listen to her." Papa's voice was strict and exacting, and despite her resistance to believing what she was hearing, she focused her attention on her mother, raising an eyebrow in expectation of answers to her question.

"What I'm telling you is, I am an angel, Poppy, and when your father was taken, a movement began, one that could destroy us all if we don't fight it." Tears came to Catherine's eyes at her daughter's look of disdain. She knew it sounded crazy, and she wanted to scream at Jill, blame her for the fact she'd never told Poppy what she knew. "You should have been told all of this sooner, but I didn't know myself, until I fell into my trance, which was obviously the only way my body could be the vessel to carry the information back to you."

Poppy scoffed. "Okay, Mama, what did the voices in your head tell you to pass on to me?"

Jill couldn't bear it anymore. As much as she wanted to keep things a secret, it would be worse for Poppy to possess the knowledge and not believe it. "It's true, Poppy. This isn't a game. Your father is an angel, too. I should know, I am the daughter of a union between an angel and a human."

Blinking in disbelief, Poppy wasn't sure which concept was more difficult – the idea of angels existing, or the idea that the stodgy old woman her grandmother had become was backing her mother up in this. "Run that by me again?"

David sat forward, deciding that the explanation Poppy needed would have to be from someone who'd lived most of his life in a human world, never knowing about the people he lived with, his own family. If nothing else worked, and Poppy felt betrayed by having been kept in the dark, she might understand and feel a connection with someone else in the same position, even if he didn't share the secret and wasn't truly a part of the world she would live in going forward.

Taking a deep breath, he chose his words carefully. "When I married your grandmother, I had no idea what she was. In fact, I had no idea about her, or your father, or your mother. I didn't learn about Richard until after his disappearance. That's why I took things so hard at the time and was a little distance. I felt betrayed by your grandmother for a very short time, and I had to get past that. But I've seen the signs, and I know it's real. If you don't believe them, Poppy, believe me."

Poppy gazed around the circle, taking in the serious expressions, as well as the skepticism on Abby's face. But even she seemed to be considering all of this with a rational mind. Poppy couldn't seem to find her rationale anywhere. How on earth was she supposed to make sense of all this?

"I don't understand why you're telling me this. I mean, how did you not know, if this is true? How do you not know you're an angel?" Poppy struggled, trying to make some sense of everything, trying to add it all up.

Catherine shook her head. "Full-blooded angels are sent down without memory, and they replace the souls of those who are not meant to survive their birth. It gives the parents joy, and it brings another good, protective entity into the world. So, I had no memory, and nothing triggered my abilities until your father disappeared. We keep the balance between good and evil without knowing, unless we are challenged."

Swallowing physically as if it would help her digest the information mentally, Poppy looked to Nana. "So, what about Daddy? He didn't know, either?"

Jill shook her head. "No, he didn't know. I watched my mother deal with her powers every day, trying to separate her daily life from her responsibilities. There are three types of angels. Messengers like your mother. Protectors, well you may have guessed that's what I am. And there are soldiers. Like Richard. I had hoped that, if Richard didn't know about it, he wouldn't seek out a life of servitude. The only reason I knew is because of my mother. Both of us were called upon before, after a calling you can sense other angels."

"And you never knew about Mama?" Poppy asked, knowing her tone was accusing.

Jill looked down at her lap, unable to meet her granddaughter's disappointed gaze. "I did what I thought was best, Poppy. In many ways, I still think it best. Your mother and father gave you all their attention, rather than having to dwell on others in need. Your mother never had to act as a channel for messages before. And whatever talent your father was blessed with never came to light, at least, as far as I know. And by keeping it from you, I had hoped we could keep the same reign on you and your powers so you were never obligated."

The impact of that statement hit Poppy hard in the gut for multiple reasons. "So, you held back from me something that I'm assuming is supposed to be a blessing. In essence, you've made me blind and ignorant to my own obligations in this world. How could you? Nana, that's so selfish." But that wasn't the worst of the shocks. "What exactly does that mean I am?" She didn't know what to think. She wanted to accept it as truth, but it all seemed as ludicrous as everyone had believed her story of a black cloud taking her father hostage to be.

"Does this mean I'm going to sprout wings now? That I'm going to hear messages from above? Does it mean I'm supposed to go out and hunt demons like some religious Buffy the Vampire Slayer? I can't even wrap my head around this, and I don't know what to think or feel. It's so outrageous, so crazy." She trailed off, unable to express in words what she was going through.

"No, Poppy, it's not like that," Catherine told her, trying to soothe her panic. "I know it's a lot to take in, but not everyone hears what I heard, and you aren't a soldier. You won't sprout wings, I don't believe. At least, no angel has so far, from what your grandmother has grudgingly told me. But then, you're a special case, so there could be things about you we don't understand."

"Catherine, that's enough. You're going to scare her." Jill's tone bit into her mother as she snapped.

"She has to know, Jill," Catherine told her, almost pleading for understanding."You have to stop pushing against this. It's better for her, safer for her to know. You tried things your way, and it hasn't done any good. It's time to open your mind and try a different way, one that makes sense in light of everything else going on."

Poppy was frantic with all the back and forth. Her eyes wide, she turned to her grandfather, who seemed to be the only one even the least bit calm and collected. He was going to be her rock in this, she could tell. "What is it I need to know, Papa? What am I exactly? And should I be frightened?"

When he spoke, Papa's voice was gruff and hoarse. "As far as anyone knows, Poppy, you are the only living product of two angels on Earth. You are a *Pure Bred*. A direct link to our maker."

Poppy blinked several times, not sure she'd heard correctly. Obviously, if all this was true, there were hundreds or even thousands or, for all she knew, hundreds of thousands of angels and half-breeds walking around on this earth. How was it possible that she would be the only individual in the entire world that was born of two full-blooded angels?

That was too much to grasp, so she shook her head. "I don't know if I'm ready to ask what that means right now.

Why don't we go back to you, Mama? I don't think you were finished."

No, she wasn't. There was far more her daughter needed to know, and she was going to get the information to her, come hell or high water, literally. Catherine squared her shoulders and sorted the messages she needed to pass on in her head, creating a list. "I think the first message I received that I could decipher was a warning." She cleared her throat and recited it, word for word. "*Souls are eaten, feeding strength, giving foot and substance to the Darkness.*"

Jill gasped, and they all turned to her, but she shook her head, her hand on her chest and her head down. "Continue, Catherine. Let's get all the information before we try to make any sense of it all, or make any rash conclusions."

Catherine nodded and presented another one. "*The Darkness consumes and grows, looking for a ladder.*" When no one responded immediately, she continued, "*The influence of the Darkness touches even the Light, and a battle must be fought.*"

"Like Armageddon in the Bible," Abby whispered, the first words she'd spoken during all of this. Poppy looked at her expectantly and shrugged. "A battle between Dark and Light. It's just the first thing that comes to mind, with all this talk about angels." They all looked at Catherine, and Abby asked quietly, "Is there any more, Ms. Applebaum?"

"Just one." Catherine nearly choked as she recited the next message. "*Richard supplies the connection. Richard is the trust and the heart of the Darkness, whether by will or by force. He must be stopped.*"

Poppy jumped from her chair. "What the hell does that mean?!"

David, too, was taken aback by the message. "The heart of the Darkness. But what is the Darkness? Every message seems to reference it, but there's nothing to explain what it is." He looked to his wife, but Jill was crying and not looking at him. "Jill, does that mean anything to you?"

Taking a deep, shuddering breath, she sat up, her lower lip trembling and tears streaking her cheeks. She swiped at them to no avail, more coating her skin. "When Satan the devil was cast down from heaven, he and his minions were the Darkness. He had hundreds of thousands of followers who did his bidding and brought in new corrupt souls. But the Redemption took his powers, and he was impotent. The souls he gets now are taken by force or given to him because they don't deserve a greater reward." She shook her head. "He is no longer the Darkness, but the ancient Dark Lord."

Still fighting against her belief, Poppy spoke in a voice barely above a whisper. "So, there's some new evil that has the powers Satan lost." She shook her head. "But what does all that have to do with Daddy? I don't understand how it's all related."

David hated that he had to deliver such news, but he cleared his throat and sat forward, propping his elbows on his knees for support. "The crucifixions. Each one of those we've looked into were angels. They are murdered in this way so the Darkness can absorb their souls."

Poppy blinked several times. "But Daddy wasn't crucified. He just...disappeared, right in front of me." She turned to her mother. "Mama, you said that Richard is the heart of the Darkness. That means he's not dead, right?"

"No, he's likely not dead, but it could be much worse." Catherine held back a sob as she started adding it all together. "But like Jill said, Satan had minions. Maybe your father's been taken for torture, or to feed the minions. Not dead, just ruined. Soulless. If we were to find him, I'm not sure he'd ever be the man he once was. For all we know, he could be fighting on the wrong side now. After all, the devil was once an angel of God that turned. Under the right influence, just about anyone would fail, have a hard time maintaining their faith." She shot a dirty look at Jill. "And especially if your father had no idea that he was an angel, it had to be difficult for him to resist anything they threw at him. His faith wouldn't have been as strong."

"I don't understand." Poppy was nearing panic mode and was thankful for Abby's hand on her shoulder to keep her grounded. "Are you telling me that, whatever this Darkness is, it eats the souls of angels? And that Daddy has either become food for them or, worse, become one of them? Are you really saying that right now?"

Jill pursed her lips. "The first message Catherine received. *Souls are eaten, feeding strength, giving foot and substance to the Darkness*. It means that, whatever evil entity is attempting to prove its prowess this time needs the souls of angels as fuel to walk the earth. Obviously, the search for a ladder means that this Darkness is searching for more than a temporary way to exist in a corporeal manner, but for what purpose, to what end, I don't know."

Catherine wanted to argue when her in-laws and her daughter told her to lay down and rest for a while, that they would go with Abby for coffee and let her regain her strength. She didn't particularly want to be alone. But she also didn't have the energy to fight and knew they were right. Her head and her heart were fine – in fact, they were ready for a fight. However, the rest of her body couldn't keep up after ten years of little workout.

So, she lay down and her eyes fluttered closed as she hoped for some untroubled sleep.

Headed back to the car, Poppy let her grandparents go ahead and hung behind a bit with Abby. "Look, I'm sorry for the disruption, and I really don't know what to say about all this. It all seems ludicrous, and I don't know how to handle any of it."

Abby shook her head. "Come on, Poppy, this is like movie stuff right here, but it's real. It's actually kind of cool, except for the fact that it means you're in danger. I just...I really think it's amazing how great your family is, even if they do have issues with each other. Plus, I think you're going to need all the help you can get." Abby nudged Poppy's shoulder with her own. "Just know that I'm here for you one hundred percent, through all of this, and anything I can do to help or make it easier, I will. I'm signed up with this army."

Again, gratitude overwhelmed Poppy, and unfortunately, Poppy knew she was right about needing help. But she didn't want to bring anyone into this unnecessarily. It seemed unfair to put all this on the shoulders of anyone who wasn't directly involved, who didn't need to know or care about the existence of things in this world that were typically mysteries or myths. And she certainly didn't want to endanger anyone.

Sighing to herself, Poppy considered the possibility of giving all this new information to Brendan. After all, he was working the case, and maybe with the facts he had access to, he'd be able to help them figure out the master plan. At the same time, Poppy didn't exactly have evidence that her and her family were angels, and they were already almost at odds, with Brendan having trust issues toward her. Why would she jeopardize what they had by feeding him information that sounded insane and reeked of cover-up?

Nonetheless, she felt the need to work him in slowly, and if she could find a way to prove to him what she knew — what her family knew — she'd do it.

She slid into the backseat of the car with Abby, giving her friend a warning look that said not to talk to Papa and Nana unless it was specifically required. Poppy still seethed at her grandmother's attitude, not to mention the fact that both of them had kept secrets and sent her away rather than preparing for this eventuality. Seriously, would there have ever been any kind of circumstances under which she could have lived her whole life without knowing the truth?

Highly doubtful.

Trying to forget about feeling betrayed, Poppy sat silently and when they got to the coffee shop, she splurged and bought the round, hoping to at least get a smile out of Nana, find that person she'd once loved. But it didn't work, and sitting around was a bit awkward. She wished her mother was with them but knew it would have been too difficult for her after such a long journey. It was really difficult seeing Mama look so vivacious and yet still knowing that, internally, she hadn't yet recovered even a fraction of her strength.

"You're off in space, Poppy." Abby's amused words cracked through the hell she was creating in her head, and she gave her friend a sad smile. "I'm just trying to process everything and decide where I can find allies and who's off limits."

Abby scowled. "You're considering bringing the cop in on this aren't you?"

Poppy shushed her adamantly. "I don't know yet, but I sure as hell don't want my grandparents to know he exists yet, especially since he *is* the investigator on the case. Okay?"

Abby nodded but it was obvious from the look on her face she had plenty of snarky remarks she was holding back. Good, Poppy wasn't in the mood for a sarcasm war right now, especially if it involved alerting other members of her family who were already too overprotective to the fact that she was interested in someone. And that this particular someone happened to be quite a bit older *and* working on the case that they specifically wanted to keep her out of.

Although, Poppy supposed, now they had no choice but to let her get mixed up in it. And that almost made her smile.

"Poppy, we'd like you to come home." Poppy and Abby had barely seated themselves at the table with her grandparents before Nana blurted the words, and Poppy's eyes grew wide. "I think it would be safer for you to be with your family so we can work as a unit."

Before she could stop herself, Poppy retorted, "That's a big change from the person who thought it best I not be anywhere near the family for the last four years." She saw Papa flinch right along with Nana, and she had a twinge of guilt, but at this point, that wasn't going to stop her from making her point. "I've made a life in Washington. I'm happy here, and I have no desire to go back with you. I'm set up to have a great education here at school, and I've got a lot of grants that are going to help pay my way. I waited forever for this acceptance letter, over all the others, and I'm not going to give away my chance to go to this school just because you're suddenly freaking out."

David rubbed his eyes, feeling every bit his age. He understood both perspectives, and it put him in a terrible position, right in the middle. "Poppy, your grandmother wants what's best for you, just like the rest of us. But sometimes we make mistakes. Whether sending you here was our mistake or bringing you home would be, something is bound to go wrong." He turned to his wife when he saw the determined look Poppy wore. "Jill, I don't think it matters at this point. What's done is done, and we can't change the course of whatever's happening just by moving around targets."

A single tear rolled down Jill's cheek. She felt cornered, as if everyone including her husband was ganging up on her. Why couldn't they listen to her? "I just want what's best for everyone, and I think that if we're all together, we're stronger than if we're apart."

"Excuse me," Abby piped up, quietly but with a degree of insistence. All eyes turned to her, and Poppy waited with anticipation to see what she'd say. "I understand your point of view, Ms. Applebaum, and it has merit. But if you don't mind me saying so, if there's someone in particular looking for Poppy or for angels in general, they obviously know where you live. They found Poppy's dad a long time ago, and if he's an angel, then it would follow for them to come back for her."

Jill considered that for a moment, against her will. "If that was true, they could have come for her a long time ago, before she came here. Richard was taken for another reason, I'm sure of that."

"She was just a child. None of the victims have been children so far. Maybe the purpose behind the crucifixions requires that it be an adult." Abby looked nervously around at all of them. Poppy looked to her grandparents. It was a sound theory, but she wondered if it would fly with her grandmother's adamant refusal to listen to reason from anyone else.

Finally, Jill sighed. "You may be right. I don't like it, but I suppose it's possible. That doesn't mean she's safe, though. Here, she doesn't have anyone to help her, to help watch for signs of danger."

Abby started to speak, opening her mouth as if to argue, but Poppy shook her head in warning, and she stopped. Was she going to mention the detective? Poppy still didn't want Nana in particular to know about Brendan. Knowing her, she'd be likely to assume Brendan was the enemy, trying to trap her. So, instead, Poppy said, "I have Abby now. I don't really want anyone dragged into this, but she's here, and she knows everything now. We might as well work together. So, I'm not alone, by any means."

David put a hand on his wife's shoulder. "There are others, Jill. We can speak to someone in the area, find others and let them know what we know. In fact, we need to let everyone we can contact know what we're dealing with."

"Not that we really know what we're dealing with," Poppy muttered. "But yes, if you know others, we should put out a mass message. They should know what Mama heard." She shivered, remembering the words, especially regarding the part her father apparently played. Even unsure of the exact role he'd assumed, the fact that he must be stopped meant he was on the wrong side. What if it came down to facing the father she'd lost to save her own life? Could she do it? Poppy wasn't sure and pushed the thought out of her head.

Jill looked around the table. She had a distinct fear that, in all of this, she was going to lose one or more of them. After losing Richard, she wasn't sure how much more she could take, especially if she had no way to step in and try to save the ones in danger. She couldn't do that from 2200 miles away. At the same time, they were all determined, and perhaps they would present less of a target if their energy was less concentrated.

Poppy alone, as the daughter of two full angels, had the most powerful presence, and that was Jill's main fear. If the Darkness was seeking out the energy of angels, she was a beacon in the black, more so than any other angel on the surface of the earth. She would have the power of a heavenly being, unlike the earth angels and that would be irresistible to anyone seeking to come out of the darkness.

But whoever sought out their kind hadn't come for her yet. And whether that was because she was here in Seattle or because perhaps she hadn't come into her full power yet, she had been safe up until now, even with the enemy preying on others in the area. "Okay, if you all feel that strongly, I can go along. But the first sign of trouble, I want you to call us. We'll come get you any time you need it."

Poppy didn't say it, but she got the impression that if she was ever in that kind of trouble, it would be over before they could reach her. But at least Nana was coming around. Poppy wouldn't say or do anything to make her question the decision. Instead, she'd find a way to get Brendan involved, and she'd contact others in the area than her grandparents knew.

And she had Abby, who, though she looked scared and skeptical, seemed to be strong and determined to help. She was like the sister Poppy never had, and she trusted Abby more than she trusted her own grandmother at this point. "I'll be alright, Nana. We just need a plan and more than just a few of us to execute it." She would also involve Brendan. He had the Intel, and if she had anything to do with it, they were going to be seeing a lot of each other. How would she explain some of the things she knew if she didn't tell him?

She wouldn't do what her grandmother had done and lie for decades. Nana had made a dire mistake. Whether it was Brendan or someone else she decided to grow old with, they would know the truth from the beginning. She believed in honesty, no secrets between her and her loved ones, and she would maintain that moral standard for the rest of her days, even if those days were numbered.

David looked at his wife again. She seemed distraught but less so than before. "We're only here for a couple of days. If we're going to get in touch with anyone you know, we'll have to work quickly. Do you have Raine's number?"

She nodded, her face drawn, her lips tight. Jill could be reasonable, but the sense of foreboding was heavy on her heart. She'd never had the gift of premonition, but she got gut feelings, and they were usually right. In this case, she just wanted to go home and be done with it. She felt as though their presence here only brought more likelihood of danger to Poppy, and avoiding that had been her sole purpose from the beginning. How miserably she had failed at that. "I'll call Raine and have her contact anyone else she knows. I'll ask them to try to meet us somewhere in the city tonight."

"Pike's Market will be pretty quiet in the evening, except for a couple of cafes down that way that are open, if you want to try that," Poppy suggested.

Abby nodded. "There are a couple of really small restaurants down that way and on First that are quiet and out of the way and won't be busy on a weekday."

"That's what we'll do, then," David settled for them. "Let's make some calls."

~~~~~~~~

CHAPTER 11

Brendan had called Poppy four times, only to get her voicemail. Frustrated, he dropped his phone on the couch beside him and stared at the television. He had no idea what was on, it was just background noise, actors on a screen dealing with some imaginary situation. This case reminded him of a movie, one with no clues. He only hoped it played out the same, with the answers coming in one big reveal at the end. What he didn't look forward to was the complete disaster that seemed like everything was hopeless prior to solving the mystery. That usually meant death and destruction.

He laughed at his own thoughts and shook his head. His imagination sometimes got the best of him, but then, what was he supposed to think about deaths that involved disappearing black clouds? All this seemed like supernatural horse shit, and he couldn't make heads or tails of it.

With a growl, he got to his feet. He couldn't just sit around in his pajama pants all day. He had work to do, and he needed to check on Poppy. It worried him that she didn't answer, and he had a bad feeling about it. He had to make sure she was okay. Her interest in his work, coupled with the fact that her father was obviously a victim of some sort, made her a special case.

His protective instincts in overdrive, he hurriedly showered and dressed, tossing all the files in a briefcase and taking it with him. If she wanted to dig deep, he'd let her. And maybe, in the process, he'd draw something out of her she had no intention of sharing, maybe even something she had no idea she knew that would help give them a lead.

As he started the car, Brendan rolled his eyes. The fact that he referred to 'them' was insane. It wasn't as if they were together and Poppy certainly wasn't his partner. She had no formal training in investigation, hadn't gone through a police academy. She was an innocent. And she was so young. He had no business messing with her at all, whether for business or pleasure. And yet, she seemed so much more mature than most of the women he knew, as if the hell she'd survived had given her perspective some people never had.

The drive seemed awfully short, and when he arrived, he cursed to himself, realizing he had no idea where on the campus to find Poppy. He didn't know which dorm she was in, and he wasn't about to just go wandering the campus, looking for her. And since she was new, he doubted anyone he might run into would know where she lived, either, should he ask. He'd just look creepy unless he showed his badge, which would make her look bad to everyone else. Why on earth would a cop come looking for her?

So, he tried her phone one more time and grew incredibly antsy and flustered when she again didn't get an answer. He got out of the car and stood there for a moment, just looking around and trying to decide what to do. He could always sit here and stake out the place. But he would bet anything the students were paranoid enough to call the police, saying he was a stalker when he was really just on a stakeout of sorts.

With a sigh, he decided to leave but looked up at the sound of a familiar voice. He blinked several times to make sure he wasn't dreaming and his stomach did a somersault in relief as he saw Poppy walking up the sidewalk with three other people. He assumed one was her roommate, looking the same age, but he had no idea who the older man and woman were. Suspicious, he took a deep breath, tucking his police issued firearm into the back of his jeans and flipping his shirt over it to conceal it, then started toward them.

"Poppy!" he called, catching her attention.

Poppy stopped in her tracks, staring in disbelief. It couldn't be...

But it was. Trying to be inconspicuous, she slid her phone out of her pocket and cursed when she saw several missed calls from Brendan's number. She should never have silenced her phone, should have at least left it on vibrate, or she could have stopped him from coming. The last thing she needed was to throw him into the mix with her family and all the madness going on. She'd planned to talk to him after they went home. Now, though, it was too late, and she would have to be very careful to control the situation.

As he got closer, she smiled hesitantly. "Hello, Brendan. What are you doing here?"

He stopped a few feet away, looking over the lot of them and assessing the expression on Poppy's face. She gave him a pointed look, and he somewhat understood, though he'd ask for an explanation later. "I thought I'd come say hello, see what you guys were doing today."

Abby raised an eyebrow at Poppy, who shook her head once again. Brendan had caught her warning, and he was trying to play it off as if he knew Abby, too. "Well, my family came to visit me today, so we're just hanging out." She turned to her grandparents. "Nana, Papa, this is my friend Brendan. Abby and I met him at a little get together a few months ago. Brendan, these are my grandparents."

Papa held out a hand with a smile. "David Applebaum. It's a pleasure to meet you."

Brendan shook it returning the smile, then turned and squeezed the woman's hand. "I'm Jill." She didn't seem to like him at all. But that was okay, he would play his cards carefully and win her over.

Poppy could tell Nana was having difficulty accepting the story. But then, her grandmother had always been suspicious of any males she'd even been distant friends with. In this case, she was looking at someone who was obviously older than Poppy and had just randomly showed up on campus to see her. And to be honest, aside from being nervous about Nana and Papa reacting, Poppy was giddy to see him.

She almost giggled when he offered a devastating, winning smile to her grandparents. "It's wonderful to meet both of you. I've heard a lot about you. Poppy's a great girl, and I have more fun with her and Abby than I think I've ever had with any other friends."

Abby nudged her, and Poppy glanced over out of the corner of her eyes, saw her friend trying not to laugh out loud. Oh, Brendan was good, and Poppy would have to ask him later if, perhaps, he'd taken theater in school.

Before Poppy could say anything, Papa chuckled. "Well, I hope you heard good things, though I wouldn't be surprised if our girl had some complaints. Either way, it's neither here nor there. We would love it if you could join us for dinner tonight. I've heard a great deal about a place called the Crabpot. I thought maybe we'd all go there tonight and stuff ourselves with seafood."

The thought made Poppy's mouth water, but she glared suspiciously at her grandfather, certain this wasn't something he'd had in mind before. Was he intuitive enough to know there was something more to it than a friendship? Or was he simply looking to discover what sort of 'friendship' his granddaughter had with a young man he'd never heard anything about?

Brendan looked to Poppy for approval, and she simply shrugged. With a nod, he turned back to her grandfather. "I think I'd enjoy that very much. I don't get to see a lot of my family, and it would be nice to be around a family that's very close."

Poppy nearly choked, and Abby spoke up. "I'm excited about it, too. I haven't seen my mother in over a year, and we've never been close anyway. I'm really looking forward to this."

What was going on with these people? Everyone had ulterior motives, this she knew. But they seemed to all be catering to her, though she knew whatever her grandmother wasn't saying couldn't be good. Taking a deep breath, she said, "Wonderful. Um, Abby, could you take my grandparents back upstairs? I want to talk to Brendan for a minute."

Abby's eyes glittered knowingly, and Poppy didn't miss the glances from both Nana and Papa as they followed Abby back toward the dorm. Feeling a bit embarrassed, she turned to Brendan. "So, how many years have you studied acting?" she asked, trying to lighten her mood.

He smiled at her and shrugged. "I think I did well, don't you?"

"Exactly," she said sarcastically. "Which only makes me wonder how I'm supposed to believe anything you tell me."

"Oh, come on. It was for your benefit. You looked like a deer in headlights when you saw me. You obviously don't talk to your grandparents much. How long have you known they were coming?"

"It was sort of sudden. Listen, Brendan. There's a situation…" She trailed off at his look of concern and instinctively took his hand in hers, gripping it a little tighter than she intended. "I'll have to fill you in later. But for now, I need you to not be a cop. I don't want my grandparents or my mother for that matter to know you're an investigator, and particularly not what case you're on."

He frowned. "Your mother?"

She nodded. "She's upstairs, resting. She…hasn't spoken since my dad disappeared, and she finally came to just a few days ago and insisted on coming here to see me. It's all part of a bigger picture, really, and I'll explain everything. But promise me you'll stay away from the subject if you're coming to dinner with us."

He nodded. "I can do that. Of course, I don't know if I can keep from doing this, though." Before she could ask, he pulled her against him and took her lips in a sensual, desperate kiss, and she couldn't help but return it, threading her fingers through his hair to press their mouths tighter together. He tasted like coffee and mint, and she reveled in it. She'd never felt this twisting feeling inside, never had her heart pound like this. And she'd certainly never tasted anything so sweet as Brendan's tongue in her mouth.

When he finally pulled away, Poppy's breath came in gasps, and she looked at him with wide eyes. "I don't know if I can ask you not to do that."

He chuckled, breathing hard himself. "Yes, well, I may have to take it a little slower for awhile. That got my blood pumping a little harder than I intended." He touched her cheek and watched her eyes dance, felt the warmth of her skin beneath his as they both delighted in the sensation. "I like you, Poppy, and I'm incredibly attracted to you. But if you want me to keep my distance, I will."

It would probably be best to ask him to do so while her family was here, but she sure as hell didn't want him distant forever. And even now, she couldn't imagine pretending she didn't want him as more than a friend, even with everything else going on. Hesitantly, she told him, "I have to warn you, Brendan, that the things going on in my life right now...they're dangerous. And anyone who gets involved could get hurt."

He searched her face, trying to figure out where her nervousness came from. Was she simply nervous because she'd never been in a relationship? Or was there really something dark in her life, maybe something related to his case, that she was afraid to share? He couldn't tell. "Whatever it is, Poppy, I'm not afraid of it. Hell, look at my chosen career. You think I have room in my life for fear?"

She shrugged, and she felt her face grow pink. "I just...I care about you, and I don't want to see you hurt. But if you're willing, I want you around. Close." Tentatively, she placed a soft, innocent kiss on his lips and whispered, "Not distant."

It lit a fire under his skin, and he took her in his arms, kissing her like it was their last night on earth. He wanted so much more, but he'd settle for this for now. Reluctantly, he let her go, and winked at her. "You'd best get upstairs. They're already suspicious of me. I'll see you tonight."

Slightly disappointed, Poppy nodded. "We'll probably be there early, maybe around 5:30. My family, I'm sure is still running on central time, and they'll be starving by then."

"I'll be waiting." With that he walked back to his car, and Poppy hurried off to her dorm, preparing herself to face the Spanish Inquisition.

To her surprise and extreme relief, Poppy found her family at least feigning disinterest in the whole thing. Her mind was still on the kiss, her lips tingling with it, and she didn't have the soundness of mind to respond appropriately to such questions.

Instead, her mother was waking from her nap, and Papa was informing her that they would be going out to dinner with some of Poppy's friends. She didn't see Nana, but Abby quickly pulled her aside. "Your grandmother's in the bathroom, but she already started asking me questions about how long we've known Brendan. I told her it's been almost a year and that we met him at a friend's party. That he's the brother of someone who went to school with us."

Poppy nodded, digesting the story. She hated lying, but in this case, it seemed absolutely necessary. "Has Papa said anything?"

Abby shook her head. "No, he seems to see through it, but he's not saying anything. I think he feels like your grandmother is way overprotective and that she's suspicious of everyone. To me, it just seems like she's used to being in control and just doesn't like that the situation calls for doing things a different way than she had planned." With a teasing look, she asked, "So, what happened after we left?"

Poppy knew she was blushing deeply from the heat on her face and neck. "Let's just say he's a really good kisser. I warned him that he'd be getting himself into a situation that could be really dangerous, but he said he was okay with that."

"He seems like a good guy. And he's still pretty, too." Abby looked like she wanted to say something else, but Nana walked in, so she just smiled and patted Poppy's shoulder. "I'm glad your family's here. I know how much you missed them."

It was interesting how, when it came down to it, everyone around Poppy seemed to fall into the pattern of excellent acting. She never felt like she was as good at it. But at least she had people to cover for her. Nodding in agreement to keep up appearances, Poppy moved toward the desk chair where her mother now sat and kissed her cheek. "Are you feeling rested?"

Catherine nodded, happy to see her daughter looking better. She'd seemed a little green at the information she'd been given, and now she seemed to be accepting. It was reassuring, and Catherine hoped it meant Poppy would be able to take care of herself. After all, it didn't make a lot of sense for her to come home. That would be the most dangerous place for her. But then, while the girls had been off whispering to each other, David had told her what a fight Jill had put up to try to convince them Poppy should return with them.

Taking a quick glance at Abby, Catherine sized up her daughter's roommate and friend. She seemed strong of will, and she gave off excellent energy. She was trustworthy. But how much help could she really be?

"I'm sorry I couldn't go with you, but I'm grateful for the time to rest. It's admittedly going to take awhile to regain my strength, but I'm determined to get there."

Poppy smiled at her. "That's good to know, Mama. Are you going to be up to dinner tonight?"

Catherine winked at her. "I wouldn't miss it for the world. I hear I get to meet more of your friends. That and the time with you are more than enough to motivate me." She motioned to Abby, who came toward her, then to David and Jill, who stood behind her looking antsy.

"Why don't we all sit down for a while, catch up with each other? I'm sure, with all the time you've spent in Seattle, you have some stories to tell, favorite places you've been."

It had been so long since she'd actually had a lighthearted conversation with her mother, Poppy wanted to cry and almost didn't know where to start. But with Abby's help, they talked and laughed about the last four years, and even Nana seemed to enjoy some of the stories. Of course, they were careful to leave out any bits about chasing down information on the crucifixion murders and the disappearances, but otherwise, there wasn't much to hide.

And by the time they caught up to the present, it was time to leave. It wasn't a long drive to the Crabpot, but there would be lots of traffic along the waterfront, and they would have to find parking. Poppy tried to keep her nerves at bay, but knowing she was going to see Brendan, and hoping that her mother approved, she couldn't help but stress. The only thing that kept her from completely freaking out was Abby's presence. Having someone who'd been by her side when her family hadn't helped her feel more secure.

~~~~~~~

Brendan stood outside the restaurant, watching people walk by, wondering if he'd made a good decision in coming here. Maybe it would be best to let Poppy enjoy her family's visit without him. Or maybe there was something going on that was family related he had no part in. But right now, he personally couldn't find the wherewithal to care. He didn't just want to be with Poppy, he needed to be near her.

Absently, he touched his lips, remembering the taste of chocolate and coffee on her, and it made him groan. He wanted so much more than a kiss, and knowing he couldn't get it tonight, or probably any time soon with her grandparents and mother in town, nearly drove him mad. Still, there was some strange connection that drew him to her, even if she was bad news. His instincts as a cop told him it wasn't her that was dangerous, but there was danger that followed her.

He supposed it could just be the connection to the case. Maybe the investigator in him saw his opportunity to solve this in Poppy. But it felt like so much more than that. He found her insanely attractive, but it didn't even stop there. He wanted to know everything about her, to protect her, and to make her happy. He frowned at that. He sounded like a lovesick teenager when he thought about it that way, and he realized it was almost obsessive.

But as he saw the group walking down the sidewalk coming his direction, a pretty sundress blowing around Poppy's legs, he had to swallow all those thoughts. She was a vision, and he didn't care how ridiculous he was being. He wasn't going to give up on this anytime soon, no matter what happened and no matter how ugly the situation Poppy referenced got.

He smiled as they drew closer, and he saw Poppy's shy smile in return. He walked toward them, meeting them at the side of the building. "Hello, Poppy, Abby. Mr. and Mrs. Applebaum." He turned to the woman he had yet to meet and nearly lost his cool. There was no mistaking her as Poppy's mother. In fact, they looked so much alike that he knew this was how Poppy would look in twenty years. And that was a beautiful thing. The woman was young and vibrant and absolutely gorgeous, just like her daughter.

"You must be Poppy's mother," he greeted, taking her hand and clasping it in both of his own. "You and your daughter look so much alike."

Catherine smiled at the pleasant young man. He was obviously older than Poppy by a few years, but it didn't really matter. She saw the way he looked at her daughter, and she rather liked it. It reminded her of the way Richard looked at her. "I'll take that as a compliment, since my daughter is gorgeous."

With a twinkle in his eye, Brendan winked at Poppy. "Yes, she very much is. I'm Brendan O'Malley, and it's a pleasure to meet you."

Poppy watched in awe as her mother blushed. No one had ever made her do that except Daddy, at least, as far as she knew. And it amused her because she knew full well she was blushing brilliantly as well. Part of her was glad to see the two of them hitting it off, but another part worried about the lasers shooting from Nana's eyes as everyone realized now that there was more between her and Brendan than friendship. And the worst part was, Poppy couldn't even define what that something more was.

But as she watched, Brendan shook hands all around, hugging Abby as if they were old friends, and then took Poppy's hand, leading her toward the restaurant with the others following behind. "How did I do?" he muttered without even looking at her.

Almost giggling at his discreet actions, Poppy mumbled back, "Impressive. Although, I have no idea how to explain all of this to my family."

"All of what?" he asked, raising an eyebrow as he finally looked at her. "You and me?" She nodded, and he snaked an arm around her waist. "I don't think they really need an explanation, do you?"

She cleared her throat, her skin warm and tingling where he touched her. "Maybe they don't, but I'd like one."

He didn't answer her, and that made Poppy nervous. In fact, he was silent as they were all shown to a table. Abby gave her a quizzical look, and Poppy just shrugged, unable to give her anything. She was incredibly confused, still quite nervous, and wildly unsure of herself. She thought about pulling Brendan back outside, demanding an answer, but she was already concerned with her family's reaction. She didn't want to raise anymore questions.

Instead, she sat down between Brendan and her mother with a smile on her face, trying to concentrate on the fact that it was a happy occasion, her family closer to whole.

As they took their seats, Brendan knew Poppy was sweating the answer to her question, and a part of him felt bad about it. But giving her that delay worked up anticipation, which could definitely heighten her pleasure when he did tell her. And while the others began ordering their drinks, he leaned over, placing his lips against her ear, and whispered, "I told you what I wanted, Poppy. I'm not going anywhere unless you push me away."

He could almost feel the shiver go through her as she turned her head and met his gaze with wide eyes. He'd certainly made an impression, and he watched the smile creep slowly across her lips, enjoying every second of it. Her beautiful face lit up, and he winked once more. "And by the way, you look amazing in a dress."

She blushed. "I never wear dresses. It's not really my style. But I figure we're celebrating tonight, so I'd dress up, go a little out of my comfort zone."

"Well, I certainly appreciate it."

Poppy's face grew even warmer, and she had to turn away from him. She had no intention of kissing him in front of her family, especially Nana, and if she didn't look elsewhere besides that charming face, she wouldn't be able to stop herself. She found Abby, who gave her a small thumbs up against her chest, and she felt a little better.

Jill didn't miss the subtle exchanges between her granddaughter and Brendan. She wasn't sure he was safe, and it made her worry about Poppy. The two of them seemed awfully close, considering that Poppy had never mentioned dating anyone, and Jill began to wonder just when she'd lost control of her granddaughter.

In fact, she wanted to figure out when she'd managed to lose track of everything going on around her. It had to be back before Richard had joined the army. After all, if she'd been able to control that, she would have saved all of them a lot of trouble. She felt like a failure in protecting her family, and that made her heart ache. She knew they all thought she was becoming a senile control freak, but it didn't matter. She just loved her family so much she couldn't let them all go down without a fight.

Deciding to put away her concerns and enjoy being with her family for now, she filed away the boy's name, knowing she could look him up later. The internet wasn't something she spent a lot of time with, but she knew quite well she could find all the information she wanted online. Pasting on a smile, she sat up straighter and joined the table conversation.

~~~~~~~~

CHAPTER 12

Seribulous eyed Richard with skepticism. He'd requested audience, claiming he had news, something he hadn't come forth with in a very long time. In fact, Seribulous had given up on receiving anything of importance from his servant and been sending out other slaves to gather information for quite some time. Moving them around the various states following a strong scent, he'd been presented with at least ten souls since they'd last met. Now he sat impatiently waiting some kind of update.

Nervous, his number one seemed a bit out of sorts as he stood before the master, and Seribulous wondered why. "Talk to me, Richard. I have not the time to sit here and grace you with my presence. Tell me what you came to tell me and let's be on with our work."

Richard stared hard at the large, ugly demon. He'd spent a great deal of time waiting during these past few months and discovered many things he'd rather not know. Nonetheless, he knew he had to play his cards carefully, especially now that he knew exactly who he was dealing with.

With a curt nod, he spoke, his voice hoarse from lack of use. He had spoken to no one for weeks. "Master, I was able to get into the house temporarily. The family is gone, traveling, and their security was easily breached without them there. I searched for the source of their protection but have found nothing so far. However, I may be able to wait inside for them to return, since the shields are down."

Squinting down at Richard, Seribulous tapped a finger on his forehead thoughtfully. "You believe the walls would simply be lifted around you if you were already inside?"

Richard hesitated, then nodded. He needed to talk to his family, to assure that Poppy was safe where she was and find a way to cover her tracks. This was a means for him to be with them and not alert Seribulous or any of his lesser demons to the fact that he knew the targets of his mission and had a vested interest in saving them.

He'd heard Catherine, his beautiful wife, when she'd come out of her silent world. And he knew where she'd received her messages. He couldn't believe that his own mother had lied to him about his heritage, nor that Catherine had never known herself what she was. Had Richard known his own background, he would have recognized it in Catherine. She'd always had that spark, that something extra. And it made all the sense in the world why, between the two of them, they'd bred such a perfect daughter. More so if he was a fallen angel then he needed to know how and why he was rejected from the path of good.

"I believe so, Master, yes. And once inside, I'll be able to hear their plans, learn all that they know, see if they have information on others. Collecting that kind of information could find you hundreds or even thousands of strong, hardy souls that will add up to the strength you need to climb to freedom."

Watching the dark light sparkle in Seribulous's eyes, Richard knew he had the demon hooked. Richard had lured enough innocent angels to their deaths, made enough of them trust him, only to watch them die in agony, to watch them pray as their souls were sucked from their weak human bodies. Today, he intended to start pushing things in the opposite direction. Somehow, he would use Seribulous's own lust for life above the underworld and whatever else he aspired to against him, to ruin him and take him down. He had to save his family and start the crusade to save them all, even if it meant losing his own life in the process.

Slowly, a rumble rose from Seribulous, a deep rolling thunder that became such an evil laugh it made Richard want to cover his ears for fear of being poisoned by it. But he stood his ground and waited while the Darkness gained control of his celebratory explosion. "Very well. Do as you wish, and I will await the information you seek. But I warn you, if you return empty handed, with neither a pure soul nor a list of strong, healthy prey, you will suffer. I have the resources to find and reap the souls of your family. I will assure you, you will never see them alive again."

Richard swallowed. Even if Poppy hadn't been his daughter, he couldn't allow Seribulous to find her. She was special, the key to assuring the demon couldn't be defeated. Richard had to make sure the Darkness never found her.

~~~~~~~

With a heavy heart, Poppy said an early goodnight to Brendan. They still had to meet with the few people – angels? – they'd managed to contact earlier in the day. And it was hard to be subtle with four other people specifically waiting on you, even when you purposely stepped around the corner, mostly out of their line of sight.

"Are you sure you have to go?" Brendan asked. Not only was he reluctant to say goodnight to Poppy, but he could also see the hesitation and anxiousness in her eyes.

She nodded. "It's some family business we have to attend to. Abby's heading home, taking the bus. It's something I have to do. Trust me, I'm not all that excited about it."

He heaved a sigh. "Alright then. Is this part of whatever you're going to explain to me later?" He caught her chill and ran his hands up and down her arms, which were covered in goosebumps.

"Yes, it is. But I can't do it with my family here. They – and my grandmother in particular – wouldn't approve of me sharing any of this information. But I trust you, and I think you need to know about it." Poppy winced, knowing she sounded cryptic, but she couldn't tell him any more right now. Not until they were actually alone.

Instead of asking questions or saying anything, Brendan simply wrapped her in his arms and held her for a long moment, pressing his lips to the top of her head. He could tell she had no idea how to react, but she put her arms around him as well and didn't pull away. "Well, if you need me for anything, just call me. I'll be there at a moment's notice."

Poppy still couldn't understand why he was so kind, why he wanted to be around her. Her life was a mess and only getting worse, and instead of running the other way, he was getting closer to her. "That means a lot," she told him, straightening and kissing him, a much more chaste exchange than earlier that day. She feared if she took everything she wanted, she'd never pull away and would get lost in Brendan.

Not that it sounded like a bad idea, but under the circumstances...

Reluctantly, she pulled away and leaned into his hand as he touched her cheek, smiling at her sadly. "You are incredibly special, Poppy. Have a good evening, and if I don't hear from you first, I'll call you tomorrow."

"Sounds wonderful. And thank you, Brendan." He gave her a quizzical stare. "For everything. For being kind and understanding and just…caring." His response was a quick kiss on the nose and a wink, and then he was off down the block, and Poppy was cold again.

Returning to her family, she saw Abby still standing with them, and her friend gave her a winning smile. "I convinced them I would need to know what the good guys look like," she muttered as they started down the street toward Pike's Market.

That made Poppy smile. The only thing she'd dreaded more than doing this in the first place was feeling alone with her family she barely knew anymore. Having Abby with her made her much more comfortable. She had no idea what to expect from a bunch of angels. It sounded preposterous to begin with, and she needed something or someone familiar to help ground her.

Squaring her shoulders, she hurried behind Nana and Papa, who had gotten a little ahead with Mama, who seemed to be regaining strength by the hour. It was really great to see, but the amount of energy she'd lost concerned her. If being an angel was such a wonderful thing, why had her mother had to suffer so much? It didn't seem right.

Catherine turned to look for Poppy, seeing her behind she stopped and walked with her daughter.

"How long have you been dating Brendan?"

The question came from her mother and, while it didn't surprise her, the tone did. Her mother sounded almost excited about it, despite her grandmother's inability to relax about it. She exchanged glances with Abby, who had nothing to offer. Trying to decide how to play this off, since she'd known Brendan for all of a few days, she hedged, "Not very long. Like I said, we're all friends. It just sort of happened."

Catherine nodded. She had a feeling they hadn't known each other as long as the girls kept suggesting, but she wasn't going to delve any deeper. She assumed Poppy was simply trying to keep Jill from freaking out. The woman had been on edge since Catherine had come to, and it was starting to worry her. But rather than back off her line of questioning, Catherine persisted in satisfying her curiosity, though she kept it light and tried not to invoke the same curiosity in her in-laws. "How much older than you is he?"

Poppy honestly didn't know Brendan's exact age, and she nearly panicked. Abby elbowed her in the ribs, and she spit out, "I think he's 25. He's not that much older, Mama. And I'm 18 now."

"Oh, I don't have a problem with it, Poppy. I'd rather you date someone older and more mature than someone young and stupid who would hurt you with their indecision and immaturity." She put an arm around her daughter's shoulders, barely able to believe how much Poppy had grown over the years. Brendan had been right about one thing for sure; Poppy was the image of herself at that age, except her daughter almost surpassed her in height.

Poppy swallowed, her eyes stinging at the thought of her mother being back, of being able to share thoughts of love and heartache and everything else. Of course, that was assuming that everything else – all the drama they faced – calmed down and stayed under control.

"Do you like him?" she asked, hoping her mother would have something good to say.

To her complete astonishment, Mama laughed out loud. "Yes, darling, I like him a lot. He only has eyes for you, and he's very respectful and mindful of those around him. He also has a protective streak, doesn't he?" Poppy looked up at her in question. "I'm guessing he offered to come with you, wherever you were headed tonight, or to whisk you away to somewhere more pleasant."

"That he did." Mama's intuition was incredible, and Poppy wondered suddenly whether that was a woman thing or an angel thing. It was something she would never have considered before, and she wondered if she'd ever be able to look at anything the same way again. "Mama, Daddy used to look at you like there was no one else in the world. I was little, but I remember."

Catherine stopped walking and smiled down at her daughter, smoothing her hair back from her face. "Yes, he did, and he made me feel incredibly special all the time. That's how I knew your father was the one. He looked at me with adoring eyes from the moment I met him." With emotion swelling inside her, she met Poppy's eyes. "Is that how it's been with Brendan?"

Thinking back to the night in the club, which wasn't so long ago but seemed like a lifetime, Poppy nodded and smiled. "Yes, I think so. Although, I didn't notice it until Abby pointed it out to me."

Abby giggled. "That's true. I don't think she would have ever realized there was something there if I hadn't pointed her in the right direction." And that was true enough.

"Well, I think there's definitely something there worth exploring." Catherine pulled her arm away and took Poppy's hand, swinging their arms as they walked as if she was still just a small child until she laughed.

But as they came up to the café, Poppy felt a niggling fear creep up her spine that made the hairs on the back of her neck stand on end. Slowing, she held her mother back, squeezing her hand tightly. "What's wrong, Poppy?"

"Something isn't right, Mama. I feel it in the air. I don't think we should be here."

Papa turned, frowning at her. "What do you mean?"

She shrugged. "I can't explain it, but it feels like something's out of place." She paused. She hated the word that was coming to mind, but she had no other way to describe it. "It feels evil."

Nana put her hands on her hips and faced her down. "You do realize you would have never thought of anything like that twelve hours ago. You're imagining things because you don't want any of this to be true."

"Jill! That's not fair, and you know it. Why don't you look back to when you first discovered what you were? Didn't you suddenly get in tune with your extrasensory powers?" Catherine practically spit the words at her mother-in-law. She couldn't believe the woman was attacking Poppy like this. "You know, if she'd always known, if *Richard* had always known, maybe he wouldn't have been targeted, or when he was, one of them would have known something was wrong and he wouldn't have been taken."

Jill shook her head. "You can blame me for anything you want, Catherine, but I've always done what I thought was right, in every situation that's been presented to me. Now, if you really believe Poppy can sense things she's never sensed before just because you told her the truth, things neither you nor I can sense, then we'll turn around and go back now. But she's being ridiculous. Meeting with the others is the best hope we all have for survival."

Seeing that her mother and grandfather were both about to argue, Poppy held up her hand. "Please, don't. I don't want to leave. If there is something wrong, the others might need our help." With Mama on the verge of protesting, Poppy squeezed her hand again. "Come on, Mama, let's do this. I can't let fear rule my life."

Feeling a hand on her arm, Poppy turned to look at a distraught Abby. "Maybe we should just go, Poppy. If you really think it might be dangerous, I feel for anyone else, but you're obviously more important than anyone. You have to be safe."

Poppy gave her a sad smile. "It's all the more reason for me to go in, Abby. You can go, if you want. I told you I didn't want to drag anyone else into this."

But she adamantly shook her head. "No, Poppy, if you're going, I'm going with you. I told you I'd stick with you through everything. So, let's go in and hope for the best."

Fortifying herself with her family surrounding her and nodding to her grandmother despite the hurt her doubt caused, Poppy led the way into the building and down the stairs into the basement café. They moved slowly, quietly, and feeling like a ridiculous movie character, Poppy pressed herself against the wall just outside the door, listening carefully.

It was practically silent, which unnerved her, until she heard a whimper, followed by a dark, growling voice in another language she didn't recognize that made her stomach churn. She met her mother's petrified gaze, her own heart thundering with fear, as a prayer went up inside the café. "Oh, Lord, do not forsake your faithful followers in their time of need. Give us strength, help us not to waiver in our devotion to you..."

Bile rose in Poppy's throat, and she couldn't wait outside any longer, not when there was a small chance she could help someone. She burst through the door against her family's protests and gasped at the sight before her. A man hung on the wall, pinned as if crucified, while two dead bodies lay on the floor, bled out – a man and a woman, their eyes staring unseeingly at the ceiling.

And in front of the man on the wall, several small black creatures, poked and jabbed, increasing the pain where they could, tormenting and toying with what was left of his life. They gave off a rank smell like sulfur and dribbled uncontrollably like babies, and squawked like mad ravens caught in poachers trap. One held a hammer, another nails. She couldn't see what the others had in the folds of hands, but it didn't matter as they all turned to glare at her with yellow puss filled eyes. Finally, she had laid eyes on the pitiful creatures of the Legion. *Soldiers of the Darkness.*

Frozen in place for a moment, she watched as one of the creatures turned and shoved a long spike in the hanging man's side, causing him to cry out in pain. At the same time, two of the figures, whose faces looked as though they had been burned in a fire, started toward her, bouncing from wall to wall with incredible speed.

Before she could move, both went down, a man she hadn't seen launching himself at the one nearest him from the other side of the café, and her grandfather flew at the other, knocking it to the ground. Seeing them wrestling jolted her into action, and she realized there were two more still posing a threat. She started for the first. "Poppy!" She turned in time to see Abby breaking the leg off a chair and throwing it to her.

She caught it, grateful for any kind of weapon to protect herself, and rushed forward to attack. For some reason, it didn't fight back, it was startled it, only sniffed the air around Poppy as she closed in on him and knocked the spike from his hand. The creature reached out with both hands, grabbing for her, but Poppy dropped to the floor, rolling behind it and back to her feet, and brought the piece of wood down across his back with all her strength.

It cried out, a shrill, ear piercing sound, and turned on her. Poppy fell onto her back, her legs up to kick at him, and it fell on top of her outstretched feet. With a quick motion, she turned the jagged end of the table leg toward it and shoved, feeling the wet, thick sensation as it drove into the creature's chest.

With a gurgling sound, it dropped to its knees and, before Poppy's eyes, disintegrated to nothing more than a pile of ash. Looking around wildly, she saw two more spontaneously combust, while the fourth, still wielding the hammer, swung it at her mother and Abby, who had teamed up against him. Determined not to see any of her family hurt, Poppy grabbed the makeshift stake and ran at the beast, driving it into his back and watching ash explode into the air.

Dropping the weapon, she brushed ash off her clothes and out of her hair, breathing heavily as much from fear as from adrenaline and exertion. She threw her arms around her mother, then reached one out for Abby, pulling her into the embrace as they all sank to the ground. Over Mama's shoulder, she saw her grandfather stand, still covered in the black shrapnel of the creatures, sweat dripping down his face. The other man who'd aided in the attack stepped up beside him, looking like he might pass out at any moment.

Remembering the man on the wall, Poppy jumped to her feet and turned to him, only to find his expression mirroring those of the dead bodies on the floor. She covered her mouth, feeling incredibly sick to her stomach, and looked away.

A hand on her shoulder soothed her, kept her from vomiting right then and there, and as she looked up at the last man standing from the café, she saw something swirl in his bright blue eyes as he smiled at her. "You'll be fine. Come, have a seat, and put your head between your legs."

Poppy did as she was told, and Catherine turned to her father-in-law, checking to see that he was alright as the other man, obviously an angel, approached. "You must be the Applebaums." His voice was rough, and Catherine didn't miss the pained glance he cast over his dead friends. A part of her, too, ached for them. They were, after all, kindred, and being so close on the tail of their deaths, Catherine could still feel their souls. Which meant that, at least, those souls had not been harvested.

"I'm Ken Warden. It's a pleasure to meet all of you. It seems you got here just in time to save my life, and all our souls." He was grateful, and his eyes shone with unshed tears. He looked like he was about to say something else, but his gaze drifted over Catherine's shoulder, his eyes growing wide. As he rushed around her, David, and Abby, Catherine turned and swallowed an alarmed cry.

Jill sat, holding her left arm, leaning against the wall in an odd position, as though her body had just collapsed there. All three of them moved forward behind Ken, who was already checking Jill's pulse. "She's breathing, but her heartbeat is erratic. We should call an ambulance. I think she might have had a heart attack."

Catherine met Ken's eyes, fear gripping her lungs. "She's one of us. Is that even possible?"

He nodded, a grim look on his face, as David pulled the cell phone out of Catherine's purse. "These bodies are vessels, the same imperfect ones that carry a human soul. They can break down, just like any other. And we are just as vulnerable as a human when it comes to sickness and injury. We're not immortal. We just have some extra means of defending ourselves, should the need arise."

"What were those things?" David asked, his voice trembling as he pulled his wife into his lap, cradling her against his chest as he handed the phone to Abby, who held out her hand to take it and make the call.

"The Darkness." The words from Jill's mouth were barely audible but they were clear. "They were the Darkness."

Poppy's head came up at that. The first thing that had gone through her mind was vampires — she'd practically staked them through the heart and watched them disappear into ash. But if they were evil, if they were the embodiment of Darkness, that made even more sense. The powers of Hell, combusting at death, burn marks on their faces. Just how long had they been roasting, she wondered, before being released to wreak havoc on earth? And how many more were there?

She didn't join the crowd around her grandmother; there were already too many people ministering to her as Abby spoke to the emergency operator. Instead, she sat there, images of the Darkness rolling through her mind. This was what she would face, from here on out. She only hoped she had the strength to do this the next time. And the next.

CHAPTER 13

Brendan was almost back to his place when the call came in. He cursed as he turned around and raced through traffic, lighting the disco lights in his front windshield trying to get other drivers to move the hell out of his way. The report of a black cloud, followed by a call regarding a heart attack victim and three dead concerned him greatly, but more than anything, he focused on one thing.

Poppy.

Whatever this phenomenon was, and whoever was behind it, he knew it had to be connected to her, and with the fact that she and her family had been in the direct area of the reports, it was more than instinct that told him she was involved in this incident. He only hoped she was okay and that he wouldn't be too late.

He screeched to a halt amidst several marked cars with lights flashing, as well as fire trucks and ambulances. He threw the car door open and bolted for the underground café, finding a mad scene inside. He stood in the doorway, searching the throngs of cops and EMTs until he saw her, wrapped in a blanket and huddled in a corner. He pushed through the crowd and knelt before her.

"Poppy! Are you alright?" He brushed damp tendrils of hair back from her face, seeing the streaks of dried tears running down her cheeks, and his heart dropped. "Your family – are they all okay?"

She nodded. "I think so, except Nana. She...she had a heart attack, they think."

He stood and lifted her into his arms, holding her tight against him. "Oh, God, Poppy, I'm so sorry." He grabbed her arms and held her away from him to look at her. "What happened here?"

Poppy didn't know how much to tell him right now. She couldn't tell him everything, without launching into a full explanation of her own life, and she didn't think she had the strength or presence of mind to do that just yet. "We walked in on a murder scene. Three people were already dead, and the fourth would have been..." She trailed off and pointed at the wall behind him.

Brendan turned and gulped. Another crucifixion. He should have known, even though no one had said anything over the radio. But he'd hoped it wasn't true. "Poppy, I want you to tell me everything. I want to know how you're involved in this, how your family is involved, other than your father's disappearance. And I want to know everything you did and saw tonight." He took note of black smudges on her cheeks and the pretty yellow dress she'd been wearing. There was no way she was giving the full story right now, and that was okay. They were surrounded by frantically working people, complete chaos, and he didn't expect her to talk just yet.

But she would. He could sense it in her.

At the moment, Poppy just felt safer and more secure in his arms and didn't want to let go. Later, she told herself. Later, they would go somewhere quiet at talk, and she'd tell him everything. But right now, she just needed to feel him. "Is there anything I can do here to help?"

He shook his head. "I doubt it. This'll be my case, so I'll be the one to take your statement. And that of anyone else who was here. But I'll check and make sure, and then we'll get you out of here, get the rest of your family on their way to the hospital to be with your grandmother."

She nodded, grateful, and sat back down to wait while he waded through all the people who had converged on the café in the last twenty minutes. She saw her mother and her grandfather standing next to the stretcher, where they were loading her grandmother to take her to the hospital. She saw Brendan approach them and wished she could hear the conversation.

Looking to the EMT's, Brendan asked, "Where are you taking her?"

The shorter of the two attending her addressed him. "Well, Harborview is the closest."

He frowned. "Is she stable?"

"Yes, sir."

"Then take her to Swedish. I want her treated like a patient, not a bunch of paperwork." He turned to the others. "How are all of you? Is everyone alright?"

While they seemed confused and surprised to see him, Catherine and David nodded and answered in turn. Catherine told him, "I'm just worried about Poppy."

David agreed. "I've had a bit of a scare with Jill, but I want to make sure Poppy's okay. And her roommate," he added, nodding toward Abby, who stood off in a corner alone, her eyes wide and frightened.

"I thought she was going home."

"She walked here with us and was about to head to the bus stop. We were going to get her a coffee to go before she left," Catherine told him, covering for what Poppy had obviously used as an excuse to send him away tonight. Of course, her daughter seemed to have taken to telling white lies naturally, which ruffled her feathers a little. After all, what difference did it really make to all of them if Brendan was a police officer?

"Okay. I'll make sure Poppy gets checked out for shock. In the meantime, I'll have one of our uniformed officers escort you to Swedish Medical Center so you can all be with Jill. We'll be along as soon as we can."

David gave him a very pointed look. "Listen, young man, I trust you with my granddaughter, even though I'm not sure I really know who you are. But I can tell you care for her. Just keep her safe, okay? It's more important than I think you realize."

Gravity seemed to make him heavier, and Brendan nodded to the older man. "You have my word, sir. Poppy's important enough to me that it doesn't matter why else she needs protection. I'll make sure she's safe."

Her teeth chattering, Poppy watched her family leave, followed closely by Abby on their tails, and then turned to see Brendan talking to the first officer who had arrived on the scene. Their exchange was brief, and then Brendan was headed back to her. "Are you ready to get out of here, get somewhere warm and quiet?"

She gave him a bit of a chuckle she didn't really feel. "You mean like the police station?"

Rolling his eyes, Brendan shook his head. "No, I figured we would start at my apartment. That way we can talk in private, and I can set the heat where it's most comfortable for you. Then, if you want, we can swing by your dorm so you can find some other, warmer clothes, and then I'd get you to Swedish to be with your family."

That sounded glorious to Poppy, and she stood, letting him guide her with an arm around her shoulders away from the gruesome scene. She caught sight of Ken as they left, returned the dip of his chin in acknowledgement as a cut on his arm was bandaged. He had given her his number and asked her to call as soon as she had a chance. She figured that, before she caught up with her family, after she'd filled Brendan in to the best of her ability, she'd call him, make sure he was alright, and find out what, if anything, he'd heard from the authorities.

The ride to Brendan's apartment wasn't long, and he blasted the heat so Poppy stopped shivering. They sat in silence the whole way, and she knew Brendan was giving her time and space to gather herself. She greatly appreciated it. As it was, she had no idea where to begin. How far back in her family line did this go? On either side? And how much did she really know?

But she would do her best and, as they parked and he cut the engine, she cleared her throat, catching his attention. "Brendan, I'll tell you right now that, more than anything else I'm afraid of, I'm worried you'll run from me when I tell you all of this. And if you do, you have every right.

But if you can stomach it and not run, just know that I appreciate everything you've done already."

More curious than ever, he nodded without responding and climbed out, grabbing the briefcase he'd taken earlier full of files, then going to her side of the car to walk her into his place. He sat her on the couch and went straight to the thermostat, needing to assure himself she was warm enough, then excused himself to brew some coffee. He guessed they'd never gotten any at the café, from the looks of things.

"The owners weren't there," she mumbled as he returned. At his questioning look, she realized she'd started at a strange spot in the story. "When we got to the café, the owners weren't there. I don't know if they were in league with the killers or if they'd been scared away before everything happened. But they were nowhere to be found."

"Okay," he spoke slowly, trying to guess where she was going with this.

"There were four creatures performing the crucifixion, and I watched one stick a metal spike like a railroad tie in the man's side while he prayed. It was sickening." She shook her head, trying to shake the image that was burned into her brain. "Another carried a hammer, and a third had a bunch of nails, which I'm guessing is what they used to hang the poor man up. The other two victims had been killed already. They weren't crucified, I don't think. At least, it didn't feel that way."

Her reference took him aback, and he considered the possibility she was an empath, able to feel or sense the emotions of others. It was something he'd heard of and knew that those who were really strong could feel those emotions in the air even after death. "How do you think they were killed?"

She thought about it. "I'm not sure. There wasn't any blood anywhere." She ran her hands over her face and waited while Brendan went back to the kitchen and returned with coffee. Even a single sip calmed her, warmed her from the inside.

"So, how did you get involved in this, Poppy? Off the record. I'm not a cop right now. I'm just someone who cares about you." Brendan hoped she took that to heart and didn't hold anything back. Whatever bothered her, especially if it had legal implications, shouldn't fester inside her any longer.

Considering his statement, Poppy decided to start at the beginning. "I've already told you what happened to my father. No body was found, and my mother became catatonic. No one's heard from him since, and my mother just broke out of her trance a few days ago." She started talking about the various murders she'd heard of and investigated over the years, about her grandmother's disapproval, and about being sent to Seattle.

Brendan had heard some of this, but this time she was more thorough, and there was a great deal more emotion.

He could sense something big coming, and he listened patiently, working hard not to interrupt. He could save any questions he had until the end. He had a feeling most of those questions would be answered before she got to the end anyway.

When Poppy told him about her mother's sudden call just yesterday, Brendan sensed her agitation and realized this was what worried her most. This is what she feared telling him. He held her hand supportively, and when she paused, telling him they'd all gathered in her dorm room, he waited for a moment, then asked, "Would you like another cup of coffee?"

Poppy chewed her left thumbnail as she waited for him to bring her another steaming cup. When he sat down, she tried to cover her hesitation by sipping at the drink, but Brendan leaned over and kissed her cheek. "Whatever it is, Poppy, you can tell me. I'm not going to judge, and I'm not going to run away from you."

Taking a deep breath, she launched into the most unbelievable part, explaining that she was an angel and how she came to be such. "In fact, I'm not just an angel. I'm the only one ever born of two full-blooded angels. I'm the only purebred alive, as far as we know. And we think the Darkness is after me because of it."

He nodded slowly, trying to swallow what she'd told him. He ran her mother's premonitions through his head, considering the impact they made, and started piecing things together in his mind. "And what about your father?"

Poppy felt the lump in her throat and couldn't answer right away. It was something she hadn't been ready to acknowledge before and so, therefore, hadn't voiced to anyone else, not even giving it voice in her own mind. But Brendan had taken her at her word so far and hadn't seemed to think her ridiculous, hadn't stalked around the room calling her crazy. He still sat next to her, holding her hand and rubbing his thumb in circles over the back of it comfortingly.

"Honestly," she said finally, "my theory truly scares me, because my father knew me better than anyone. And I think that my father is behind this in some way. Based on what Mama said, the things she heard, my father is the key to the Darkness being able to reach us. I don't know if he's being forced to do it or if he's turned on his own kind, but I think that whatever power controls the Darkness is relying on my father to find me."

Brendan felt the same fear. Who better to find Poppy than a member of her own family? But even so, he wasn't sure that anyone was fully on Poppy's trail just yet, or she would likely have already been dead. Maybe, just maybe, her grandmother's lack of honesty with her had saved Poppy's life in the past. Switching modes, Brendan rubbed her back. "So, the Darkness is behind the crucifixions. And it sounds like that's the way it takes the souls of the angels."

Poppy looked up at him with amazement. "You're not going to question anything I've told you?"

He scoffed. "Why should I? There's obviously something special about you, and everything you say adds up, even if it's a little unorthodox to believe. But really, who are we kidding? There are lots of unexplained phenomena in this world, and you've just given the most logical possible one for this particular situation. What else would crucifixions be other than some form of biblical occurrence?"

Poppy shivered at the thought. "I just wish I knew exactly what it wants. The Darkness. I want to know who exactly is behind it, and what the ultimate goal is. Why am I the one? What is so important about a purebred?"

Brendan stood and began to pace, going into investigative mode. Facts and files floated around his head, as theories presented themselves randomly. Most would be pushed aside, he knew from experience, but somewhere in the sorting he'd find an answer that they could build on, something that would give them more direction.

"You said the Darkness is taking the souls of angels to give foot to the earth. So, it has to feed on angels to be able to walk above ground." Poppy listened as Brendan mused aloud, fascinated by him and his movements, as well as his mind. How had she managed to find the one person who not only had background information on the murders but also was willing to believe in the supernatural?

"That's right. I'm guessing that either all the minions have to feed, or that one soul isn't enough to last very long," she said between sips of coffee.

"And that's very limiting. What if," Brendan continued as he walked circles in his living room, "a purebred would give the Darkness permanent residence on the earth, if this being never had to return to the underworld with the strength of a soul like yours?"

The foreboding in Poppy's chest froze her in place with her cup halfway to her lips. He was right. Something inside told her this was the reason she was a target beyond all others. Of course, that raised so many more questions. "If that's true, and he's using my father, why haven't they found me yet? I don't think it has anything to do with me not knowing what I am. I mean, whether I know or not, my father must know."

"Did he know about your mother?"

"No," she whispered, her hope deflated. Poppy had considered the idea that Daddy was only working with the Darkness under the guise of loyalty, using his position to help protect her. But if her father wasn't aware of her mother being an angel, there was no way he could know that Poppy was the spawn of two angels. "No, he didn't."

Brendan rubbed his chin, feeling the stubble that was coming in and randomly thinking that he needed to shave. "Maybe this is still a hunt. I'm betting, if we talk to the guy who survived tonight, we'll be able to find out if there was any kind of interrogation before they started killing everyone. Sure, they needed the souls, but what if they wanted information first. You know, something about two angels breeding."

Drawn into the possibility, Poppy perked up slightly. "'Excuse me, but do you happen to know any people like you who've gotten it on and spawned a child?'"

"Exactly!" Brendan pointed at her and smiled, finally standing still for a brief moment. "When are you supposed to call that guy?"

She looked at her watch and realized it was after midnight. How long had she been talking? "It's late, but Ken said to call him any time." She took out her phone and dialed the number she'd just saved. He answered on the first ring. "Ken, it's Poppy. Are you alright?"

"Hanging in there. How about you? I saw you leave with the cop. Did he get you home okay?"

"We were just going over what happened tonight. Listen, Ken, we still need to talk. I have a lot of questions I need to ask, if you're up for it. But right now, I'm about to head to the hospital to check on my grandmother. Can we get together early tomorrow and talk over a cup of coffee?"

There was a brief silence. "I'm not sure there's much of anywhere that's safe to meet."

Poppy raised an eyebrow at Brendan, who was watching her expectantly. "I know, Ken, but I don't think holing up in our houses is any safer."

He heaved a sigh into the phone. "I guess you're right, but maybe somewhere more public, with more people, would be better. What time can you be at the Space Needle?"

Relieved that he agreed to meet her, Poppy said, "As early as you want."

"Okay, meet me up in the observatory at 9 am. And be careful getting there."

"I will. And thank you." She hung up and told Brendan the plan. "I'll go with you. And don't worry, I'll be discreet. I'll even stay downstairs if you want me to."

Feeling a bit selfish and needy, she said, "I'd rather have you go up with me." With a shy smile, she stood and made her way across the room to where he stood, stopping a few feet in front of him. She gazed up into his eyes, not sure whether her fear or her desire gripped her tighter. Either way, she instinctively knew this man held the answer, could give her something to satisfy her.

Brendan read both in her gaze and closed the distance between them, placing his arms lightly around her waist and enclosing her in a safety bubble, as her mother called it. She placed her palms on his chest and stood there, maintaining eye contact, even as he bent his head toward hers. He watched her lashes flutter closed just before his lips brushed hers, and every nerve ending in his body caught fire as she kissed him back, her tongue intertwining with his.

He tightened his hold on her, and Poppy wrapped her arms around his neck, drawing him down further as she rose on her tiptoes to taste more of him. He felt his own physical reaction, throbbing as his entire body burned and tingled with need, and Brendan roamed her back with his hands, feeling her goosebumps rise beneath his touch.

Poppy threaded her fingers in his hair, not wanting any space between them, no breathing room at all as she pressed her body to his. He was hot, his heart pounding, and parts lower on his body were as needy as she was. She knew she had things she needed to do, but she wanted to be with Brendan tonight, wanted him to hold her as if nothing else in the world mattered to either of them.

And in Brendan's world, nothing else did matter. They could deal with the Darkness and any other supernatural creatures in the morning. They could form a plan of action to protect Poppy and take down evil tomorrow. Tonight, the only thing he could think about was the way she felt against him, in his arms, and the way she tasted. He broke the kiss, only to trail his lips over her jaw and down the side of her neck to her shoulder, feeling her breath as she panted against his throat.

Brendan's teeth nibbled at her collarbone, and Poppy let out a sigh, things low in her body tightening at the sensation of his mouth hot on her skin. So this was how it felt to want someone, to want to crawl inside them, to want someone to be one with you. Her nails scratched at his scalp, and he groaned against her shoulder, the sound vibrating through her, and she pushed herself harder against him, wanting to wrap herself around his body and never let go.

Ever so slowly, Brendan began walking, moving Poppy carefully backward and supporting her weight should she stumble, until he reached the couch. He laid her gently down and lowered himself on top of her, holding himself above her with his arms so he didn't crush her as he took her mouth again.

But he was too far away, and Poppy wanted his weight on her, so she grabbed his shoulders and pulled him down, reveling in the feel of his body on hers. They seemed to fit just right, her slight curves molding into to his hard, muscular body. He felt even better than he looked, and she found herself reaching under his shirt, wanting to feel his skin on her fingertips.

He trembled at her touch, and for some reason, that gave her an incredible sense of satisfaction as Brendan licked at the corner of her mouth, his hand caressing her cheek as he lifted his head to meet her eyes. "Tell me what you want, Poppy. I won't do anything you don't want."

Honestly, Poppy wanted everything. She wanted to feel what it was like to make love to someone, wanted to erase her fear and her loneliness, but she didn't know if she was ready. Could she just be clinging to him because of the crisis they were involved in together? She'd seen enough movies to realize that relationships founded under duress didn't last, and she didn't want to make a mistake. Her intuition told her this was more, but she couldn't risk having her heart broken, not when there was so much else at stake. Right now, what she needed most was Brendan's trust and companionship. She didn't want to ruin it.

Kissing him tenderly and running her hands over the smooth skin of his back, she pushed back the desire to take off the clothes that were still between them. "I want you, Brendan, but I think we both know it's not the right time."

Struggling against disappointment, Brendan tried to put away his desperation for her and nodded. "You're right. He brushed her hair back and gazed down at her emerald eyes, which had a sheen that almost looked like moisture but he recognized as unsatisfied desire. Kissing her again with less need and just a little seduction, he pulled himself away, sitting up and running his own hands through his hair as he worked to calm himself.

Slowly, Poppy drew herself up to sit next to him, wrapping her arms around herself to curb the empty feeling. It wasn't like rejection, but she'd turned down the only chance she'd ever been given to connect with someone on a sexual level. She wondered if that would be a permanent mistake, but as Brendan sat back and drew her into his lap, she somehow doubted it.

They sat like that for a long time, Poppy's head tucked under Brendan's chin, as they both let their flesh cool. Finally, she felt Brendan heave a deep breath. "Would you like to go see your grandmother now?"

She nodded and then laughed, feeling his head bob up and down as she did so. "Sorry, I didn't mean to bang against your chin."

He chuckled and kissed the top of her head. "It's alright. Come on, we'll go to the hospital. Then, we can either stop at your place and get you some clothes, or you can sleep in one of my t-shirts and a pair of my pajama pants, and we'll get your clothes in the morning. You're not staying alone tonight."

She stood and looked down at him as he gave her a challenging look. "I wouldn't be alone. Abby will be there. And I'm sure either my mom or my grandfather would come back with me."

He stood and crossed his arms. "But you won't ask them because you want them to be there for your grandmother. And don't get me wrong, Abby's a great person, but I don't think she's strong enough to hold her own against a vampire-like demon. I'm sure she'd put up a good fight, and I would be willing to bet she'd offer you comfort, but I have weapons, and I'm trained in combat."

She swallowed. "I don't want you hurt, Brendan. I—"

"Not to mention I think my place is safer anyway, since it's not connected to you. Keep in mind, there are plenty of public records that can trace you back to the campus." He smiled triumphantly as her shoulders drooped, and she realized he was right. "Now, do you or do you not want to spend the night curled in my arms? Because I, for one, would love to wake up with you next to me."

As if to prove his point, he pulled Poppy to him, just holding her, and she buried her face against his chest. Yes, that did sound lovely. And the idea of wearing his clothes was comforting. There was something about the baggy, oversized feel of men's clothes that made everything better, and knowing they would smell like Brendan was the icing on the cake. "Okay, you win," she agreed, her voice muffled against his skin. She pulled back and kissed his cheek. "Let's get going. I'm exhausted."

~~~~~~~~

Jill had just woken up when Poppy and Brendan entered the hospital room. She felt much better, though quite weak, and as she looked around, she was almost surprised to find her family there after how difficult she'd been for the past couple of days. "Nana" Poppy asked hesitantly as she entered the room, holding the young man's hand.

"I'm alright, Poppy." But even her voice was weak, as though she couldn't put enough oomph behind it to sound like herself.

Poppy looked around the room. "Where's Abby?"

Her mother came forward and hugged her. "She went home. One of the officers gave her a ride. She just left a few minutes ago. She was falling asleep on her feet."

Poppy moved toward the bed and her grandmother, still holding Brendan's hand and placing the other on Nana's leg. "What's the word from the doctor?"

"It was a mild, stress-induced heart attack. She should make a fairly fast recovery," Papa replied, stepping up beside her.

"Now, would you like to tell us who this young man really is?" Nana motioned weakly to Brendan, but when Poppy caught her expression, it wasn't irritated or belligerent. "I'd like to know who's taking care of my granddaughter."

Poppy and Brendan exchanged a meaningful look, and Poppy nodded. "He's the lead investigator on the crucifixion homicides in Seattle. But that's not how we met. That's just a coincidence."

Catherine gave her daughter a sympathetic look. "Honey, if there's nothing else to learn here, it's that there are no coincidences. I met your father for a reason. Your grandparents sent you to Seattle for a reason. And you met Brendan for a reason."

"If it makes you all feel any better, I know all about the situation," Brendan piped up. "And I'll do anything I can to help. I've got the files on most of the disappearances and murders, and I know Poppy's got more information. Between all of us, we can figure out what the Darkness is trying to do and how to stop it."

But Jill shook her head. "Boy, I'm less concerned with solving the mystery and more concerned with protecting my granddaughter. The question I have is, do you care enough about her to risk your own life to keep her safe?"

Poppy would have turned bright red, but Brendan took her chin in his hand and turned her to face him. There was something in his eyes that made her heart jump in her chest. "Mrs. Applebaum, I've never cared about anyone the way I do about Poppy. I'm falling in love with her, even if we've only known each other for a very short time. And yes, I would give my life to keep her safe. I would sacrifice just about anyone's life for that."

At the satisfied look on his wife's face, David smiled at Brendan. "I think that was the right answer, son."

~~~~~~~

CHAPTER 14

Having slept soundly with the scent of Poppy's hair surrounding him as he cradled her soft body with his, Brendan woke with a bit of a start, realizing his arms were empty. He started to panic, but the smell of fresh brewed coffee hit him, replacing that of the woman who'd been in his bed, and a smile curled his lips.

Rolling over and stepping into his slippers, he stood, smoothing down the hair he knew was sticking up in eighteen different directions and plodded toward the kitchen, not even stopping to pull on a shirt with his pajama pants. He stopped in the doorway, taking in the view – and the aroma – of Poppy cooking breakfast in his kitchen.

The sleeves of his shirt fell over her hands, and she had to keep pushing them up out of her way. His bottoms hung low on her hips below the length of the shirt and were scrunched up at her ankles, covering most of her bare feet with the exception of her painted toenails, which were glinting a bright blue at him under the fluorescent lights. Her hair was pulled up in a messy bun at the top of her head, several tendrils falling loose around her face, which he only caught in a minimal profile as she moved about aptly.

The smell of bacon wafted to him with the coffee, and he grunted in appreciation, which caught Poppy's attention. She looked at him over her shoulder with a brilliant smile that would have melted even the most frigid heart, and he moved up behind her, curling his arms around her waist and nuzzling her neck.

Poppy giggled. "Stop it! That tickles!" When he finally released her, Poppy pointed in satisfaction to the bacon and eggs on the plate and the pot of coffee on the counter. "They should be edible. I haven't cooked much in a long time, unless it was in a microwave, but it's sort of like riding a bike, isn't it?"

"Yes, I suppose it is. And when was the last time you did that?" he asked playfully as he piled his plate high with food.

She stuck her tongue out at him. "Shut up and eat. We need to leave in half an hour so I can change and we can get over to the Space Needle on time."

He glanced at the clock for the first time and realized he'd slept later today than he had in months. And he felt more rested than he remembered feeling, even as a child. As Poppy sat across from him, bringing two mugs of coffee, he gave her an appreciative look. "I'm apparently a very lucky man."

She snorted. "You really think so? Here we are, headed out into the world to fight off supernatural powers that have the upper hand in all this because they know more than we do. You slept in a bed last night with a girl who, even if she had been ready to get intimate, was far too tired to do so. If you continue to spend time with said girl, you inherit her father, who is apparently on the wrong side of the war, a mother who is just now ambulatory and vocal again, and a grandmother who hates everyone who doesn't agree with her. Something about that doesn't strike me as good luck."

He shrugged. "I said I was a lucky man. I never said that was good luck." She flung a piece of bacon at him and he laughed. "Seriously, though, Poppy, you're beautiful, intelligent, talented, kind, and a fabulous cook who spent the night in my arms, smelling wonderful, and woke me up to the smell of breakfast I didn't have to cook for myself."

Poppy blushed. She wasn't used to compliments, and Brendan was always full of them. And now, with everything going on, he still appreciated her. What man still ended up in such a good mood in the morning when a woman left them wanting? Not to mention the fact that he was going to run her where she needed to go, be there with her in case she needed help. Frowning, she thought of something. "Don't you ever have to report to work?"

He nodded. "Today, I do. But that's going to involve a phone call to the chief to let him know I'm following up with witnesses to last night's murder. He'll be perfectly happy to have me away from the office. He hates when I mope around, unable to make two and two add up to four."

A little relieved – and wondering how the hell she was going to deal with it when Brendan did have to go into the office, or when she had to start class, for that matter – Poppy finished her breakfast and washed it down with the last of her coffee. "Do you mind if I use your shower? I really just want to run in and out of the dorm, if that's alright with you."

Brendan knew she could read the heat in his eyes at the thought of her in his shower, the hot water running down her skin, the soap slick on her body. He swallowed, relying on every last bit of willpower to stop the images and to tell himself he couldn't join her. "Of course you can," he said, and even he could hear the gruff quality of his voice. He wanted to kick himself in the ass. "The, uh, towels are in the cupboard just outside the bathroom."

Her face heated and her mind swirling at the things that must have been on Brendan's mind, Poppy walked away without responding, not trusting her voice. But even as she climbed into the shower and thought of that firm, bare chest she'd stared at all through breakfast, she couldn't help picturing Brendan in here, shaving his face, showering, completely nude. She pressed a hand against her stomach, trying to stop the twisting, tremulous desire that almost cramped inside her at the idea.

She showered and put the dress from the night before back on as quickly as possible, sure she'd finished her cleanup in record time, then combed her fingers through her hair, making a mental note to run a brush through it quickly before heading back out of the dorm. With a final look at herself and the suddenly ever-present rose-colored spots on her cheeks, she rejoined Brendan in the kitchen, where he was just finishing cleaning up after her cooking.

"Wow, a man after my own heart."

Brendan started, not having realized Poppy was back. "I figure it's only fair. You cook, I clean, or vice versa." His teasing eyes found hers, and he gave a mischievous smile. "It's my understanding that's how couples do it."

A shockwave poured through her body at the term 'couple'. Is that what they were now? Poppy didn't have enough experience to know what constituted a couple, but she liked the sound of it. And even better, she could now talk to her mother about these things.

As he placed the last dish in the dishwasher, Brendan stepped toward the door. "Give me about ten minutes to shower and shave and I'll be ready to go."

Poppy nodded, watching him walk away. Even in pajama pants, his bottom looked good. Of course, she couldn't decide whether she'd rather watch that or the muscles that moved like pistons in his back with the swinging of his arms as he walked away. Everything about him was sexy and enticing, even when he wasn't trying. But maybe she was prejudice. She shrugged to herself, not knowing why she even cared.

Last night, Brendan had told her family that he was falling in love with her. Of course, that thought gave her the warm fuzzies, and when she evaluated her own feelings, she could easily feel herself falling for him as well. But what if he was just saying that to reassure her grandmother? What if he cared but it wasn't something as deep and meaningful for him as it was for her? Dropping into a kitchen chair, Poppy worried at her bottom lip with her teeth. How could someone who made you feel so incredibly special, so important, also make you so insecure?

She wanted to beat her head against the table. This wasn't what she should be thinking about. She was going to meet with Ken, and she had questions she needed answered. As far as anyone knew, Ken was the first one to have walked away alive from an attack by the Darkness, and he certainly had insight no one else could provide. But he was also scared, and so Poppy would have to be gentle with her questioning.

Of course, once she had the answers, she didn't know what she would do with them. She only hoped that working together with Mama, Papa, and Nana, and maybe with the outside perspective Abby could offer and the professional opinion she could expect from Brendan, they could find a way to stop the killing, discover what the final goal was, and just maybe save her father from a fate Poppy felt was worse than death.

When Brendan returned, smelling of soap and aftershave, he bent down to kiss her, and Poppy couldn't help touching his freshly shaved cheek, smooth as a baby's behind. His dimples showed as he smiled down at her. "Do you like that?"

She stood and considered. "Yes, I do, but I also like the feel of your stubble." She tilted her head toward the front door. "Are we leaving?"

"If you're ready." He watched her grab her purse and sling it over her shoulder, enjoying even the smallest movements like the tiny wiggle of her hips and the shake of her head as she meant to move the hair from her face. He opened the door and followed her out, hoping like hell he could keep his promise to keep her safe.

~~~~~~~~~

Poppy unlocked the door to her dorm room as quietly as possible and tiptoed in, trying not to wake Abby. But as she opened the top drawer of her dresser, her roommate groaned and rolled over. In a sleep-filled voice, Abby asked, "So, did you do the deed with the cop?"

With a shake of her head, Poppy couldn't help but smile at Abby's choice words. "No, I just spent the night over there because he wanted to make sure I was safe."

"Uh huh, sure he did." Sitting up and stretching, she spoke through a yawn. "So, where are you off too early in the morning?"

"It's not that early, we just went to bed really late. It's already nine. And I have an appointment to meet with Ken, the angel we met last night. I have some questions for him." She stood and started to change as she filled Abby in. "Believe it or not, Brendan and I spent most of the night hashing out possible theories back and forth. We have a lot of questions we need answers to before we can start putting things together in a way that makes sense and actually gets us somewhere."

"Just like every other cop, looking for the big break that will solve the case." Poppy shot her a surprised look, wondering if maybe Abby was jealous, but all she saw was teasing in her expression. "Come on, Poppy, the boy is sprung hard for you. I'm assuming he knows everything now, but even before you filled him in, he was willing to lie for you. And obviously, now that he knows everything, he's still around? Don't let that one go."

Poppy stood for a moment, absently reaching for her brush and pulling it through her hair thoughtfully. "Abby, he told my family he's falling in love with me. Isn't it too soon for that? I mean, could he just be saying that?"

But Abby adamantly shook her head. "For some people, it's far too soon. But I see the way you look at each other. And I can almost feel the connection between the two of you. It's like static electricity and an unbreakable cord, all at the same time. Friction and binding. You two are meant to be together."

"I think that's what Mama was trying to say last night. She said there's no such thing as coincidence." Shaking off the sudden seriousness, she pulled on a pair of sneakers with the jeans and hoodie she'd already donned, feeling ever so much more comfortable and normal. "Whatever it is, I think I like it. And I think I might be falling in love with him, too."

"That's awesome, Poppy. I'm really happy for you, and I hope it works out. Just don't get distracted and do anything stupid that could get you hurt." Abby's concern touched Poppy, and she touched her roommate's arm before she left, noting that the girl yawned and laid back down as she shut the door behind her.

Poppy hurried back downstairs and walked hand in hand with Brendan back to his car, and they drove quietly toward the Space Needle, finding parking close by and heading to the ticket booth downstairs. Poppy tried to protest as Brendan bought the tickets, but he held up a hand. "Get used to being courted, darling," he said in a smooth, Irish accent. "Even in the most desperate of times, a man wishes to provide for and woo the woman in his heart."

He took her hand and danced with her, with no music at all, and Poppy couldn't help but laugh. "Alright, I get it. You are incorrigible."

"I think the word you're looking for is infatuated." He kissed the tip of her nose and took her hand again, this time leading her toward the front door of what had to be the most well known icon in all of Seattle. They followed the small crowd, thin because it was a weekday, down the hall and toward the elevator that led to the observation deck. Poppy found herself excited, having not been here yet and wondering just what the city would look like from such a height. She concentrated on that anticipation to keep her from getting overly nervous about this meeting.

Brendan watched her carefully, could feel her pulse getting faster as she tightened her grip on his hand while they rode the elevator. Her eyes shone with what Brendan read as excitement, and he was glad she wasn't focused on the negative aspects of this little outing. A part of him worried that Ken wouldn't show or, worse, he was being tailed. But as they stepped off the elevator and he looked around, he couldn't see anything that looked out of place.

Poppy instantly pointed to the exterior door. "Ken's right there." He followed her directions, and he saw the man as well, breathing a sigh of relief to find him present and alone. "Let's go take a look and have a chat."

In awe of the view, Poppy couldn't find her voice at first, even as Ken turned and gave her an almost imperceptible nod of acknowledgement before turning and leaning on the railing again. Poppy stared out over the unbelievable beauty of the city she called home, with water in two directions and the buildings of downtown in between.

"It could all fall apart." Ken's voice was grave, as if he'd given up hope. Poppy turned to him and he shook his head. "Don't look at me. I think they have human helpers that tip them off about where to find us. I don't need anyone suspicious of our conversation. My nest is empty except for me now."

Looking back down as Brendan came up on the other side of her and put an arm around her shoulders, Poppy frowned. "What do you mean, your nest?"

"There are several of us who choose to live together, so we aren't alone. We call it a nest. The other three in my nest died last night." Out of the corner of her eye, Poppy saw Ken brush at his eyes as if wiping away tears. "They were essentially my family, and I don't know what to do. Living in that house alone, full of memories, is a nightmare, but leaving and going somewhere else alone could be dangerous."

Poppy glanced at Brendan and mouthed, *my family*. He nodded, and she said, "You should stay with my family. My mother and grandmother are both…special. You'd be welcome with them."

"And why were you sent away?" he asked, sarcasm dripping from his voice.

She cleared her throat. "Well, that's why I needed to talk to you. Before those *things* killed everyone last night, did they ask any questions? I mean, all I heard was some strange language before I burst in. We think they're after something, and it just makes sense they would have tried to recover any information they could before they murdered anyone."

"They want our souls, kid." He lowered his head even further and looked away, making it difficult for Poppy to hear him. She strained to listen without turning in his direction. "They don't need anything else. They just want our souls. But yes, they did ask one question."

Brendan clasped her hand tightly in his, and Poppy felt a surge of hope make her heart start to pound. "And what question was that?"

"They wanted to know if any of us bred." He shook his head. "They asked if we'd ever produced a purebred, and said if we could point them in the right direction, they would let us live."

"And what did you say?" Poppy's heart was in her throat.

"I told them the truth that angels couldn't breed together. We're incapable of having children that are pure, we cannot fall in love with another angel, it just doesn't happen. But they didn't seem to believe it. And it's not like they cared. They wanted our souls."

"Why didn't they take the first two?" Brendan spoke up.

His voice seemed to irritate Ken, who shivered and turned slightly toward them for the space of a heartbeat. "They were messengers, the weakest of the angels. Neither of them even had any powers. They were like victims who didn't belong. We took them in because, after all the reports of crucifixions, they needed protection. They still gave off the scent but couldn't protect themselves. Their souls wouldn't have given the strength it would have taken to consume them." Pushing away from the railing, he moved directly behind Poppy. "If I were ever to find a purebred, if such a thing did exist, I would turn the vile thing in. It's unnatural. And it might make these demons stop coming for the rest of us. I would advise you to do the same."

He went inside, and Poppy started to go after him, but Brendan held her back. "He's not a friend, Poppy. He may have been before last night, but now, even if he believed what you were, he'd be more likely to turn you over to the Darkness for whatever they had in mind rather than to help hide you. He's bitter and afraid of death."

Her stomach sinking, Poppy knew he was right. "But I thought angels were the good guys."

"Living in a human world isn't easy, is it, Poppy? We all become selfish. His reaction is just a form of self preservation. I just think he's not considering the implications of the possibilities should the Darkness get its hands on a purebred." He rubbed her arms as he saw the chill run over her.

But Poppy was focused on something else. She wasn't cold; she'd just had a thought. "Brendan, he said that angels can't breed together. If that's true, how is it possible that my parents had me?"

He turned Poppy to look at him and pressed a kiss to her lips. "Because you're a miracle, Poppy. Angels also work miracles, don't they?" She seemed skeptical, but he just smiled. "If you can believe everything else, you can certainly believe in miracles, Poppy."

She nodded and hugged him, and as she did, a familiar sensation crawled over her skin, a sound she'd heard before, and she watched as a black mist began to form over the ground below. Leaning over the railing, she wanted to call out, to shout to Ken as he walked right under it, to try to save him, but it was too late.

"Dammit!" Brendan followed her gaze and saw for himself as the black fog overtook the man, passersby oblivious to it and Ken, and as he turned towards the cover of some trees it all began to dissipate, taking Ken with it. He looked at Poppy. "We've got to go, now."

They raced into the elevator, both of them willing the infernal device to move faster, and took off at a dead run through the gift shop, out the door, and back to the car. Poppy tried to catch her breath as Brendan drove and called in Ken's name, getting an address and heading that direction. "What are you doing, Brendan?"

"They haven't killed him, Poppy. They took him, and I'm betting they plan to use him for information. And even if they don't, they'll take his soul."

Confused, Poppy scowled. "I don't understand, Brendan. Why are we going to his house?"

"Because most of the crucifixions have taken place in the home, Poppy. Maybe they've taken him there and we can save him."

Understanding dawning on her, Poppy began to will traffic to get out of the way as Brendan followed the directions on his GPS. When it finally opened up, they had a straight shot, and Brendan pulled to the curb of the northern Seattle home as another black cloud began to surround the building. "Stay here, Poppy."

"No, Brendan, you aren't going in there alone." She slammed the car door and ran up the steps behind him, following as he threw the door open. But Brendan stopped moving, and she ran into him, like a brick wall that wouldn't let her through. "Brendan…"

He turned and wrapped her in his arms. "Do you trust me, Poppy?"

Suddenly frightened, she nodded. "Of course I trust you."

"Then don't look. Please." In one quick motion, he turned her away, drew his gun, and shot the man pinned to the wall, meeting his eyes and seeing the plea he sent out just before the bullet struck home. The beast in front of him cried out with a shrill noise that made Brendan cover his ears as the soul he was in the middle of drawing out of the body on the wall retracted from him and began to ascend, even as the black cloud lifted.

The beast turned on him, and he pointed the gun at it.

Poppy spun and grabbed his arm, pointing the gun up in the air. "No!" Before Brendan could get the gun back down, she was rushing the beast, a sharp, pointed object in her hand. She shoved it straight into the beast, and with one more screech, the beast exploded into ash that rained down on Poppy. Brendan grabbed her as she dropped what appeared to be a broken piece of wood, and she motioned absently to a picture frame from the entryway. "It worked before. The table leg. I didn't know if a gun would do anything."

He gathered her to him as she looked up at Ken, and a wail arose from her throat. "I got him killed, Brendan. This one is my fault."

"No, Poppy, you didn't." But somewhere in the back of his mind, Brendan wondered if there wasn't an inside source, someone who'd infiltrated and begun to feed information to the other side, as Ken had suggested. A human, an angel who had turned. How could you tell a friend from an enemy? Obviously, Ken would have been of no assistance to them.

"Why did you shoot him?" Poppy asked as tears spilled over unheeded.

"To save his soul," Brendan answered, holding back tears of his own. "And it worked."

Poppy nodded. "Thank you."

Brendan didn't respond, just held her for another long moment. "Come on, Poppy, we can't stay here. We need to relocate you and your entire family. They may have someone following all of you, we need to find a way to get you to a safe place and lose any potential tail in the process."

Leaning back and searching his face, Poppy panicked. "What about Abby? I don't want her hurt or mistaken as one of us."

"Don't worry, we'll move her, too. I don't think they'll mistake her because Ken said something about a scent. But she would be identified as someone who could give them information. So we'll protect her, too." As he led her out of the house, he said, "We were right, you know."

"About the interrogation? Just one question," Poppy answered, drying her eyes. "They're looking for me. Or rather, they're looking for a being that's not supposed to exist and no one knows about that I happen to be." She dropped into the car and buckled in as Brendan went around, took the driver's seat, and started the car. "I'd still like to know how my mom and dad apparently pulled off a miracle that no one else has."

"Right time, right place," Brendan muttered. "Your mother said there are no coincidences. If the Darkness was planning this…whatever it is, then maybe a higher power fated that you'd be born. For which, I might say, I'm incredibly grateful."

Blushing again, Poppy took his hand and watched the buildings go by as Brendan drove through the city toward Swedish Medical Center. She was anxious to go back and get Abby, pack her things to leave, but she knew he made the right choice as soon as she walked into the hospital room and hugged her mother. Her tears started again and she laughed at herself. "I don't think I've cried as much in my entire life as I have the last few days."

Catherine held her daughter and let her unload the emotions as Brendan told them what they'd been through this morning. Terrified, Catherine wrapped her arms tighter around Poppy, both taking and drawing strength from her. She held her cool even at the pain of having lost yet another angel in Ken, but she wept when Jill called Brendan over and hugged him, thanking him for releasing their brother's soul. "That's compassion and love, and you are an incredible man for saving him, the good Lord will truly reward you."

Poppy watched Brendan sniffle as he winked at her, and she knew Nana's thanks meant as much to him as it did to her. It meant acceptance and trust, and Poppy took pride in being connected to someone of whom her entire family approved.

Eventually, the conversation wound around to the search for a purebred and the fact that one shouldn't exist, and Catherine was floored. She looked to her mother-in-law, who pursed her lips. "This is why I never questioned you, Catherine. I didn't believe you could possibly be an angel, especially not after you and Richard had Poppy. She's a beautiful, special girl, but Ken is right, and her existence shouldn't be possible. The lack of belief even among our own is going to be on our side. It means that, if questioned, there won't be any possibility of anyone talking because no one will even think someone like Poppy exists."

"And it also protects her from those like Ken, who would turn her in to save their own skin," Brendan added.

Catherine shook her head. "They would never actually be able to save themselves. The Darkness would take them anyway. Greed and power. It knows no mercy."

"Yes, well, the first Dark One was the world's best liar," David reminded them. "It would follow that any other Dark power would be able to convince anyone of just about anything." He turned to Brendan specifically. "You, in particular, will have to watch out for that. I know for a fact that humans are more easily swayed."

Brendan exchanged glances with Poppy. "I'll always have Poppy to help me see the light," he assured them. Holding out his hand to her, Brendan asked, "Would you like to go gather your things and your roommate so we can find you a safe place?"

Poppy nodded and hugged her mother. "Are you getting out soon, Nana?"

"They're releasing me this afternoon."

Poppy looked to her mother. "Call me as soon as you check her out. Don't go back to the dorm. I'll let you know where to find us, and you can come there. It'll be safer." She kissed Mama's cheek. "I love you," she whispered, then took Brendan's hand and followed him out of the room and down the stairs.

At the dorm, Poppy rushed up the stairs, Brendan right behind her, deciding the rules didn't matter. If anyone questioned her, Brendan could flash his badge and it would all be good. Even if it wasn't some things were more important than not pissing off the resident advisor.

Abby blinked at them, looking a little surprised to see both of them, but Poppy didn't stop moving as she reached under the bed for her bags. "Pack up, Abby. It's not safe here."

"What happened?" Abby asked, not wasting a moment as she, too, began throwing clothes, books, and everything else she owned into her own luggage.

Brendan wanted to help but didn't know where to start, so rather than get in the way, he waited until bags were filled and closed, then moved them into the hallway to make more room. Poppy explained the morning's events to Abby, whose eyes grew wide and liquid with tears. "Are you serious? Oh, Poppy, I'm so sorry!" She glanced at Brendan over her shoulder. "So, where are we going?"

He stood scrolling through his contacts, looking for the chief's number. He wanted to give the guy a head's up on the latest victim and let him know he had two witnesses he was taking into protective custody. Brendan realized the chief likely wouldn't be happy with his lack of forthcoming regarding details, but he'd push his advantage and remind his boss that it appeared someone was following these people and could very well be tapped into the phone line, hearing anything that was said.

To answer Abby as he hit the button to dial, he shrugged. "I'm not sure yet. There's not much of anywhere I would consider safe at this point, but at least we can try. If we move you all somewhere unexpected, somewhere they haven't tracked yet, we'll at least buy some time. The good news is, they don't know it's possible to create someone like Poppy, so they're on a wild goose chase at this point."

The chief answered with a grumpy rasp, and he stepped into the hallway to speak, leaving Poppy staring around the room, trying to take note of anything she might have missed. She felt like she'd packed everything of consequence, however, and was satisfied with how quickly she'd managed to consolidate her things and get them packed. Turning to watch Abby, she realized her roommate was working just as efficiently and not far behind. "How's your grandmother?"

"Doing much better, thanks. The doctors think she'll make a fast recovery." As Abby closed up the last bag and they gazed around the stark, empty room which had only been home for a few days, Poppy realized she wasn't sure she'd miss it. After all, she hadn't really become attached just yet. And on top of that, if they couldn't figure something out soon, she most likely wouldn't be able to return to school at UW, or anywhere, for that matter. A profound sadness at that thought fell over her, but she wouldn't let it bring her down or stop her.

This thing was bigger than her, bigger than her family. Even if she couldn't save herself, she wanted to find a way to save everyone else. Other angels didn't deserve to die, and she intended to do everything in her power to make sure the Darkness was thwarted. With harsh resolve, she shouldered three of her bags and dragged the last two, both on wheels, as Abby grabbed all her luggage, and they met Brendan in the hallway.

He finished his conversation quickly, and they headed down to the car, where they played Tetris with their bags in the trunk. Brendan was a spatial genius and made everything fit perfectly, and Abby seemed impressed. "I don't think I've ever seen anyone pack that efficiently."

He gave a goofy, lopsided grin in return. "Well, at least you ladies are pretty good about not over packing. Is this all your stuff?" When they nodded, it was his turn to be impressed. "So, there it is. A little teamwork in making things fit and not being packrats."

For a while, Brendan drove aimlessly, trying to decide the best course of action. Where on earth could they go that would be at least relatively secure long enough for them to put together a game plan? His apartment would likely be tagged now, which meant he needed a bag of his own. There was no way he was going to leave Poppy in the middle of all this. Making the brief stop, he ran inside, leaving the girls in the car and the engine running.

"If anything at all seems out of the ordinary, I want you to get behind the wheel and drive," he told Poppy. "Call me when you're safe, and I'll find a way to meet you there. Otherwise, I'll be back in less than ten minutes."

Gnawing on her thumb nail as she waited nervously, Poppy glanced back at Abby. "I'm sorry I'm taking you away from life as you know it. I'm sure Brendan could find a way to reinsert you into society without you being a target, if you'd rather."

But her roommate looked almost offended. "I have a mother who hasn't spoken to me in months, even when I told her I was heading to UW. I don't have a father because he ran out on me. I have no brothers or sisters because, let's face it, my mom didn't even want me, much less a whole slew of kids. I don't even know any of my aunts or uncles, and my grandparents died before I was born. I don't have a life to be taken away from. You are my family, Poppy. What else do I have, school? What kind of a career could I possibly build in a world that's stalked by this Darkness? Better to fight the good fight than to sit at home acting like I'm oblivious and be miserable."

Some of what Abby said made Poppy sad. Yes, her parents had been absent for many years, but not by choice, and she'd always had her grandparents, even if they were distant. At the same time, she was incredibly touched for Abby to refer to her as family. That kind of bond, that level of friendship, was the sort of thing to fight for, the reason for living. Abby was right, and Poppy understood her well.

She started to say more, but Brendan was already on his way to the car, and she simply closed her mouth and turned back toward the front of the car. He tossed a single bag in the back floorboard, making sure not to put it in Abby's way, and they were off again.

As he'd filled his bag, Brendan had considered a number of options. They'd gone to a public place this morning in hopes that the crowd would be a deterrent but seeing as the passersby hadn't noticed a thing, such tactics didn't seem to be helpful. Of course, isolating themselves could be just as dangerous, with no way out should the enemy find them and attack. Still, at least, if the Darkness found them, there would likely be no other casualties in the battle as there would amidst the throngs of the city.

So, he'd reached a decision and put in a quick call and found a cabin they could haunt for a few days. It was big enough for the three of them, plus Poppy's mother and grandparents, as soon as they could come up. "Have you spent any time at Snoqualmie Pass?" he asked the girls.

Poppy shook her head, and Abby sat forward in her seat. "I haven't been in years, but when I was little, I went with my mom once or twice. She handed me over to the babysitters on the bunny slopes, went and got her drink, and spent all day on the bigger slopes. It's a beautiful place."

Brendan didn't know what to say to that, so instead, he turned to Poppy. "I think you'll love it. I got a cabin up in the mountains, in a resort area but a little off the beaten path. It's isolated enough to keep most of the civilians out of danger but still busy enough to not feel completely alone, like if we disappear, no one will ever notice. You should text your mother the address so they can get up here. I'll pay for a cab."

The kindness, generosity, and fast thinking never ceased to amaze Poppy as she stared at the handsome man driving the car with determination toward Route 90 over the mountain pass. She didn't think she'd ever be able to thank him for everything he'd already done, and decided the best way to show her gratitude was to keep him alive and unharmed.

Taking the small piece of paper from his hand, she dialed her mother's number, knowing Mama wasn't likely to respond to a text, and waited for an answer. All she got was voicemail, so she left the address Brendan wrote down in a message and asked her mom to call her immediately upon receiving the message. If she didn't hear back within an hour, she'd call again.

Feeling a little burnt out on the topics weighing on their minds and knowing there would be a lot more discussion in the very near future, Poppy didn't try to make conversation but rather cranked the radio so they were soon singing along as they made the awe-inspiring drive through the mountain pass. It completely defied reason that it could be 65 degrees outside, with snow just a few hundred feet up in elevation and a frozen lake just below. It made Poppy wonder just how solidly that lake froze during the winter months to maintain a solid surface in these summer temperatures.

To Brendan's relief, there was no patchy ice on the roads. The pass was clear, and they managed to maintain 70 miles per hour or better the entire trip, shortening what could have been an extensively troubling day. Upon arrival, he once again asked Poppy and Abby to stay in the car while he checked in, giving no more than his badge and that there was a 'police matter involved' before he got the keys to the cabin as they drove a little further up the dirt path into a clearing between trees where there were four large, almost identical cabins.

The raw beauty of nature struck Poppy, and as she stood, she couldn't help turning circles, taking it all in as she breathed the fresh, crisp mountain air. If she'd thought Seattle was refreshing, she'd been sorely mistaken by comparison to this paradise. Brendan came up behind her and wrapped his arms around her waist, placing his chin on her shoulder as Poppy covered his hands with hers. "This is absolutely perfect."

"I've always liked it up here," Brendan told her. "It's quiet, peaceful."

Abby stepped up beside them, seeming to take in the scents and sounds as well. "If things keep going like they are, it may be the last peaceful spot on earth."

That was a reality check, and Poppy switched into high gear, getting the bags of hers that Brendan hadn't already grabbed and following him and his overload inside, with Abby and a single suitcase trailing just behind. They dropped their things, not even caring to determine who would sleep where just yet, and Poppy frowned as she checked her cell phone. "I don't really have a great signal up here. I don't know if Mama will be able to reach me or not."

"Don't worry, she has my number, too," Abby told her, "and my signal looks pretty good."

"And you can give her mine, if she needs it," Brendan offered. "I get wifi and roaming, so I almost never lose signal."

Hoping that was good enough and grateful for her friends, Poppy explored the cabin, finding a huge kitchen, four bedrooms, a giant living space with a fireplace that could blaze with warmth at night in the winter, and two bathrooms. She began to count and frowned. Looking back and forth between Brendan and Abby as they took separate bedrooms on the same side of the cabin, she didn't know what to do. She desperately wanted to place her things in Brendan's room, but she feared that would offend her family and hesitated to do so.

"Hey, Ms. Deliberation, check this out," Abby called from the room she'd taken. Reluctantly, Poppy brought her things with her, only to find Abby standing in the center of the room with a mischievous smile. To Poppy's great surprise, she walked over to the wall, which appeared to be made of wood paneling, and slid open a quiet door that separated her room from Brendan's. "That's why I chose this side. There's no secret doorway on the other side." She winked at Poppy, who gave her a look of eternal gratitude as she walked over to where Brendan stared out the window beside the bed in his room.

"Your friend's a sly one," he said, his voice full of mirth.

"Good. That means I can be where I want to be when I fall asleep and still not worry about upsetting my family." When he raised an eyebrow at her, she blushed. "It's not like they have a problem with you, but my family is very old fashioned, and I don't think they'd appreciate me even spending the night in a bed with a man I'm not married to, especially since I'm…"

She trailed off, blushing even deeper, and Brendan chuckled as he finished the sentence for her. "Eighteen? Poppy, you may be young physically, but you're incredibly mature, and that makes a difference. Don't for once think I've ever had much appetite for young girls. Like I've said before, you're special." To emphasize his point, he pulled her into a tight embrace, kissing her with all the pent up emotions of the day.

When they came up for air, he took a deep breath. "We'll need some food and supplies. I'm going to run down to the general store and get what I can. Will you girls be okay here without me for about an hour?"

Abby rolled her eyes. "We're not helpless, you know. I'm sure it's a lot of fun being a hero, but I don't think we'll need rescuing in the next few minutes."

Poppy rolled her eyes as the two of them playfully squared off. "We'll be fine, Brendan. Go do what you need to do. I'll just unpack a few of my things, make it comfortable here. I'm sure Abby would like to do the same." Giving her a roommate a meaningful stare, she let Brendan out the door, locking it behind him, then shoved Abby into the room. "You, my friend are a pain in my ass sometimes."

Giggling, Abby retorted, "What are friends for?" With a wink, she asked, "Do you think Brendan would be pissed at us if we just explore around the outside of the cabin? This is such a gorgeous place, I don't necessarily want to be cooped up inside just because we're trying to come up with a way to stop the end of the world."

Aside from being rebellious, Poppy knew Abby was trying to lighten the mood, and she appreciated it. With a shrug, she said, "I don't think we have to wonder away or anything. In fact..." she trailed off and moved toward the large kitchen in the back, finding exactly what she expected. There was a sliding glass door that led to a wooden veranda that extended across the entire back side of the cabin. "That's what I thought. We could even hang out on the back porch and soak up some nature."

"Fantastic!" Abby commented breathily, shoving the glass door open and stepping outside. "I'm almost sad it's not covered in snow up here right now. Have you ever walked barefoot in the snow and crunched it between your toes?"

Poppy laughed out loud. "I can't say I have. Honestly, I'd never seen snow before I moved up here. I'm from Texas, remember? In central Texas, it's rarer than the way you eat your steak." She put on a heavy southern drawl that had them both doubling over in fits of laughter. Sure that stress relief and exhaustion played a part in it because it hadn't been that funny, Poppy was just glad to take a brief moment in time to pretend everything was back to normal.

But as they calmed, even Abby grew serious, staring out at the snowcapped mountains surrounding them. The ski slopes had fresh powder, and it made quite the scenery. "Where do you think your father actually is?" Abby asked as though she were musing out loud.

Tilting her head as she considered, Poppy followed Abby's gaze up the mountains, finding just a couple of lone skiers making their way down the mountain like large insects sliding down a wet car window. "I'm not sure. But I know he's got to be miserable."

"If you think about it, he'd be less miserable if he'd succumbed to the Darkness. It wouldn't be as painful as being forced into service. I mean, I know that it's painful for you to think that he'd turned against his true nature, but what if it made his life easier, kept him from hurting?" Abby asked her questions hesitantly, obviously concerned she would anger Poppy with them, but her words made sense on the surface.

"Yes, Abby, that's probably true, but for how long would he avoid the pain? I think that the Darkness is eventually going to betray everyone he makes promises to." She thought back to Brendan's words about lies. "The last time a dark entity tried to take over the world, he lied, and he was good at it. And it takes people away from their families, makes them suffer every day, regardless of how great the rewards seem on the surface, initially. If my dad truly believes in himself, as an angel, he'll hold out and bide his time. He'll take the punishment now so he can reap the reward later for being faithful in his heart."

Poppy realized she sounded like she was preaching and laughed nervously. "I feel so strange talking like that. I mean, I never even went to church as a child, and now, here I am sounding like some minister preaching fire and brimstone."

Abby's laugh was soft and humorless. "I guess you're right, though. If I had a family, I might have a better understanding of that point of view. I've just never had anyone protect me, and I've never felt obligated to protect anyone. At least, not until now." Her tone held a sense of longing and sorrow, and Poppy really empathized with her best friend, who rested her elbows on the railing and leaned her head on her hands, a far off look in her eyes. "What was your mom like when you were little?"

"A lot like she is now," Poppy said. It was true. "Her and Daddy both played with me and catered to me, to the point that I was more than happy but not quite spoiled. I didn't ask for a lot, and my dad and I would take special trips to the candy store. That's why we ended up there the day he got back from the war. The day he was taken." Poppy swallowed past a lump forming in her throat. "Do you know how long I've truly wondered whether or not he was alive? I mean, in my heart, I always felt like he was, but then, I wondered why he wouldn't have come back. After all, he made it out of a war prison in Afghanistan. Why wouldn't he be able to escape now?"

"You actually questioned whether he might have actually abandoned you, and if you had just made it all up in your mind." It was a statement rather than a question.

"Actually, yes, even though I always thought my family believed me. No one else did, and so, from time to time, I would wonder."

"I wish I could wonder about that. I wish I could have seen what you saw, had my father taken away. I know that sounds really petty and selfish, but one of my earliest memories is my third birthday. My mom had baked me a birthday cake, the only one she ever made that I could remember, and they started fighting in the kitchen. My dad went in the bedroom and a few minutes later came out with a bag. As he walked out the front door, he told my mom he never wanted to see either one of us again, and my mom threw the cake in his face and told him not to leave her with a child she hadn't wanted and only had to try to save their marriage."

Poppy was appalled at the memory. She'd known Abby had issues with her home life, but this was the first time she'd talked about how far back they went and how deeply they cut. Her roommate's face was drawn in agony at the memory, and Poppy moved closer, putting an arm around her shoulders, trying to comfort her. "I'm so sorry, Abby. That's awful."

Abby scoffed. "Yeah, well, I'm glad he left when he did. I'm sure it would have turned into an abusive situation eventually, whether for me or my mom or both, I don't know. What I do know is my mom hated all men after that and tried to make me hate them too. But I always felt safer at school making friends with the boys. I think I realized even then that my mom was manipulative, and I never wanted to be around other girls who could act the same way."

Poppy nodded sympathetically. "I can imagine."

There was a brief silence, but Poppy could tell Abby had something more to say in the tension she felt in her friend's shoulders. It hung in the air with a sense of foreboding, and Poppy wished she would just come out with it already. Finally, Abby asked hoarsely, so quietly Poppy could barely hear her, "You're not going to just walk away from me at the end of all this, are you? I mean, when you and Brendan ride off into the sunset together, are you going to forget about me?"

Poppy was taken aback by the desperation and rejection in Abby's voice, and she shook her head. "No, Abby, you've become my family. You've been here for me when I had no one else. I trust you with my life. I'll never walk away from you, and I'd give my life to protect you."

A sick look on her face, Abby stood, almost shaking off the arm Poppy had around her. "Thank you, Poppy, that means a lot." Sniffling a little, she said, "I think I'm going to go lay down for awhile. All this action is killing my energy, and I need to be awake when Brendan gets back so we can do what needs to be done. Come get me if you need anything."

Poppy nodded, realizing this was taking a toll on everyone involved. But they didn't have time to rest, not really. She had no problem with Abby lying down for now, but she knew instinctively there wouldn't be this kind of down time later. She expected a full on battle, chasing down the enemy and destroying them as quickly and efficiently as possible. Who knew how many more of them there were, or if the ring leader could simply wave his hand in the air and make more? Hell, for all they knew, the Darkness dripped demons like rain so there were millions of them, disposable and replaceable at any given time.

That idea made Poppy shiver, and she rubbed her arms, not against the breeze that had kicked up off the mountain, but against the internal chill that crawled through her flesh. How were six people supposed to face legions down?

Suddenly, a thought occurred to Poppy, and she wondered if there was Wi-Fi in the area. She'd heard Brendan mention he could pick it up on his phone, so with hopeful strides, she crept into her room, where Abby rested and grabbed her laptop bag and then rushed into Brendon's room. She pulled out the computer, suddenly anxious, and plugged it in, waiting impatiently as it booted up.

As she crossed her fingers, she did a search for available networks and threw her hands up in triumph as she found one for the resort and connected. Instantly, she pulled up a Google window and stared at the search bar, trying to decide what to start with. She typed in 'Darkness legends' and hit enter but didn't like the results it returned so started over with 'legends of Satan and his legions'.

These results looked more promising, and she began clicking on results. The first listing simply recounted biblical information, running through the creation of the devil, his falling from heaven, and his determination to take faithful servants of God with him. The next few weren't much better, though some of them referenced Satanism and its practices. There were references to the instance in the bible where Jesus had driven the cattle off the cliff to destroy *Legion*, the army of demons who had possessed a man, but little else other than movie references appeared.

Becoming frustrated, she backed out her search terms and tried one more time. Muttering to herself, she typed in, "Satan and Darkness legends". For a moment, as her computer seemed to think much too hard, she was afraid she'd lost her connection. Then, about five references popped up, and her eyes widened. This was what she was looking for, and the third listing down caught her attention the most.

"Son of Satan – Real or Fiction" was the title and the summary reference below offered her even more hope. "...sometimes called the Darkness, Satan and his demons...legends regarding Satan having spawned a son...hidden from the world due to Satan's embarrassment..."

With rabid anticipation, she clicked the link and found a site that, while many would assume it was a hokey Satanist site, she recognized as something more. It was reference material, with quotes from various mainstream books as well as the bible, along with texts found during excavations near the location of ancient Babylon, in Israel, and more. All the references were listed. Whoever had put this together was a scholar, not a radical, and she scrolled through the pages and pages of material, reading intently.

Poppy didn't even know Brendan had returned until he placed a hand on her shoulder, making her jump and cry out. She covered her mouth, hoping she hadn't woken Abby, and turned to give him a harsh look. "How long have you been here?"

He smiled sheepishly at her. "About two minutes. Long enough to drop the bags in the kitchen and come to check on you. Sorry I scared you, but you look awfully intense. What are you looking at anyway?"

Giddy with her findings and almost sure she'd discovered a lead, she pointed to the screen. "I had a thought early and it sort of snowballed and led me here. But I think I've found something that will help us. It's sort of an out of the way reference, and I haven't really checked the author's credibility, but it all makes sense with what we're facing."

"Well, let's hear it," Brendan told her, plopping down beside her where she sat at the edge of the bed.

With a deep breath and an excited smile, she began. "Well, the first thing I thought was that there could be far too many of those creatures of Darkness for the six of us to do battle with. You know, the bible talks about legions. And that made me think of Satan and references to a Dark Lord versus the reference to the Darkness. So, I started searching terms like that and it brought me to this." She knew she was going a mile a minute and couldn't seem to slow down, but she couldn't wait to see if Brendan would validate her theory. "What if Satan gave up, feeling like he failed, because after all these millennia, he still hadn't turned mankind against God? And what if that failure was driven home by the fact that God had sent angels to earth to protect people against any further machinations?"

"Okay, I can see that, but how does that lead to the current situation?"

"There are scrolls talking about a secret son of Satan, a son the devil never wanted to acknowledge, who is referred to as the *Son of Darkness*. What if that's the Darkness we're facing today? Maybe, just maybe, this secret son is trying to impress his father, win his heart, like any other child with a parent who rejected them, and to do so, he's started these attacks, trying to get rid of the angels? Isn't it possible that he wants to prove to Satan that the world can be won? That all men can be turned from God, and that he will be the one to do what Satan couldn't?"

For several long moments, Brendan blinked at her, taking in what she said and chasing around stories he'd heard and read over the years, everything he'd ever heard during his brief stint of going to church, and he wrapped it all up into a neat little bundle in his head. Nowhere had he heard anything about the *Son of Darkness* or the *Son of the Devil*, but he had heard the term Satan's spawn. And it had to come from somewhere.

Looking at Poppy with new respect, Brendan smiled. "Poppy, that's brilliant. So, the question is, how do we find information on a child of the devil that no one knows exists?"

~~~~~~

A vote for the library was quickly shot down, for being too public and too far, as well as having little or nothing more to offer than the World Wide Web. But it was frustrating having just one machine, and eventually, Brendan took his out as well, and together, they sat, enthralled, searching anything and everything they could think of, clicking on links to other sites, and taking pages and pages of notes. Poppy wasn't sure it would all add up to anything, but every little bit counted.

When Abby shuffled into the room with heavy eyelids and a big yawn, it didn't take long to wake her up, with Poppy energetically reiterating where her thoughts had led and what they were doing. Becoming quite animated, Abby went to the kitchen, coming back with chips and sodas, then headed back to the bedroom and returned with her laptop to join the search.

Poppy read until her eyes were crossed and still felt like they were getting nowhere, simply reading the same regurgitated material they'd come across at first. Finally, on a whim, she decided to try something out of the ballpark. Logging into Amazon, she searched under books for 'son of the devil', pulled up a second window and searched 'son of Satan', and a third to search 'the Darkness+angels'.

As she scanned the last page, she sighed, realizing it was going to get her nowhere, but when she clicked back over to her first search, she let out a triumphant cry that got everyone's attention. She pointed to the screen and to one book in particular, titled "*Seribulous: Fact or Fiction*". She read the description aloud. "'Many question the truth of the Bible, but it's hard to refute the evidence provided by ancient scrolls found alongside those chosen for the grand work. This includes evidence that Satan not only took down a number of angels when he fell from heaven but also a family. While many have tried to hide the son of Satan, or Seribulous, from the eyes of the greater religions, others have blown off the evidence as fiction written for entertainment or even to inspire fear of God in children. This work explores the writings and translations of the scrolls, as well as interviews with scholars who have made it the work of their lives to discover and ascertain the meaning of such information, as well as the implications on life and religion as we know it.'"

"You know, that would make for a great dissertation, or a senior paper," Brendan muttered. "That would be great, but we don't really have time to order it, do we?"

Poppy smiled smugly. "No, we don't have time for it to be shipped, but Amazon has the digital copy so all I have to do is pay and download. Information Age speed!" She turned to get Abby's thoughts, but her roommate stood, a slight tremble in her hands and a gray-green tint to her skin. "Abby, are you alright?"

Shaking her head, Abby grew more ashen. "No, sorry, I think I'm gonna be sick." With that, she rushed toward the bathroom, slamming the door behind her.

Poppy gave Brendan a look of alarm, and he waved her on. "Go check on her, and I'll get this taken care of." He pushed her out of the chair, and she hurried after her friend, knocking on the door and opening it all in the same breath. "Abby, what's going on?" Her friend had her head over the toilet and was breathing hard. Feeling sympathy for her, Poppy gathered Abby's long blond hair in one hand to hold it out of the way while rubbing circles on her back with the other.

Eventually, Abby lifted her head enough to wipe her mouth and running nose with the back of her hand. "Sorry, I just…something about that made me ill." She sat back on her bottom, reaching for a towel to clean herself up, and gazed up at Poppy with watery eyes.

Something specific, Poppy thought, recognizing the pain and sorrow, as well as the fear in Abby's expression. "Tell me, Abby. Tell me what bothered you."

She shook her head, bursting into tears. "I don't want it to be true. I mean, why is it that even the devil can have a family of his own and I can't? How is that fair?" She sobbed loudly, and Poppy wrapped the girl, who seemed very young and fragile all of a sudden, in her arms and just held her, rocking her gently.

"You have a family now, Abby. We've talked about that. And no, life isn't fair. If everything we've read so far is true, Satan rejected his son, when my father and mother were taken from me against their wills. When Mama and Daddy would have done anything for me, I don't understand disowning your own child."

For just a moment, she felt guilty for saying that, remembering that Abby's parents had all but rejected her. But Abby coughed out a laugh between sniffles. "You know, my mom always called my dad the devil. I guess that could make me the rejected spawn of Satan, too, couldn't it?"

They had a good laugh, and Abby held onto Poppy's arm where it wrapped her shoulders. Finally, a little calmer, Poppy let her go and stood. "I'm going to leave you to shower and clean up. Brendan should have the book downloaded by now, so we'll be in there checking it out and waiting for you. Okay?"

"Thank you, Poppy." The tears still streamed down her cheeks, but Abby seemed to be calmer, and Poppy anxiously returned to the computer.

"Well?" she asked as she took a seat.

Brendan smiled and kissed her. "Hello to you, too. Is Abby okay?"

"I think so," Poppy told him, though to be honest, she wasn't quite sure. It seemed like maybe she was taking an *'end of the world'* perspective and confessing all her deepest, darkest fears and pains. All of this was unhealthy for Abby, and Poppy wished she could take it all back, keep Abby out of the circle of people involved so she'd be safe at home in the dorm, assuming Poppy was just spending time with her family.

"She's chosen to stay with you," Brendan reminded her, reading the guilt on Poppy's face. He pulled her against him and into his lap, similar to the way she'd just held Abby, and rested his chin on the top of her head, just smelling the orchid and lavender of her shampoo. "She's your best friend, Poppy, and she's not abandoning you. That's special. It's something that doesn't happen very often. And I know you want to protect everyone, but you have to let it go because all the people you want to protect are the ones determined to keep you safe."

Poppy's heart clenched into a tight bunch in her chest at Brendan's words. Of course, he was right, but that didn't make it any easier. In fact, if she was honest with herself, that was the hardest part. Being selfish had never been in her nature, and taking the support others offered without second thought, risking their lives, seemed the epitome of selfishness.

But being in Brendan's arms helped her release some of that tension, and she relaxed against him. After a few minutes, she leaned back and spoke softly into his ear. "You know, Abby will be out here any minute, and I told her we'd be looking at the book, waiting for her. Right now, we look like total slackers."

Cupping her face in his palms, Brendan kissed her, long and slow, until he felt her shoulders loosen. Then he pulled away. "No, we just look like lovesick teenagers who can't seem to find enough time in the world to satisfy our need for each other."

"Oooh, you should have been a writer," Abby quipped as she came into the room towel drying her hair.

Brendan made as if he was shining his knuckles on his chest. "Yes, I know, but it was a tough decision. Overall, I decided I was an even better investigator than writer, and I figured that hiding this body behind a computer and never sharing it with the world would be a travesty."

His sarcastic self-importance had Abby throwing her towel at him and Poppy wrapping her arms around his neck with a bit of a growl. "I don't know about the rest of the world, but I sure think it would have been tragic to never have seen this beautiful face."

"You almost didn't," Abby reminded her as they all crowded around Poppy's laptop where the newly downloaded file sat open and waiting.

CHAPTER 15

Richard bent under the pain and weight of the fiery chains that struck him across the back yet again. The human flesh tore and burned, but he refused to give the satisfaction of crying out, whether in agony or for mercy. On his knees, he wanted to cover his ears against the assault of the shrill screams and curses that rained upon him, the inside of them feeling as though blisters and welts plagued his skin.

"Your lies are intolerable!" Seribulous thundered with enough rage that boulders rattled and pebbles began to pelt those around him. "I would see you skinned, drawn and quartered, and your beating heart ripped from your chest as I drank of your soul, but that wouldn't be punishment enough!" He punctuated each sentence with a violent blow that threatened to rip Richard's body in two. Any lesser man would have passed out from the pain or begged forgiveness by now, but Richard gritted his teeth and kept silent, forcing his consciousness to stay with him.

"How dare you betray me, with all that I have done for you?!" Another lash and a grunt escaped his lips without permission. It fed Seribulous and made him laugh, the evil sound echoing through the caverns with such racket it would be a wonder if a mild earthquake weren't reported on the surface. "To think that all this time I trusted you, as if you were worthy! And you have returned to me with false information, led me astray. I should peel the flesh from your bones."

The force of the metal whip drove Richard to his hands and knees, unable to hold up against the pressure and pain any longer. He could feel the blood soaking his shirt, feel it running in rivulets down his back, and even as he struggled to breathe, he held on, envisioning his wife, mother, daughter. Poppy. He'd finally seen her, and she was the image of her mother, absolutely angelic.

The pun made him laugh, and he choked, spitting out blood where he'd bitten his tongue multiple times. But it served to renew the Dark Master's anger with fresh vengeance. "You dare laugh?" he roared, the blows coming faster and with every bit of strength he wielded, until Richard was face down on the floor of the cave. Until his sight blurred, and gazing around that the audience of lesser demons, he saw them trembling, biting their claws, some of them even whimpering.

When the beating finally let up, Richard dared to raise his head, meeting the Dark Master's eyes. "I ask you, Master, what you would do to protect your family, to assure they were safe. And then I ask, what you would have of me now." His voice was weak, his heartbeat thready, but he was still alive, and he intended to stay that way, at least until he assured his daughter was safe.

Sharp, yellow teeth smiled out at him, and black orbs glowed with malevolent delight. "I hand out a simple punishment, something I could imagine for someone like yourself was easy to take, and you scold me?" His voice dripped with false sweetness, still holding the grit of the damned. "Your betrayal has been all in vain. You will no longer be able to protect your family from me, Richard. Instead, I give you a choice."

Knowing there would be no possible path to take among the choices offered, Richard steeled himself, even raising up on his hands and knees with valiant effort to face off against the beast who had held him in submission for more than ten years. "Give me my options, Dark Lord."

Steepling his hands in front of his face, Seribulous seemed pleasantly satisfied by his own decision as the lesser demons and servants watched. All except Richard, the man in question held their breath. How Seribulous loved a captive audience! "You have the option of bringing your daughter to me of your own volition."

Richard snarled. "I would choose death first!"

"Death is not an option!" Seribulous snapped. "However, if you should bring me the purebred, I will make her death, as with the others, swift and painless. I will not bring any suffering to your family upon taking their souls."

"And if I refuse?" Richard asked through clenched jaws, his heart sinking.

Revulsion shot from the Dark Lord's gaze as he looked upon the man before him. How was it that the same man who had been so easily contained over the past decade also be so stubborn and persistently strong now? It truly disgusted him. "Should you refuse the offer, I will have my minions recover your entire family anyway. And under your watchful eye, I will torment each and every one of them until they beg me to take their souls, or perhaps turn on each other. And you will be the last to die, perhaps after centuries of my toying with them, taking them to within an inch of their miserable lives, only to bring them back again."

At last, Richard could no longer protest. He'd failed. In his one and only mission that had ever mattered personally, he'd failed, and his family would die because of it. If only he'd been more vigilant, or taken the risk of going to Poppy sooner, alerting her to the danger...

But it was too late for any of that now. Head low as he swiped at tears with bloody hands, Richard nodded. "Then allow me to take my family. And allow me a final goodbye, a chance to apologize to them."

The raucous laughter that ensued from Seribulous rocked the floor, making Richard dizzy with his blood loss and the motion. It seemed hours before the ugly beast recovered his cool. "Oh, it is the least I can do for your faithful service, is it not?" He snapped his fingers, and four of his *Legion* rushed forward with a bow. "Take him, clean him up. Feed him, and give fresh straw to lay upon. Then, leave him alone to heal. Once he is well, he will be off to a bittersweet reunion with his family."

"One last thing, Lord." Richard hesitated.

"Speak you imbecile, out with whatever it is. Now you test my patience." Enflamed with rage Seribulous leaned forward, daring Richard to make his final demands.

"Why me? Why did you take me?" Bellowing with laughter Seribulous stood and turned to walk away, several of his servants close behind him. "You've never realized why? Because you took the life of an innocent. A murdering angel. You give off a signal to my army like a beacon in the dark. You were the key, Richard. Without you none of this would have been possible." Walking away Seribulous's entire body shook with pleasure as he wallowed in Richards's pain.

Allowing the vile creatures to carry him out of the main hall and into the chamber that had become his home so long ago, it seemed almost forever, Richard closed his eyes and said a prayer. He prayed that, if Poppy was the key to the survival of heaven and earth, she be spared, and that his life be taken as pittance. He prayed forgiveness, and he prayed his death would keep Poppy safe, give her the time she needed to find the weapon or weakness that would bring the Dark Lord to his end.

~~~~~~~

Deciding it was a waste of time for all of them to stare at the same laptop, Poppy had emailed copies of the book file to both Abby and Brendan, and they'd divided the pages into thirds, each taking a section. They'd been at it for more than an hour, and Poppy knew she was on the verge of uncovering the final secret when Abby's phone rang and she stepped outside to answer it, her signal weak indoors.

Poppy rubbed her eyes and continued, but Brendan put a hand on her shoulder. "Come on, sweetheart, you need to give yourself a break."

She tried to shrug him off, but he stood behind her, massaging her back and shoulders, and her eyes closed automatically. She moaned aloud, leaning into his touch, savoring the moment of relaxation. As he worked, she sighed and told him what she'd found so far. "The scrolls speak of a Chosen One, a child bred of two angels that is a gift to either side, good or evil. I think I'm right up on what a Dark Lord, like Satan or his abandoned son, Seribulous, would stand to gain from someone like me above any other angel."

"And when you find it, we'll celebrate and figure out how to use that against him." He leaned down and whispered in her ear. "But for now, save your eyes. It's just a few moments, Poppy, and it could mean more rational thinking when that time comes."

She barely registered his words, too taken by the feel and smell of him so close to her. Without thinking, she turned in her chair and took his face in her hands, caressing his cheeks and kissing him hard, pressing fully against his lips, delving into his mouth with her tongue. She licked and savored his taste, her whole body buzzing as his hands ran over her arms, pulling her to her feet and dragging her against him.

Brendan ran his hands through her hair, loving the silken feel of the strands threading through his fingers. It was light and feathery, soft and supple like the rest of her body. He wanted her desperately, especially now when even he feared the outcome of the battle that was sure to come. But he wouldn't push her, especially with the stress she was under, not to mention the presence of her friend and, he guessed, her parents arriving sometime that evening.

But damn, she felt good against him!

Having trouble breathing with her heart throbbing and her body demanding satisfaction, Poppy felt as if her life support had been cut as she pulled away from that kiss. She may have never dated before, but she couldn't fathom any other man kissing her like this, making her feel this way. It was like heaven on earth, and if she could just have Brendan for the rest of eternity, she'd give up just about anything else in her world.

"I'm sorry about that," she told him through her gasps. "I couldn't help myself."

She felt the vibration of his low, deep, sensual laugh rumble in his chest. "You have no reason to ever apologize for something like that with me, Poppy. It's welcome anytime." He kissed her nose and willed various parts of his body to behave as he heard the door to the back porch open.

Abby breezed into the room, looking drawn and tired. Poppy was really becoming concerned and thought about asking Brendan if there was a way to get her checked out by a doctor before they went any further, dragging her along. But Abby had a determined stride and came right up to them. "Hey, lovebirds, the rest of the family is on their way. They want us to meet them at the base of the mountain, or at least one of us. The cab's going to drop them off there, and they need a ride up."

Brendan blew out a long breath, relieved that Jill had been released but also a little disgruntled that he would have to leave Poppy again. "I'll go down in about half an hour. That should give them plenty of time to get here." Taking one briefer but thorough kiss, looking forward to having everyone together again. It would be more protective. "You can stay here and find what you're looking for, talk it through with Abby, and maybe even have a plan between your brilliant minds before we get back."

Poppy sent Abby a worried look, and the girl smiled at her, though the curve of her lips didn't light her eyes but rather seemed to make her look paler and more drawn. "I'm fine, Poppy, stop your belly aching. Brendan, fetch the family whenever you're ready. And if you wouldn't mind, I'll give you some cash, if you can bring me back some nausea medicine, Emetrol or Pepto Bismol or something of that nature."

"Sure thing." Brendan ran the pad of his thumb over the line of Poppy's jaw, admiring her face. Poppy was easily the most beautiful creature, inside and out, he had ever known. Leaning in to brush his lips one more time over hers ever so softly, he whispered, "I love you, Poppy."

Trying not to let the tears she felt threatening to spill from her eyes, Poppy blinked several times, then threw her arms around him, whispering in his ear, "I love you, too, Brendan." It didn't make any sense; they'd known each other less than a week. But it was an undeniable connection, and Poppy wanted to spend the rest of her life or forever, whichever came first, with Brendan. Somehow she knew he was her perfect mate.

With a quick sniffle, she hugged him and pushed him away. "Go on, then. You might as well head down now and be waiting for them. It's getting dark, and I don't want to take any chances with them being out there alone." Sure, her mother and grandmother were capable individuals, and they had Papa, but that didn't mean much. Nana and Mama were both still weak, and Papa wasn't an angel, so he wouldn't have the same intuitions.

Brendan nodded and headed for the door, calling back over his shoulder to Abby, "Watch out for her, okay? Don't let anything happen to her!"

"I'll keep her right here, Brendan, don't worry." Abby winked at her as Poppy sat back down, pushing herself to finish her reading and find that last little detail that kept evading her. "I'll be right back," Abby told her, but Poppy barely heard her and just waved in acknowledgement without looking up.

And there it was! Poppy nearly squealed out loud as she found the passage she'd been looking for. She read it three times over, her chest tightening and her determination growing with each time through.

While the souls of angels are said to give the Darkness – *or Seribulous and his Legion – the ability to walk* *temporarily on earth, they do not provide a permanent* *solution. Only the soul of a purebred, the Chosen One, son* *or daughter of two angels, can give the spawn of the devil* *freedom from the realm below. In fact, the power of the*

Chosen One is enough to help Seribulous ascend to Heaven with his army of minions and take over both Heaven and earth.

The scroll which references this use, however, also points to the fact that only one with a pure soul, that of two angels who have managed to have purity of heart enough to produce offspring, has the power to reduce the son of Satan to a 'cowering beetle'. According to the written word found in one of the deepest caverns of the desert outside ancient Mesopotamia, the Chosen One will either give Seribulous all-encompassing power that rivals the power of God or will use his or her own power to destroy this rebellion, much as Michael and his army crushed Satan himself and cast him out of Heaven.

Bursting with excitement, Poppy spun in her chair with the intention of shouting the news to Abby, but before she could say anything, something jarring caught her in the face, burning her cheek and knocking her to the ground. She hit her head, and it bounced off the floor, making her nauseous and, for a second, she thought she would pass out.

Then, she was face down, her hands behind her back, and someone was tying them together that way. She raised her head to try to look over her shoulder, but whoever it was pushed her back down with a hand to the back of her skull. "Don't fight me, Poppy."

Abby? She was crying, blubbering really, but she continued with her work, then used the rope to yank Poppy to her knees, the rough material biting into Poppy's wrists painfully.

A little dizzy, Poppy couldn't even struggle just yet. "Abby, what the hell are you doing?"

"Shut up!" she screamed in a maniacal voice. "Don't talk to me, Poppy. Don't. I have to do this, and you're just going to make it harder."

Not knowing what was happening but certain she didn't want to make it easy, Poppy struggled to pull away, only to find that Abby was a lot stronger than she looked as she started tying Poppy's feet as well. "Abby, please, I don't know what the point of this is, but if it's a prank, you have to stop it."

"A prank? No, definitely not a prank." She pushed Poppy down on her stomach again, then rolled her over on her back, which tore at the muscles in her arms with how tightly they were stretched behind her. Looking down at her with an expression Poppy couldn't read, Abby shook her head. "I don't want you hurt, Poppy. I just want for you what I never had."

"What are you talking about? Abby, you've lost your mind."

But she shook her head vigorously. "No, I'm perfectly fine. And in just a few minutes, you'll thank me for what

I've done." She sat in one of the chairs, nonchalant even with a swollen, red eyed face, and waited as if there was nothing out of the ordinary going on.

Poppy did her best to hide her panic and swallow her tears. She tugged at the rope, but there was something wrong with it, a black stickiness that felt as if it clung to her skin and wouldn't let go. And with a gulp, she realized it was the same sensation she got from the dark cloud of mist that surrounded its victims. Realization hit her and she stared up at Abby in utter horror. "You're working with the devil."

But Abby wiped her nose and glared at Poppy. "No, I'm not. I'm working for you. Your father came to make sure you were safe, more than once. And he talked to me, Poppy. He stayed and talked to me, the way a father should talk to a daughter. So I asked him why he didn't talk to you, and he said he couldn't yet, that he wasn't strong enough. But he said he would be soon, and that I couldn't let you destroy the man who was keeping him alive. That Seribulous was important and he couldn't live if Seribulous died.

"So I told him I'd try to keep you from finding out how to beat Seribulous. Your father told me that, when you were close, it would be time, and I'd have to stop you and make sure you didn't find the way, and then he could come and be with you. Then he would be strong enough." She sobbed in the middle of her tale, placing her hand over her heart, while Poppy looked on in terror. "And then he told me he loved me like a daughter, and when the two of you were together, he'd take me away with you, too. We could be a family."

Something didn't make sense, and Poppy tried to make the words fit in her head, tried to wrap her thoughts around them. And she hit on a single point that sounded odd. "What do you mean, he would take us away? Abby, my father wouldn't take us anywhere. He'd come home, to the whole family. And yes, he would welcome you in like the rest of my family. But he wouldn't take us anywhere."

"You're lying!" Abby huddled in on herself, rocking back and forth, and as she did, Poppy felt a frission in the air, something unworldly and definitely not safe. The space to her left began to look wavy, like the horizon outside when heat pours up off the concrete.

Abby caught sight of it, too, and they both went rigidly still as the vision became corporeal.

"Let me go Abby, you've been tricked!"

~~~~~~~

Healing of the physical wounds took little time. His own powers, combined with those of the Dark Lord that had unwontedly been bestowed upon Richard assured that it took only hours rather than days or weeks for the ragged openings on his back and arms to close, leaving behind not a single visible scar. But for the first time since coming under the control of the son of Satan, Richard's spirit had shattered.

He was led to an underground pool; they wanted him clean and presentable if he were going to convince angels to trust him. After washing all the blood and grime from his body, he dressed in the long sleeved black button-down shirt, the black slacks, and the boots that had been brought to him and stared at his reflection across the water, barely recognizing the shell of a man who stared back.

His face was pale and drawn, sunken with defined cheekbones that were too sharp. His dark hair fell in shoulder length waves around his face, and he thought he looked like the quintessential vampire, minus the fangs. Even his eyes had lost their luster.

He thought about the time he'd spent here, with no memory of his past, thinking only that he'd been born into misery, into the service of the Dark Lord. That ignorant, pathetic life had been better than the pain and cruelty dealt him now. To see his own family's death...that was, as Seribulous had guessed, the ultimate punishment, and if any of them died at the hands of the Darkness, Poppy especially, Richard refused to live. He would beg for death, be it torturous or quick and painless.

He held to a single thread of hope that something would go wrong for Seribulous. While he didn't know the extent of his daughter's knowledge or understanding, he had to put some faith in her ability – as well as that of his wife and mother – to find a way to defeat the monster. Richard bore no false hope for himself; he was well aware that, if Seribulous was destroyed, he would take all he could with him, and Richard would not survive. But dying with the devil was preferable to living with the heartache of losing his family.

With hatred and despair wringing his guts, he turned as the boulder enclosing the space was rolled to the side and Seribulous stepped in, two of his most dim-witted worshippers by his side. Richard almost felt sorry for them; they blindly followed and trusted the beast simply because he was the only one who feigned tolerance of their idiocy, and they performed menial tasks for the Dark Lord that helped keep him from losing his patience with them.

Now, they stared up in rapt adoration at the vile creature bent on reaching the gates of heaven, just to run them down, while Seribulous gazed at Richard with a curiously amused expression. "Your disdain for them is much too obvious, Richard."

Richard shrugged. "I don't suppose it matters anymore. You've made clear my use to you and the task I must perform. I doubt my feelings will matter now."

"True enough." Seribulous's lipless mouth curled into a farce of a smile. "The time is upon us, Richard. Are you well? Are you healed?"

Glancing back at the water now behind him, Richard answered in a disinterested tone. "My body is well. You've succeeded in achieving your desired results with me."

Narrowing his slit eyes even further, he cocked his head to the side, considering Richard's words. "No need to be glum, Richard. You will see the rewards in time. Even you, born of miracles and clouds and brilliance and light – " Seribulous mocked it all, his enormous body wavering and fluttering his hands in the air " – will not be able to deny that the fruits of these labors far outweigh those you would reap in your previous role."

Unwilling to respond to the obvious taunt, Richard simply motioned to the two Legion, indicating his disapproval. "Is this the army we're taking?"

"Oh, by no means is this a suitable escort for our journey," Seribulous said. If he'd had more than holes for a nose, Richard was sure it would have wrinkled with disgust. There was, at least, the one point of view they shared. "We don't actually need an army. However, we will be taking one. These are so that I may have sustenance to enjoy my walk on earth. After all, I can't leave this underworld without something to ease my soul into the light." He snorted at his own form of humor, then grabbed the first of the two followers around the neck.

Opening his mouth until his head looked like nothing more than a gaping hole, Seribulous squeezed the lesser demon, who was ripe with having freshly fed, until his head nearly blew apart. Then, Seribulous placed the demon's head fully in his mouth, sucking at it until the body was wrung dry. The second minion started to creep away, but Seribulous caught him with a claw in his neck, then placed his mouth around the hole in his throat and sucked the essence from him as well.

Smacking his makeshift lips, Seribulous threw the bodies against the wall to his right and watched the ashen explosion with mirth. "So worthless, those two. I apologize for my earlier comment. It's impossible to hide revulsion for such infidels."

Gagging and heaving but trying not to throw up, Richard leaned his hands on the wall to the side of him. After all these years, he had no soft stomach, but with the impending doom the Dark Lord dangled before him and the scene he'd just witnessed, what little was in his stomach threatened to overflow right now. With deep breaths, he specifically ignored Seribulous and his murmurings, getting control of himself. In his current state, he wouldn't be able to help anyone and might just stumble the wrong way and get someone killed.

Seeming to understand the situation, the Dark Lord gave him a moment for recovery, and when Richard finally stood straight, the Dark One crossed his arms over his chest and gave him a piercing stare. "It's time now, Richard. We will join the small army convened yonder, and we will all ascend so you can do right by your family."

And that was Richard's plan. He had his doubts, but those were outweighed by hope and confidence in Poppy.

~~~~~~~~

CHAPTER 16

Brendan checked his phone and cursed. Something was wrong. The Applebaums should have been here by now. Reaching into his pocket, he pulled out the slip of paper Poppy had written her mother's number on and dialed it, hoping that maybe they'd just taken a wrong turn or gotten stuck in traffic. Something in his gut, though, felt wrong.

It took several rings before there was an answer. "Hello?"

"Catherine, it's Brendan. Are you guys almost here? Abby said you were on your way an hour ago."

There was a brief silence. "How would Abby know where we were?"

The hairs on the back of Brendan's neck rose and a tingle of fear crawled down his spine as he turned and ran for the car. "Didn't you call her? Poppy said you couldn't get through to her cell phone."

"No, Brendan, we never called her." Catherine began to panic. "We'll be there in about twenty minutes, but we didn't tell anyone we were coming. I was going to call you when we got there."

"I'm on my way back up the mountain now, Catherine. Just stay calm and don't come up to the cabin till I call you. It's not going to be safe." Brendan started the car and revved the engine, shooting out of the parking space and into the road, barely looking for traffic, knowing there was little likelihood of anyone coming.

"Don't even think about it, Brendan. We're coming. You can use us." Catherine began talking to Jill and David in a low voice that, Brendan assumed, the cab driver couldn't hear. "We'll be there as fast as we can."

"I have to go, Catherine. Stay safe." He hung up, winding up the path at dangerous speeds until he reached the turnoff for the cabin. He found himself instantly in a black fog as thick as pea soup and wanted to scream in frustration. The high beams wouldn't cut through it, and he couldn't see where he was going. He slammed the car into park and decided to go it on foot, keeping low to the ground and looking for landmarks, praying he was moving in a straight line that would lead him to at least a corner of the cabin and not have him miss it entirely.

There was no sound, no light, and his heart thundered, fearing he would be too late. Had Abby lied? Or had she been tricked? Either way, they were out of time. Brendan knew, deep down, that this wasn't some random visit by several ugly demons. This was Seribulous, coming to claim Poppy. And if he was too late...

He couldn't even think about that and let out a breath he didn't know he'd been holding in relief as he stumbled over the rocks around the garden area at the front of the cabin. He followed the stones to the front steps and stood in front of the door, listening, not sure if it would be safe to go in. What if they'd laid a trap, some sort of setup that would kill Poppy if the door opened? He had no idea what to expect, and it was terrifying.

At first, he couldn't even hear voices inside, but he could feel something and sense the vibration of people moving and speaking. So he stood there, silently, trying with all his might to focus on those sensations until they turned into voices and words.

~~~~~~~

Abby's eyes grew wide as the beings materialized. These were nothing like the man who had visited her so many times in the last few weeks. Of course, she'd been warned that the Dark Lord would be terrifying, both in appearance and in strength, but she hadn't expected something almost profane. Not to mention the lesser demons surrounding him, their scarred faces making her cringe as they salivated to the point of dripping on the floor.

"Where is he?" Abby asked, her voice trembling. "Where's Richard?"

One of the demons spoke, and she recognized the voice, completely in horror. "But I am right here, darling Abby. I told you we would be together once I had Poppy." A maniacal laugh exploded from the creature, and Abby shielded her face. What had she done?

Seribulous tilted his head and attempted a frown in mocking pity of the girl. "So young, so innocent." He patted the demon who'd spoken on the head. "So clever." He turned to Poppy, who had wriggled to a seated position but still sat, bound in ropes, on the floor. "I am pleased to finally make your acquaintance, Poppy Applebaum. I am the Dark Lord Seribulous, and we are about to become quite intimate."

Poppy spat at him, but he ignored it. She listened to his words, looking for an opening, a hole in his plan, and counted the army surrounding him, wondering how outnumbered she was. Even with Brendan and her parents returning, they were 2 to 1, and she would be willing to bet there were plenty more who could instantly join the ranks where they'd come from.

With a grin, Seribulous continued, "You should really kneel when addressing me." With a wave of his hand, Poppy was on thrown to the floor. Her hands remained tied, but her ankles were free. To Seribulous's surprise, she didn't rush him or do anything rash. "Very good. Now, to show my gratitude for the gift you are so generously going to bestow upon me, I have brought you a peace offering of my own." He snapped his fingers, and another hooded figure stepped from behind him, having been completely shielded by his large body.

Two human hands reached up and lowered the hood, and Poppy gasped. She would know that face anywhere. "Daddy!" It was the man she'd always known, thinner and a little tired, but just as handsome. She thought about running to him, but something held her rooted to the ground. He seemed different, as if he'd been stripped of everything that made him golden and loving and kind. Tears welled in her eyes. "Daddy, what happened to you?"

He shook his head. "Don't worry about me, Poppy. It's you that matters." Slowly he strode to her, one foot in front of the other, and it seemed an eternity before he stood directly in front of her. Looking down at the beauty of his child, so much like her mother, he had to swallow a sob. "I want you to know I have never betrayed you, never left you, and always carried you and the family in my heart, even when I've been at my worst."

She wanted to hug him, but the smell of sulfur clinging to his clothes repulsed her, even though she caught the faint scent of him – earth and trees and grass – behind it. Her lip trembling, she was suddenly an eight-year-old girl again, standing on the porch of a candy store and clinging to her father's wallet, wishing with all her might to have him back. "I love you, Daddy. I've been trying to find you. I didn't know…"

He placed a finger over her lips to stop her, unable to bear the pain and longing in her voice. "Poppy, I want you to listen to me." Finding his inner strength, the last of it he possessed, he tapped into the one talent that had kept him going all this time, the one piece of him that Seribulous couldn't touch. Aloud, he said, "I want you to be strong, and I want you to close your eyes and let yourself go. It's the easiest, least painful way."

But as he spoke, he relayed a silent message in her head, directed only to Poppy, in desperate words.

"Don't fight me. I need you to pretend to be draining your soul and power into me, but instead, I want you to take mine. With your power and mine, you can defeat him. You have to do this, Poppy. Don't worry about me, I'll be alright. Just do what needs to be done to stop him. If you destroy him, you'll destroy all his creatures and all his plots."

"No!" Abby screamed, pushing Richard away from Poppy. "I can't let this happen." She looked Poppy in the eye. "I told you I'd rather die than see anything happen to you, and I meant it. I'm so sorry, Poppy, I never meant to betray you."

"You fool!" Seribulous lashed out and struck Abby across the back with an invisible whip that tore her shirt and left a welt across her back as she cried out and fell to her knees. "You are mine now. You have promised your services to me, I will take your soul once my work here is done."

Poppy watched in horror as Abby looked around frantically, back and forth between her and Seribulous. Her eyes grew dim, and Poppy sadly watched the hope fade from her eyes. Lowering her head, she looked as though she was ready to submit, but her head whipped up, her face distorted by anger and determination. "You can't have my soul if I take it myself!" Before Poppy could scream her protest, Abby reached out and grabbed a knife she hadn't seen from beneath Richard's cloak. She looked at Poppy. "I'm so sorry Poppy, really! I love you."

Richard lunged for her and the knife, but it was too late as Abby drew the blade across her throat and slumped to the ground. "Dammit!"

Poppy just stared in horrified fixation at her best friend's body as it jerked around bleeding out on the hardwood floor. Bile seeped up her neck into her mouth and she shook her head in disbelief. "Oh my god." It didn't even matter that Abby had been the one to bring this scenario on; it hadn't been malicious. And now, the person she'd leaned on for the past four years was gone, in an instant. She looked at her father, who knelt, praying over Abby's body.

Seribulous rumbled with evil laughter. "You idiot. After everything you've done, do you truly believe the heavens will hear your prayer? It's all for nothing. I have told you to put your faith in me. We will reap greater rewards than imaginable."

Richard finished his prayer, unaffected by the Dark Lord's words. Then, he stood and braced himself. "It is one of the last things I will do of my own volition, so I felt the need to try." He was a brave man, but even he feared death now, after, as he had just been reminded, all the miserable things he'd done, the lies he'd told, the lives he'd helped take.

But this was the only way.

Poppy didn't understand what her father meant for her to do, and she imagined the worst. She would take his power, he would die in front of her just like Abby had, she'd again lose the father that had just returned to her, and she wouldn't even know how to use the power to defeat the monster she faced. Her whole family would die when they arrived, followed by every other angel and human in this world turning their allegiance to darkness.

How could she possibly be the key to all of this when she didn't have any clue what she was supposed to do? She wanted to scream out how unfair it was. But then, whoever had thought life was fair didn't know jack about it. Regardless of fair or easy, she would do her best and fight to the end.

Taking a step forward, she nodded to her father, pride and courage mixing with fear and resignation in her heart. "I'm ready, Daddy."

Richard held out a hand to his daughter, and she laid her much smaller one over his palm. Rather than intertwining their fingers, he pulled her into a tight but gentle hug, almost crying at the feel of his strong, grown little girl in his arms. He cradled her head under his chin, reveling in the idea of just being with her, even if it was only for a few moments. At least it would be the last memory he had, and that would be a sweet thing to take to his grave.

~~~~~~~~~

Brendan stood outside, squinting through the window. He had barely held back a shout of betrayal at the idea of Abby giving them up, followed by a cry of rage and grief when she'd taken her own life. He wished there had been something he could have done, but busting into the cabin just then would have been the death of them all, so he shed a few tears as he gazed on, looking for his opportunity.

He nearly lost it when Richard pronounced Poppy's death sentence, and had reached into his jeans for his gun when she'd simply agreed. But he took a good look at her face, at the confusion there, and something stopped him. He believed in Poppy, knew she wouldn't go down without a fight. So what was she doing?

Using his willpower to create a level of patience he didn't really possess, he watched Richard pray over Abby's limp body, and though he couldn't hear the words, Brendan knew they were said with full sincerity. He could read the emotion on Poppy's face through the window, could feel the energy around the prayer as if it were a blanket that covered him and warmed him.

And then, Richard pulled Poppy into his arms. This was the time!

But somehow, Poppy caught Brendons' gaze, made the briefest eye contact. And as she did, she shook her head, ever so slightly, almost imperceptible, but Brendan had watched her closely enough to catch even the tiniest gesture. He was sure what she meant.

He had to wait; there was a plan.

Brendan gritted his teeth, watching in agony and waiting, watching to make sure no one else made a move before Poppy was ready.

~~~~~~~~

"Perfect," Poppy heard Seribulous utter in a tone that, by all rights, should have been too deep for the human ear to perceive. Of course, logically, she realized she wasn't exactly human, and maybe that was the difference. Either way, he was watching and savoring the idea of Richard usurping all of Poppy's powers and stealing her soul.

As she felt a surge of warmth flowing into her where her father's arms were around her, she heard his voice again in her head. *"Don't utter a word, Poppy, and don't look invigorated. I want you to slowly slump against me, like I'm draining you of everything you have."*

Unsure if she could respond, she focused a thought back to him. *Have you done it, Daddy? Have you taken souls?*

Never taken, she heard and almost cheered that she'd managed to communicate with him. *But I've helped them be stolen. And I will eventually pay the price for that. I'm not scared anymore, Poppy. I get to hold you now, and I get to watch you bring down the most vile, evil creature in the universe, the beast who has forced me to do things unimaginable for our kind.*

A wave of panic flooded Poppy's heart, but per her instructions, she allowed her body to sag slightly in her father's arms. *If you keep feeding me energy, you'll die, Daddy.*

No, sweetheart, I'll be okay. Unfortunately, I have enough of the Darkness inside me to keep me standing. Just do as I say, and together, we'll make sure Seribulous never takes another soul.

Her head was spinning, her body on fire, and Poppy felt like she could fly over the mountains, run through the Sahara Desert and still have energy on the other side. Still, she sagged further, so it appeared as if Richard was holding her up.

Good girl, Poppy, she heard and nearly sobbed. She'd wanted to hear those words for so many years, and now, she couldn't even express her emotions at the pure joy of being with her father again. He continued, *I love you, Poppy, with all my heart. Now, close your eyes, and I'm going to carry you to Seribulous. He's going to take your hands and try to take your soul. But I want you to wait for my signal, and when I give it to you, I want you to open your eyes and push your power at him until you feel the souls he carries released.*

Poppy had no idea what to expect or how to accomplish so large a feat when she'd never attempted any such thing before. But she silently agreed and let her eyelids fall closed, gave up her entire body weight to Daddy's arms, and he cradled her against his chest like a child.

"Bring her to me now, Richard!" Seribulous bellowed, so anxious and full of excitement he created a brutal wind that stirred through the house. A picture fell from the wall and papers in the notebooks on the desk fluttered.

Steadfast and ready to lose the last of himself, Richard did as he was told, using the last of his strength, the part that belonged to the Darkness, to place Poppy on her feet, standing and staring at Seribulous. With everything in place, Richard smiled viciously at Seribulous, his entire body light and airy without the burden of an angel's conscience to guide him. He felt free, for the first time in his entire life.

"She's all yours, My Lord." Poppy heard the words, knew they came from her father's mouth, but didn't recognize him at all. This sounded like one of the monsters they sought to destroy. She wanted to look at her father, reassure herself that Daddy hadn't switched places with anyone else, but she didn't dare. Instead, she stood there, as Richard placed her hands in the slimy palms of Seribulous and the defiled beast closed his sharp-clawed digits around them.

Instantly, she felt weakened, but she held her ground and waited for her father's signal, waited to hear his voice in her head telling her it was time to fight back. Seribulous wasn't just draining her soul; he was feeding on her power first. She had to stop it, but how? She couldn't wait much longer for Daddy to tell her what to do. She felt as if she was slipping away, and she shouted in her head. *Daddy! What am I supposed to do? I think I'm dying. Daddy, help me!*

All that came was a dark laugh, and Poppy's knees buckled, only the power of the Darkness holding her in position now, her feet not even touching the floor. She was floating, and so was her mind. Maybe her father had been right and giving herself over wouldn't be painful after all, she thought. *Daddy? I love you.*

The thought was weak in Richard's mind, but it caught his attention. *Daddy? I love you.* This wasn't just some creature to feed on, someone to give the Dark Lord a way to ascend to heaven. This was his daughter, Poppy, and they'd had a plan. Alarm rose in each of Richard's limbs, reawakening him and putting his thoughts in motion. *Now, Poppy! Now!*

Brendan watched in horror as Poppy looked like she was going to lose consciousness. He couldn't wait any longer for Poppy to signal him, and he burst through the door, ready to fight down the legions.

At the same moment, Poppy's eyes flew open, and the dissipation of her power ceased. She was weak, but she stared straight at Seribulous, her eyes making contact with his and not wavering. Slowly, the circuit turned around, and she felt her power – her father's power – returning to her, making her strong, and she almost broke the link with the nasty creature as her feet touched the floor.

"No, Poppy, you've got to keep holding!" Richard's command rang out as he dropped to the floor and rolled toward Abby's body, taking the knife she'd stolen from him, and rising to his feet. He looked on as the man who'd just entered the cabin in a rage used the pistol in his hand more like a bludgeoning device than a gun, not shooting, just throwing harsh punches and slamming the butt into the lesser demons.

Richard turned a circle standing in place as demons swarmed him, and he ripped the knife through the middle of five inhuman chests, turning them to ashes. Then he lunged at another, headed toward the other mans back, stabbing it straight through the heart.

Brendan tossed the gun aside and reached for the nearest chair, breaking off one leg and wielding it like a bat, then a sword and finally, stabbing it through the heart of the demon before him, a stake. The demon was gone instantly, but three more stood in his place.

Seribulous roared in absolute rage, and still, Poppy held on, her hands burning as she took back the last of the power he'd drained and felt something more enter her. The powers of the angels he'd consumed. She recognized it unerringly, and it came as a shock that names flooded her mind, sorrow filled her heart at all the loss but also pride in the faith and service these angels had shown. The more determined she became to win the stronger she felt.

A movement in her upper shoulders and back stirred her. It felt warm and comforting, like she was about to be born in her mother's womb for a second time. Closing her eyes Poppies head fell backwards and without warning two beautiful white feathered wings burst open from her body. Rising upwards they swamped over Seribulous's huge body shadowing him, ready to contain the beast in their grip.

"Stop!" the Dark Lord cried, shoving Poppy away so hard she hit the floor with a thud halfway across the room. She was up on her elbows instantly, scooting away from him as he stalked toward her. "You can't release the souls. I must have them all. And I will take yours!" He leaped at her, and Poppy rolled to the side, then jumped to her feet and climbed up Seribulous's back as he tried to stand.

With her hands on his skin, she felt dirty, slimy, unwell, but she had to do it as she felt lives – souls – restored and watched the brilliant light of them ascending to heaven as they were removed from within the Darkness. And then it stopped as one of the demons pulled her off the broad shoulders and she landed on the ground with such a thud it knocked the wind out of her.

"You can't fight if you can't breathe," the raspy, demonic voice whispered as he pulled her head up by her hair and held it there as she lay on her stomach, waiting for the end.

A knife swept across the evil demon's throat, and he disappeared. About to thank Brendan and look for some sort of weapon to join the fight, she stared in awe at her mother wielding the weapon with grace and confidence. Her mother simply shouted at her and said, "Finish it," before returning to the battle in the center of the room.

Brendan let out a cry as one of the demons swung a clenched fist making contact with his forearm but lifted his makeshift spear and finished the demon as retribution for his suffering. He turned just in time to see one of the larger demons headed straight for Jill, who was creating small fireballs with her fists to unnerve and, in some cases, burn to death some of the attackers. Behind her, David had come in and gone for broke, a cane in one hand and another leg from the chair Brendan had used in the other. He taunted and teased and trapped the beasts until they practically threw themselves onto his weapon in a wish for death.

Poppy got to her feet, searching the room that had become a battlefield, seeing Mama and Nana fighting side by side, with Brendan and Papa back to back across the room. And then she found her target. Seribulous crouched in a stance readying himself for the final attack, and she faced him with murderous intent. He seemed larger, more menacing, a huge hulking beast, and he came at her with the force of an angry two-ton bull.

She braced herself, planting her feet firmly and leaning forward to take the assault dead on. But as he rushed her, she waited and leapt before he made contact, catching him in mid air, her wings swirling around him in a vice like grip, her arms wrapped around his neck. Thinking of her family – all those who fought now, and all those who had died – she found his eyes with her hands and covered them, letting the love for them flow out of her, pushing it into the Dark Lord, until he screeched in agony, the devoured souls pouring out of him, each one racing around the room for its freedom.

Poppy pushed harder, feeling weak and tired but determined to free them all, until Seribulous dropped to his knees and the screaming stopped. Around her, things grew quieter, but she closed her eyes, focusing the last of her will on her task. She felt the body under her crash with a thud, and a great deal of the impact hit her and knocked the wind out of her.

Before she could protest, there were arms pulling her off the beast, and she started to scream, but she knew the feel and the smell of Brendan and gave in, letting him cradle her sore, worn body. "It's over, Poppy," he breathed into her hair as he kissed the top of her head, and Poppy blinked back tears, barely able to process his words in her exhaustion. Her wings closed and disappeared leaving no trace at all.

But suddenly, an image came to mind. She'd seen her whole family fighting…except for Daddy. She remembered feeling his weakness, knowing she'd taken all his power, and fear gripped her, driving her into motion. She opened her eyes and pushed away from Brendan, searching the room and crying out at what she saw.

Her mother and Papa knelt next to two bodies on the floor, everyone covered in ash and blood. Crawling toward them, she choked out a sob as she saw her grandmother, looking pale and sickly, lying next to her father, the dark shadow that had seemed to dwell over him gone but his breathing shallow and his eyes dull. Poppy could barely see past her own tears as she looked up at her mother, who held Daddy's hand, her own tears raining down her cheeks.

Richard reached weakly for Poppy with his other hand and sighed contentedly when he held both his girls. But they both looked so sad. "Daddy, you said you'd be alright."

He forced a smile. "When you released the souls from Seribulous, his strength faded from all of us. I have nothing left." He coughed harshly, cursing internally at his lack of breath.

Glaring at him in anger, Poppy said, "You shouldn't have given me everything! I don't have any of it left. Please, take some of mine."

He shook his head the best he could. "No, Poppy, I won't take your life force. I gave you mine so you wouldn't die, and that's how I intend for this to end."

"Wait." The croak came from Nana, and Poppy turned to her, feeling torn. She wanted every minute she had with her father before it was too late, but it was obvious Nana didn't have much time either. She reached for Nana with her free hand.

"I love you, Nana. So much." She wept unabashed. She was losing three people today, and it was almost more than she could handle.

"Don't cry, child." Jill squeezed her granddaughter's hand with what little strength she had. "Listen to me, Poppy. I need your help. My body is tired, and my heart is done. But my power – the spirit that keeps my soul alive – is still strong." She rolled her head to the side to look at her son. It had been so long, so many years, and after tonight and the sacrifice he had made, she couldn't be prouder. "I don't have the ability you do to transfer power."

"No, Mother!" Richard choked out. He knew what she planned, and he protested.

Poppy looked back and forth between them, not sure who to listen to. But Nana nodded and spoke again. "Poppy, I made selfish choices in not telling you about your heritage, and I would pay for that if I didn't do something selfless to atone. And I want my son to live. I want you to have the father you've missed for so long, and I want your mother to have the husband she loves. I want you all to live the happy, full life I've had.

"So I need you to take my spirit and transfer it to your father." Poppy's eyes bulged, and she started to shake her head, but Jill laughed weakly. "Poppy, you aren't taking my life. That's seeping away anyway. I told you, this body is done, and I can't live without it. Trust me, Poppy, I want this. I love you all."

Looking for guidance, Poppy turned to her mother, but Mama's eyes were filled with tears as she looked down at Daddy with so much love in her eyes it made Poppy ache. Then she turned to her grandfather, and Papa rained kisses over Nana's hand as he squeezed it between his own and let a few tears roll down his cheeks, even as he smiled upon her. "I love you, Jill. You've always been headstrong, but you're not selfish. You never have been. You are a beautiful woman, and I will miss you."

The words were barely more than a whisper but as she heard Papa saying his goodbyes, Poppy knew Nana wasn't lying. She was dying one way or the other. Poppy felt a presence behind her and looked up to find Brendan limping over to her. "It's okay, Poppy. Do it. Your grandmother's not going to a bad place, you can save your father. Let her go."

Brendan gave Jill a salute, and she tried to smile, but only one side of her mouth lifted. "Thank you, Brendan. Take care of my granddaughter."

Feeling terrible but doing as she was told, Poppy opened herself to her grandmother, deciding that maybe she would just act as a conductor, and let Nana's power flow through one hand straight through her into her father's hand where it rested in Poppy's. Nana felt weak, and her hand drooped, so Poppy had to hold tightly, but Daddy gasped and clenched a fist around Poppy's right hand, squeezing almost to the point of pain. She could feel him gaining strength, saw the color return to his cheeks, the luster to his eyes.

Brendan placed his hands on Poppy's shoulders for support, knowing how difficult this was for her, and he could feel the energy pass through her body, the heat of it warming his hands and rising to his chest so his heart did a little flip of joy. It was amazing and indescribable, and he smiled despite watching as Jill's eyes closed and her breathing slowed. He knew the instant she was gone, feeling both the end of the circuit Poppy was completing as well as the sag in Poppy's shoulders as she realized it was over.

Richard sat up almost instantly, throwing his arms around Poppy and Catherine. He would be angry with his mother later. Now, he would celebrate the fact that, because of her, he could enjoy the life he'd wanted for so many years, could forget about all the hell he'd literally endured, and get to know his daughter and wife again. Relearn who he was.

Poppy sobbed for the loss of her Nana but with hope for the future. She had the mother and father she'd longed for, and her Papa was still there. She would bury and mourn Abby as well, but as she thought about family, she backed away from her parents' arms and stood, latching onto Brendan with all her might. She also had a new best friend, not just someone to talk to and joke with but someone who loved her and would stay by her side, as Mama and Daddy intended. As they would be able to now that all this was over.

And that thought drew her eyes back to the mess around them. The demons had all disintegrated into ashes, but the body of Seribulous was gone. Vanished from the place it fell. Poppy wondered if maybe he had disintegrated into ash just as the demons had. Of course, Poppy didn't trust that. It was too easy, and while she may have destroyed his corporeal body, she didn't believe for an instant that his being had been killed. He was supernatural, and the odd disturbance in the air spoke volumes as to his influence on the world. Whether he came back or not, a part of him was in existence, somewhere.

Brendan moved toward Abby, checking her pulse just in case. He looked up at Poppy, feeling profoundly sad. "I'm sorry about this, Poppy. I wish we could have stopped her."

Richard nodded as he stood and drew his wife to her feet. "I tried, Poppy. You know I did. She moved faster than I expected."

Sniffling and kneeling to touch her roommate's hair, she shook her head. "Her guilt was too much. I don't think she could have lived with herself. I think she would have ended up in an institution. You didn't hear her when she was tying me up. She was barely making sense. I wish I'd never brought her into this, but I'd like to think she's not hurting anymore."

Brendan put an arm around her shoulder, and her father squeezed her hand in sympathy as her mother hung onto him as if she was afraid he'd evaporate once again. "Should we call her family?" Catherine asked.

"No, she doesn't really have any, except for us," Poppy told her mother. "We'll take care of this. We'll take her and Nana home and do this right." She looked around again and groaned. "Of course, there is an incredible mess here we'll have to clean up."

"Don't worry about it," Brendan said, kissing her temple. "I'll hire a cleaning crew to come out here tomorrow and get it done. I don't know how we're going to explain all this, but for now, we need to get the authorities out here to confirm times of death and do all the legal stuff before the lines get anymore blurred and making sure everything's cut and dry."

TWO MONTHS LATER

Her mother, father, and Papa had stayed with Poppy for two weeks, just getting to know each other again, and then the family returned to the farm after the coroners released the bodies for burial. Poppy and Brendon spent a few days with them wanting to say their last goodbyes to the fallen. Richard talked somewhat about the last 13 years of his life, he didn't dwell on it and got a haunted look every time he did make mention of it, so everyone else tried to avoid the topic. Poppy recounted how the last four years in Seattle had been and, though her family begged her to come home, she told them that as much as she loved Primrose Farm, this was not her home anymore.

Poppy kissed Brendan goodbye as she climbed out the passenger side of the car and took off for class. She'd moved back into the dorm, much to his disappointment, but she wasn't about to quit school, not now that everything was back in order. Nor was she ready to move in with him as he'd hoped.

Poppy was crazy in love with Brendan, but she was young and unsure what she wanted to do with her life. She certainly felt like she and Brendan would be together forever, but she wasn't ready to make the commitment yet and was relieved he hadn't mentioned marriage so far, although he did reiterate on a daily basis how much he loved her.

Which Poppy didn't mind at all and returned with fervor.

Mama and Daddy seemed to be doing well, and they were courting each other like young teenagers falling in love for the first time. But then, they looked younger and happier than ever. Poppy couldn't help but wonder if their angel heritage had something to do with it. At the same time, she didn't want to think about that part of herself at all, so she refused to ask. She'd had enough of the supernatural to last her a very long time.

While Brendan remained listed as the lead for the crucifixion murders case, when months passed without incident, it was filed with cold cases, and Brendan was assigned fresh cases. He loved his job, and it made him happy to go back to being useful. At the same time, he worried about Poppy, even though she was currently busying herself with school.

Every week they would go to their favorite restaurant and over dinner he would start the evening with the same conversation. "Do you know yet?" Brendan asked.

And Poppy shook her head. "I have no idea what I want to do with my life yet, no. But it doesn't matter right now. I have plenty of time to decide."

After that, they would bounce ideas back and forth while they ate, some legitimate, others teasing and ridiculous. But it would all end in a decision that nothing would be decided just yet, and they would continue to mull it over until Poppy absolutely had to choose a career.

Whatever the outcome, it would be an adventure, and they were more than happy to face it together.